A Life Twice Given

a novel by

David Daniel

BERWICK COUR'

Chica

Berwick Court Publishing Company
Chicago, Illinois
http://www.berwickcourt.com

Publisher's Cataloging-In-Publication Data
(Prepared by The Donohue Group, Inc.)

Names: Daniel, David, 1956-
Title: A life twice given : a novel / by David Daniel.
Description: Chicago, IL : Berwick Court Publishing Co., [2016]
Identifiers: LCCN 2016932550 | ISBN 978-1-944376-00-0 (print) |
   ISBN 978-1-944376-01-7 (ebook)
Subjects: LCSH: Cloning--United States--Fiction. | Names, Personal--Religious
   aspects--Judaism--Fiction. | Psychiatrists--United States--Fiction. | Loss
   (Psychology)--Fiction. | Nuclear explosions--Fiction. | Jewish fiction.
Classification: LCC PS3604.A55 L54 2016 (print) | LCC PS3604.A55 (ebook) |
   DDC 813/.6--dc23

To David Gordon Louis Daniel, whose wise and understanding heart should have beaten for a hundred years.

"Those who are born are destined to die, and those who died are destined to live."

- Ethics of the Fathers, 4:22

"The past is never dead. It's not even past."

- William Faulkner, *Requiem for a Nun*

Prologue

IT WAS SNOWING HEAVILY IN the Staré Město when the astronomical clock struck midnight. On cue, the famed skeleton flipped the hourglass, the apostles marched behind Saint Peter, and the cock crowed. Below, in a sidewalk café protected by an awning and warmed by infrared heaters, two Americans and a Czech sipped pilsner from heavy glass mugs.

The old scientist's wrinkled face drooped with age, but his eyes sparkled like robin eggs. "We can give you your son back, but it will be very expensive."

Rachel straightened her posture abruptly, a thinly veiled expression of sadness passing across her face. Joseph watched tears well up in her eyes, and then she seemed to compose herself. She seemed to realize that there had to be some kind of deal made and it had to be surreptitious. The ends justify the means.

Joseph was willing to pay anything and realized the man knew that. Unwilling to tip his hand so early in the game, Joseph passed on the payment question.

"Aren't you putting the cart before the horse? First tell us what you can do."

The old Czech covered his mouth with both hands and coughed vigorously. The air escaped upward, blowing wisps of thinning white hair back over his temples.

"Assuming you brought us good material, we can provide you early embryos of identical cell lineage to your son."

"By early embryos, you mean?"

"One hundred cells or so. It's called the blastocyst stage. It's just at the maturity level ready to implant in your wife's uterus."

"And then what?"

"They should grow, but there's no more guarantee than there would be with a natural embryo."

"We haven't had any issues so far. You really have as good a record as a natural embryo?"

"That's why we're so expensive. What tissue of your son's did you preserve? Something with stem cells, I hope."

"I thought you could do it from any cell."

"We can, but it's dicier. Stem cells are much easier to grow. What kind of tissue did you save?"

"Taking tissue samples from your son for purposes of cloning him doesn't exactly have the Good Housekeeping Seal of Approval. I did the best I could under the circumstances."

Joseph looked at the old Czech a long time, then at Rachel. He summoned the waitress, ordered a whiskey straight up, and downed it greedily. The alcohol burned his throat.

"I got hair follicles."

"Is that it?"

Joseph's heart fluttered. He considered ordering another whiskey. *No*, he thought, *I need my wits now, all of them. This is Joey's only chance to come back.* He turned toward the man.

"I got the earlobes. I had to make them look the same. It was very difficult. The nurses were watching me. I made do with a pocket knife." Joseph closed his eyes and fought back the tears.

For a moment, he was lost in time, remembering the words Rachel had whispered just before she was airlifted to safety: *"May God be with you. Whatever it takes, bring Joey back."*

Part

I

The Vow

1

Examination

Washington, District of Columbia
May 9, 1990

THE EXAMINATION ROOM WAS DARK, lit only by the subdued gray light of the ultrasound monitor.

"The gel on this probe may feel cold," warned the obstetrician.

"That's OK." Rachel was more excited than nervous. It was her first pregnancy. She would find out today if the baby was healthy and if it was a boy or girl.

"I'll have to press it firmly to get a good picture. It may be a little uncomfortable. Now, please be very still. This works like sonar, kind of like a bat sending out a vibration and listening for the echo."

Her back on the table, her belly bare in the darkened room, Rachel held Joseph's hand. Their eyes were fixed on the video monitor, searching for their baby. A shadowy figure appeared on the screen.

"So far, so good!" said the obstetrician. "Here you see the heart with four chambers. Extremities and spine look normal, ten fingers and ten toes."

Joseph sighed. "Hallelujah."

"Is it a boy or a girl?" Rachel cut in.

"Well, let's see," the doctor said and squinted at the screen. "Now, I have to inform you that there's a 3 percent chance of error in visually gauging the sex at this age."

"That's a 97 percent chance of being right," Joseph said in a reassuring tone.

Rachel cut them both off. "Yeah, yeah, yeah. What do you see?"

The obstetrician moved the probe over the fetus's groin. "It's moving around a lot. It's hard to tell from this angle."

"What's moving around?" asked Rachel.

Joseph laughed. "That's got to be a boy, right?"

"Looks like a Jacobson to me," Rachel said.

"Almost certain it's a boy. Have you picked out a name?" asked the doctor.

"Joey Jacobson," Rachel and Joseph said in unison.

"Named after you, Dad?"

"Yes. My grandmother, who grew up amid the pogroms in Smolensk, Russia, always said it was bad luck to name after the living. Dangerous, in fact. She said that, when it's time for the father to die, the Angel of Death – she called it Malach HaMavet – could take the younger by mistake. She said it could take many forms."

"So she was superstitious?" asked the obstetrician. Joseph thought he heard faint traces of a Central European accent underneath the doctor's nearly perfect English.

"I suppose that's one way to look at it," said Rachel, looking protectively at her husband.

"My people from Prague hold the same beliefs," the obstetrician said. His dark, neatly trimmed beard framed a soothing smile. "And you, Dad, are you superstitious?"

Joseph thought for a moment, torn between the scientifically acceptable "No, of course not," and something else he felt in his gut. He could see his grandmother's face.

"I don't know," he finally said, almost in a whisper.

2

The Covenant

AT THE JACOBSON HOUSE IN the bucolic Virginia suburbs of Washington, DC, friends and family waited for the bris to begin.

"My stomach is queasy." Joseph chuckled uneasily. "This reminds me too much of Rosemary's Baby."

He held 8-day-old Joey in his lap lovingly, but with a twinge of empathy and dread for what his son was about to feel. The mohel, the religious figure who performs the circumcision, soaked a napkin in red wine and put it in Joey's mouth to blunt the coming pain. Joey sucked it robustly, as if in gratitude.

"You know, there are scientific articles about the long-term traumatic effects of this," Joseph said with some anxiety.

"Well, we have to do it," Rachel responded. "The Torah is pretty clear: you can't be a member of the tribe without a circumcision."

"You're not the one having your foreskin removed, though,"

Elisabeth mused. Elisabeth, in her early 30s and married, was one of the more empathic psychiatrists who worked with Joseph.

"They say it may be what makes Jewish men neurotic," Caitlyn said. Caitlyn was the administrative manager in Joseph's neuropsychiatry research office. She was approaching 30 and happily single. "It seems like a shame to crop that thing," Caitlyn whispered to Susan, Rachel's mother, in a tone of womanly camaraderie.

"Rachel said that at the ultrasound there was no mistake about him being a male," Susan whispered back with a wink. "I think he'll have plenty and then some."

Izzy Rosen, the good-natured mohel, had overheard all the conversation. Standing in the center of the room, his ceremonial white smock, high brow, frizzy salt-and-pepper hair and bushy mustache gave him the look of a mad scientist. Ready to begin the ceremony, he spoke up. "The wine and the topical anesthetic will keep him from feeling a thing," he said as he removed Joey's clean diaper and uncapped the tube of anesthetic.

"That's what we would *like* to believe," Joseph said. "Don't be stingy with that stuff. He's got to develop basic trust one of these days, you know."

The mohel slathered Joey's penis with a clear, heavy ointment, wiped his hands with a thick ornamental white and blue tasseled towel, and said, "Praised be Thou, O Lord our God, King of the Universe, who hast sanctified us with Thy commandments, and commanded us concerning the rite of circumcision."

He then applied a device with a striking resemblance to a medieval torture instrument to Joey's penis. He turned a dial and adjusted it. With dexterity, he removed the noodle-like foreskin, producing a grimace of agony from Joseph and profuse but short-lived bleeding from Joey.

Joseph kissed his son with love and sympathy, and recited in a triumphant crescendo, "Praised be Thou, O Lord our God, King of the Universe, who hast sanctified us with Thy commandments, and hast bidden us to make him enter into the covenant of Abraham, our father."

The non-Jews watched with interest. The Jews in the room responded in unison, "As he has entered into the covenant, so may he be introduced to the study of Torah, good deeds, and long life."

The wine was blessed, Joey was bandaged, and a napkin freshly soaked in wine placed in his mouth. The mohel said, "Creator of the universe, in Thy abundant mercy, through Thy holy angels, give a pure and holy heart to Joey Jacobson, the son of Joseph and Rachel Jacobson, who was just now circumcised in honor of Thy great Name."

3

A Cold Spring

IT STARTED OUT LIKE ANY other day, but oddly cold for a spring that had followed a very mild winter.

"Brrrrrr," sputtered Rachel with an exuberance that said this was nothing for a native of Buffalo. She slammed the car door forcefully against the brisk, frigid wind and checked the straps holding Joey close to her in the BabyBjörn papoose. Then she and Joseph sprinted the 50 yards from the parking deck to the entrance of Aji Nippon, a small, chic Japanese restaurant near the Georgetown section of Washington, DC.

"I thought this town was supposed to have Southern character," carped Joseph playfully after they were seated at a table near the entrance. His face was red and his breathing rapid from the frigid wind, even after only a few moments of exposure.

"But you did notice we crossed the Potomac River driving up here? That puts us back in the North, you know."

Their faces beaming, Joseph and Rachel raised their cups of warm sake in a toast: "To our family!"

Before they could drink, the door opened again. A huge blast of cold air swept in from outside, obliterating the cozy warmth of that happy moment. Rachel reached down to pull the hood over her son's head.

"My God, what happened?" Rachel said, her voice aghast, pointing to Joey's face. Her own face twisted in fear and horror. "His eyes are as red as a beet! What happened to his lips? Could the cold have made them crack so fast?"

Joseph felt a pitch of anxiety in his gut, but like any physician in a crisis, he put on a mask of calm and a steady voice as he examined his son. Having picked up on his parents' angst, Joey was squalling loudly now, mouth open wide. The first thing Joseph noticed was that his son's tongue was red and speckled. *Like a strawberry*, he thought. Then an unpleasant memory from pediatrics in medical school began to dawn on him. He rolled up Joey's pant legs and took off his shirt. The skin was swollen with a raised crimson rash, covering his lower legs and arms like socks and gloves, but the tips of his fingers and toes were blue. He felt Joey's forehead. *Hot as a hare*, he groaned to himself.

He ran his fingers under Joey's armpits. There was something leathery, shaped like a bean. The same sort of tiny object was in his groin. Quickly, he opened Joey's diaper. The tip of his penis was peeling. The awareness of what was happening to his son hit him like a punch in the stomach. He turned to Rachel, equanimity shattered, shaking his head in disbelief. His eyes were wide in surprise, his face contorted into a look of consternation.

"Kawasaki disease," he choked out.

Forty-five minutes later, they were in the crowded waiting room of Dr. McDonniel, a very distinguished, albeit aging, DC pediatrician.

Despite being hassled and behind schedule, she maintained a dignified and upbeat bedside manner.

"What's his age?"

"Five and a half months," Joseph answered.

"How's his behavior been?"

"He was fine this morning, but now he's completely miserable," Rachel answered, having recovered her composure in the reassuring atmosphere of the doctor's office.

The pediatrician removed the rectal thermometer. 104.9 °F. Her expression was somber under the veneer of her warm professional smile. "It's good you got him here so quickly. We need to do a blood test and an echocardiogram to be sure, but it's looking an awful lot like what your husband fears: Kawasaki disease. Time is of the essence if we're going to prevent the worst."

Before Rachel could ask what the worst was, the doctor continued, "We still don't know the cause of Kawasaki, but we know if we don't act fast, the arteries that feed the heart can swell and burst. Your son is about six months old. That's within the most dangerous period."

Rachel nodded grimly, setting her jaw and pursing her lips while stifling a scream.

Dr. McDonniel spoke rapidly, pausing only to suck in little gasps of air between words. She smelled like cigarettes, Joseph thought. Teetering slightly, the doctor steadied herself with both hands on the cabinet top. "The danger increases with every hour that passes before treatment. I took the liberty of calling the Georgetown Hospital pediatric cardiac clinic and you need to take him there immediately."

At Georgetown Hospital, attendants were expecting Joey and quickly took him into a treatment room while Rachel and Joseph signed the necessary papers. They entered the treatment room as the technician was checking Joey's pulse and blood pressure. He drew several tiny vials of blood without a hitch. Joey's shirt was quickly stripped off and his chest slathered with a cold gel that smelled of alcohol. The lights were turned low and the stub of a small wand was pressed firmly to his chest over his heart. Joey thrashed about restlessly, miserable from the fever and rash. The technician stared intently at the lighted monitor and didn't speak or smile.

Joseph's eyes were glued to the shadowy ultrasound images on the screen.

"What's he doing?" Rachel whispered quietly to Joseph.

"He's measuring the diameter of the arteries that feed the heart muscle to see if they're swollen," Joseph whispered back, without taking his eyes off the monitor.

Rachel shivered, stifled her anxiety and, in a voice as calm as if she were inquiring about a mosquito bite, she asked, "Does it look OK?" She was trying not to panic, Joseph saw, admiring her resolve.

"It's been a long time since I've looked at one of these," Joseph hedged, thinking of how to best tell Rachel. He had already drawn all the conclusions he needed. In a quiet tone, he added, "Let's wait and see what the cardiologist says."

But his voice cracked subtly, and Rachel picked up on the stress in his tone immediately. She slowly turned her eyes away from her son and back toward her husband, just catching the faraway look of resignation in his eyes.

4

Treatment Resistance

Washington, District of Columbia
April 3, 1991

T HE GRIM-FACED CARDIOLOGIST'S TONE reminded Rachel of a judge leading up to a death sentence.

"The echocardiogram shows severe acute swelling of the coronary arteries, called aneurysms," Dr. Aaron explained. "They're only 3 to 4 millimeters wide now, but it's very early. They will probably get much worse. If they reach a certain size, they won't get better and may burst or close up from a clot."

Rachel implored, "Doctor, what on God's earth is causing this?"

"Something has convinced Joey's immune system that an invader is hiding in the linings of his arteries, and the immune system has launched an all-out assault on his blood vessels in order to destroy the intruder. The endothelium, that's the inner lining of his blood vessels, are very inflamed and weakened from the attack. Some of them, especially around his heart, are so damaged they're swelling into aneurysms. A blood test we use to measure the amount of inflammation is already more than ten times what it should be."

"All things considered, what's his prognosis?" Rachel asked, stifling a sob.

"You need to accept that he has a 50 percent chance of dying," the cardiologist said pointedly, without a trace of empathy.

"Fifty percent chance of dying when?" Joseph asked, looking into the doctor's eyes, too worried about his son to show his exasperation for the doctor's lack of bedside manner.

"In the next few weeks or months," Dr. Aaron said matter-of-factly.

Before the conversation could go further, there was a knock on the door and the Jacobsons were instructed to rush to another part of the hospital to meet with a specialist in infectious disease. Their escort was a nursing student with a long ponytail and sleepy blue eyes.

"Can you excuse us for a moment?" Joseph asked.

The young woman smiled faintly and nodded. The situation was wearing on Rachel, Joseph realized. He drew her into a corner off the crowded corridor and kissed her tenderly on the lips. Then he stepped back, swallowed hard and set his jaw for a moment. He looked into her eyes softly but intently enough to hold her gaze. "The three of us are going to get through this together and we're going to be the same as we were before."

Rachel closed her eyes and tried to squeeze back the tears but they ran down her cheeks. She rested her head on Joseph's shoulder for a moment before taking a package of Kleenex from her purse and drying her face. She stood up very straight and took a deep breath. "Let's go."

For a few days, the immunological armament factory stopped making the antibody smart bombs that had been exploding on the inner lining of the blood vessels that fed Joey's heart. His erythrocyte sedimentation rate, an early warning system for the destruction of his coronary arteries, drifted back down to normal, as did his temperature. Both were signs of a general demobilization of his immune system. His ready smile and infectious laughter returned. His brown eyes sparkled from his round face as he sat on his mother's lap, entranced as she turned the pages of a picture book.

They were with Rachel's parents, Susan and Don. Don's eyes shone through his glasses as he lifted his grandson over his shoulders for a game of horsey. "Just like new!" he said.

"Better than new," declared Susan, beaming proudly.

Joseph rubbed noses with his son. "That's an Eskimo Kiss."

Joey laughed.

"Do you know how to play peekaboo?" Joseph asked.

Joey giggled again.

"Cover your eyes like this." Joseph covered his own eyes, leaving enough space between his fingers to watch Joey's eyes widen curiously. *Like little quail eggs*, Joseph thought, smiling. "Now you."

His son stared expectantly, not having picked up the game yet. Joseph covered the infant's eyes. "Peek a Boo!" When Joseph removed his hands, he looked away briefly, then looked back again quickly, holding the infant's gaze. The corners of Joseph's smile slowly turned down and his brow knit. He felt a sudden stinging in his armpits.

"Shit!" he said under his breath. He cleared his throat and steadied his voice. "Rachel, can you please come here for just a second?"

Rachel was on the phone, chatting gaily with a friend. "I'll call you right back."

She walked over quickly. "What?" Her voice was a choked whisper, as if she was asking a question she didn't want to know the answer to.

"What do you see in his eyes?"

Rachel knelt and gently brushed Joey's light brown hair to the side. "Nothing."

"Don't they look a little red?"

"Nothing special."

"Don't they look a little pink to you?"

"What are you getting at?"

19

"It may be nothing, or it may be an early sign he's getting sick again. Remember how red his eyes were?"

Rachel took his temperature rectally and it was 100.3 degrees. "That's *nothing* for a baby," she said, searching Joseph's eyes for confirmation.

"Let's just keep an eye on him," he replied, trying to sound upbeat.

At lunch, Joey wasn't hungry. By afternoon, he was grumpy and Joseph thought his eyes were a tad pinker. That evening, he started to squall. His eyes were red.

"It's because he's crying," Rachel said as she checked his diaper. It was dry. She dipped the thermometer into the Vaseline, gently slid it into her son's rectum, closed her eyes and waited three minutes.

Mere hours earlier, she had gushed to Joseph how nice it was to have Joey home. Everything seemed perfect. Soon it would be summer and they would take him to the Cape. He would love the sand and the water. There were so many things to show him. She looked at her watch. It had been five minutes. She held her breath, carefully removed the thermometer and held it close to the light. She exhaled slowly.

"Aghh!" But then she muted her voice to avoid alarming the infant. "It's 104.2," she said under her breath. Rachel opened the door of the study where Joseph was searching medical journals online. His eyes meet hers and fell to the thermometer. Then she saw the title of the journal article on the screen: "Treatment Resistant Kawasaki Disease."

5

The Vow

S CIENCE AND MEDICINE APPEARED TO have failed Joey, Joseph was forced to conclude. The treatment options were exhausted. Now he and his baby son were alone in the treatment room waiting for the definitive echocardiogram that would reveal Joey's fate. Joseph felt the weight of the world on his shoulders as he blinked back his tears. He took an egg-shaped stone out of his pocket and rubbed it in the tiny palm of his son's hand. It was a good luck piece that a family friend, Mac Levy, had picked up from a dry streambed in western Canada while hunting with Joseph. Mac likened it to the stone used to slay Goliath. The stone was special to Joseph because Mac was a local hero in Mississippi for standing up to the Ku Klux Klan.

Joseph, seldom religious, felt a strange, unfamiliar energy come over him. He found himself lifting his head and eyes upward and starting to pray, silently at first, then a whisper, and then a chant rising in a muffled but ever more intense crescendo: "Dear God, I pray you notice a young boy who needs your help."

Then he called upon his deceased relatives who he felt might have access to God. "Come Beverly, come Fanny, come Papa, Ada and Granddad. Come Ida and Sarah, come Bailey, come Lynn, come Marion and Dan. There's a child who needs God's help. Please call God's attention to your grandson, your great-grandson, your nephew, your great-nephew, your cousin! Come…"

Then he implored each ancestor individually. "Dear Bailey, please hear me, your help is needed, please call God's attention to my son, your cousin."

Then in a whisper, he added, "Malach HaMavet, take my life, not the life of the child."

Finally, after a pause, he thought, *Malach HaMavet, do what you will to me if it saves the life of our child.*

Joseph was actually unsure if there was a God, but he had exhausted everything else he knew to do for Joey medically or scientifically in this world. If there were a God, Joseph assumed he was too busy to notice everything that needed his attention on earth. But if there were a way to connect to God spiritually, he would do it now if he could. His last hope for his son was to try to send a spiritual telegraph, to summon someone in heaven who might implore God to help Joey.

Like any worshipper or shaman attempting to reach a transcendent state, he used repetition, chanting, and ultimately a mild self-induced trance to create a subjective sense of connecting to God.

Rachel and the technician entered a few minutes later. They had given Joey 12.5 mg of a sedating antihistamine, diphenhydramine, an hour earlier to keep him still during the procedure. Joey was sleepy but didn't sleep. The cold liquid on his chest made him shiver. They turned down the lights so the technician could see her screen, and she pressed the wand hard on Joey's chest, moving it around. A ghostly image appeared on the screen. Joseph and Rachel peered closely as the technician measured Joey's coronary arteries and the percentage of blood ejected from his heart with each beat. But the numbers didn't show up on the screen. The technician had been instructed to give no feedback, but Joseph and Rachel tried to pump her.

"How does it look?" Joseph tried to sound stoical.

"Dr. Aaron will go over it in detail."

Joseph, unabashed, waited a few moments, then said, "No one will hold you to it."

"We're not allowed to comment because the doctor has to interpret it, but..." She stopped herself in mid-sentence.

"But?" Joseph said softly.

"Dr. Aaron will tell you all about it," she said apologetically, then pursed her lips.

Joseph gave up on her saying anything explicitly and studied her poker face for clues but saw none. She carefully repeated several of her measurements, saved the results to a disc, switched off the screen, dried Joey's chest, and told Joseph and Rachel they could stay in the exam room until Dr. Aaron reviewed the results and filled them in.

Rachel pulled Joey's baby Lacoste shirt over his head and arms. She took him into her arms and he dozed off.

Joseph took a deep breath as the door opened and Dr. Aaron stepped in.

"Good news. The echocardiogram shows his coronary vessels are indistinguishable from normal."

Many individuals and prayer groups of many faiths had prayed fervently for Joey's recovery. Joseph and Rachel were never sure whether it was the science or the religion, but they were strongly biased toward the science and the novel treatment.

To try to prevent any undetected but subtle damage invisible to the echocardiogram, Joseph saw that Joey took once-a-day baby aspirin, fish oil and putative cardioprotective B vitamins. He also hoped these would reduce Joey's vulnerability to later onset of coronary artery disease. Yet, given how swollen Joey's coronary arteries had been, along with the cardiologist's earlier prediction of a 50 percent chance of survival, the speed of his recovery raised the possibility of a miracle. Regardless of the cause, Joseph and Rachel kept their vow to live every day with their son to the fullest. Moreover, Joseph remained as sincere as ever in his vow to sacrifice his own life for his son's.

The chance came in mid-summer, seven idyllic years later.

Part

Pegasus

6

Bedtime

ALTHOUGH IT WAS NEARLY TIME for bed, the Jacobson summer home in the mountains near Luray, Virginia, was still full of life. After giving his father a pretty good scare in chess, 7-year-old Joey had managed to put off bedtime by engaging his mother in one more game of Sorry. His younger sister, Bevy, and the twins, Noah and Teddy, had fallen asleep in their bunks. Joey had just put on his pajamas and was negotiating with his mother for a bedtime story when the phone rang.

"It's awful late," Rachel said. "Who's calling?"

Joseph ran downstairs to answer the phone and fell into a hushed conversation.

While waiting for Joseph to return and complete his nighttime ritual with Joey, Rachel read to her son from a book called *The Golem*. It was set in medieval Prague and described a mythical creature created by a rabbi in the attic of a synagogue to protect the Jews of the ghetto.

"Mommy!" Bevy called from the other room.

"I'm coming, sweetie."

As she brushed her lips gently over Joey's head, Joseph came upstairs to tuck him in.

"This is how my mother did it," Joseph said as he gave his son loving pats and tucks. "Then she would say, 'Gay schlafen,' and kiss us goodnight."

"What does that word mean, Daddy?"

"It's from a language Nana Beverly, my mother, spoke called Yiddish. It means, 'go to sleep.' She died before she could meet you, but her other grandchildren were the light of her life."

"Daddy, why did she die?"

"No one ever knew for sure. Her heart stopped working and then her kidneys. We couldn't keep her alive. She was too young to die, and she wanted to live. Her body fought very hard to live."

Joey could see that this was very hard for his father.

"As she died, I told her that I would see her again, that I would find her someday."

"Did you mean in heaven?"

"Yes. I would have done anything to give her the life she deserved. She certainly sacrificed for me. Science and medicine have come a long way since then, though. There might be things that could be done now if you were determined enough and had the resources and the right connections. But there was nothing else that could be done for her at the time."

Joey wondered what his father was talking about. "When I get older, I'm going to have an office with you so we never have to be apart." Joey saw a wetness creep into his father's eyes.

"That would be wonderful, Joey, if that turns out to work for you," Joseph said as he planted a kiss on his son's forehead. "You don't have to be a doctor, you know. Whatever you pick, you should always be hungry to learn more about it and it should come naturally for you. Like riding a bicycle. Do you remember what kind of doctor I am?"

"A psychiatrist."

"That's right. Granddaddy and your uncles and aunts and cousins are internists. They take care of the body. A psychiatrist takes care of the physical brain and the mind. A good doctor's like a detective. Your granddaddy was considered a great internist because he would consider everything on earth that might cause a patient's medical problem, and then whittle it down like he was solving a mystery. A psychiatrist does the same thing when it comes to the brain, but pays more attention to the way the patient was brought up and how the patient's view of the world affects his or her illness. A really good psychiatrist can step into the patient's shoes for a while, so to speak, and then step out again."

"I'm tired, Daddy. Can I go to sleep now?"

"I'm sorry, son, I'm being too technical."

Joseph kissed his son goodnight, lingered for a moment with their cheeks touching, then turned out the light.

Joey woke up just before midnight. He padded past Rachel, who had fallen asleep with Bevy, walked across the hall, and crawled under the covers next to his father.

"Joey?" Joseph asked sleepily.

"I don't want to be apart," Joey whispered.

"What's wrong, Joey?"

"I had a bad dream."

"What did you dream?"

"I had a dream about Nana Beverly. There was a gate that led back to earth, but she couldn't go through it."

"Joey, sometimes I think you come from another world," Joseph mused.

"She wants to come back, but she can't," Joey said with gravity.

"Where did you get that idea?" Joseph asked.

"I don't know. It just came to me in the dream."

"Have you ever heard it before?"

"No. Daddy, will you take my glasses?"

Joseph set them on shelf and Joey quickly fell back to sleep. But then he woke up in the middle of the night.

"I peed in my sleep!"

"Don't worry, Joey, it can happen to anyone. Give me your pajama pants."

Joseph ran the faucet in the upstairs bathroom until the water was warm and dipped a washcloth under the spigot. He returned to the bedroom and gently washed the pee off of his son, dried him, and put a fresh dry towel over the spot on the sheet. There were no spare sheets in the house. He handed Joey a clean pair of pajamas.

"Do you want some water?"

"Yes, please."

Joseph trotted down the steps. Upstairs, Joey heard the refrigerator open and the snap as his father broke the seal of the bottled water. The Jacobson family used an ultraviolet water treatment system to sterilize the well water but only drank it if they had to. It carried a smell somewhere between that of a hard-boiled and a rotten egg.

Joey took a few sips. Joseph set the glass by the side of the bed, turned out the light and said, "I love you very much."

"I love you, Daddy."

"Goodnight, Joey."

"Goodnight, Daddy."

Lying next to his father, Joey remembered the last time he had peed in his pants. His father had taken him to visit his very old great-great-Aunt Sarah in a huge nursing home on the Hudson River near Riverdale, New York. When he had first met Aunt Sarah, she lived alone in a majestic country home in Mississippi surrounded by beautiful things she had collected in the eight decades since she had left her birthplace in Smolensk, Russia. Now she shared a small room with a blaring television in a hospital-like setting with another very old lady. Despite her stroke, Aunt Sarah was lucid and appreciative of their visit, and she reminisced with his father in great detail about Nana Beverly. Joey could never remember Aunt Sarah's name and referred to her afterward as "the very old lady."

After the visit, Joey had wet his pants while they waited for a taxi. He was very embarrassed as they entered an elevator at their hotel because his pants were obviously wet and he was very close to the other passengers. Despite his father's reassurances, he started to cry. A very attractive, expensively dressed woman in her 30s asked him with a sympathetic, motherly look, "What's wrong?"

"I wet my pants."

She seemed to take a moment to gather her thoughts. The crowded elevator stopped and people got on and off.

"Sometimes I pee a little in my underwear as well," she whispered.

"You hear that, Joey? It can happen to anyone, even an adult," Joseph said.

The door opened at their floor. Joseph looked at the woman gratefully, both a little in awe and a little ill at ease as well. "Thank you very much," he said in his warmest tone as some kind of parent-to-parent communication passed between them.

After the elevator door closed, as they walked toward their hotel room, Joseph added, "That was a very thoughtful lady, Joey."

A sadder memory came as Aunt Sarah died soon after their visit. His father had spoken about it very differently than Nana Beverly's death. He said Aunt Sarah had lived a long, fulfilling life and had always done what she wanted to do. He thought she would rest in peace.

Joseph was already downstairs making breakfast when Joey woke up. Rachel was still asleep upstairs with Bevy and the twins. They had a breakfast of "Daddy toast," which was thickly sliced white bread sautéed in a skillet with a little butter. It was good and satisfying comfort food.

"Look, son, there's a deer."

A doe about the size of a full-grown Great Dane strolled past the open kitchen window with no more caution than a typical suburban-ite strolling out to pick up the morning newspaper.

"Why isn't she afraid of us, Daddy?"

"It's not deer hunting season."

"So she doesn't need to hide from people?"

"Not this time of year."

"Does she need to hide from mountain lions?"

"Well, maybe. The park ranger said they get reports of mountain lions around here sometimes."

"Is that why Shane was so scared last night?" Just after dark, there had been a sound like a young woman screaming in terror in the woods. Shane, the family's Australian shepherd, who heretofore had a reputation for fearlessness, dropped to the ground as if paralyzed in fear. "Could that have been a mountain lion we heard last night?"

"Maybe. More likely a bobcat or a barn owl. Your mom thought it sounded like a bird of some kind."

"Or a person?"

"There shouldn't be any people around here making a noise like that."

The others had come downstairs.

"Who called late last night?" Rachel asked.

Joey heard his parents fall into a hushed conversation.

"It was Izzy Rosen. He called to tell us that he had a feeling about this place."

"I'm not sure what that means, coming from a superstitious mohel." Rachel chuckled doubtfully. "What kind of feeling? Some kind of vibe?"

"Sort of a vibe, at first. But he said he had confirmed it by re-searching the history of the land. Something about 'bad ground.' He was called away by an emergency but said he would get back to us." Joseph turned to the kids and gave them a reassuring smile. "Joey and Noah, put on your bathing suits. Mommy, Bevy and Teddy are going to get the car tire fixed. We need to get onto the river before it gets too hot."

7

The South Fork

"JOEY AND NOAH, PUT YOUR life preservers on," Joseph ordered.

There wasn't a cloud in the cobalt blue sky. The air was warm but not yet oppressively hot on this late July day. Joseph buckled their life preservers and pulled them tight across their chests.

"Do I have to wear this? I'll be in the boat." Joey tugged at the neck of his life preserver.

"What if you and Noah fall out of the canoe?"

"We'll hold on or you'll get us."

"What if you can't hold on and you all go in different directions and I can't get you?"

"But it's so hot with it on."

"I'll splash you with water. Do you know what to do if you get swept downstream?"

They had just watched the canoeing safety movie on the outdoor VCR and screen at the Adventure Raft Company.

After a moment of silence, Joseph answered his own question. "Put your feet in front of you."

"Why?" Noah asked.

"So you don't hit your head. Now, Joey, you're the oldest so if we turn over, you hold on to the boat. I'll probably have to get Noah first. But don't hold on to the downstream side of the boat because the current could push the boat on top of you. The best way to never turn over is to stay low in the boat."

"Why low?"

"It keeps your center of gravity low."

Joseph knew he sometimes used words that were too old for them, but he enjoyed teaching them what they meant. Still, sometimes people looked at him strangely and disapprovingly when he did this. But he had explained why. Between their father and mother and Rachel's parents reading to them, they knew lots of words for a 7- and a 4-year-old and often surprised people.

Joseph had clearly expected Joey to ask what center of gravity was, but before he could, Noah chimed in, "What's center of gravity?"

"For our purposes, it's the level of the boat that's stable. It means you want to keep low in a canoe, because the center of gravity is low and if you get above it, it will tip. Maybe even capsize. Joey, you sit in front and keep the paddle on your lap. I'll let you know what to do. Noah, sit here in the middle."

"What does capsize mean?" Joey asked quickly.

"It's a term for a boat turning over." Joseph dragged the wide-bottomed Olde Towne canoe with the children in it down the concrete boat ramp just below Bixler's dam. He walked them into the water, pointed the boat into the current and then sat down.

The river was constantly changing. This time of year, they could be paddling hard in deep, slow-moving water one minute, only to turn a bend and be dodging huge boulders and small but deceptive rapids with deep drops below them the next. Just below the rapids, the smooth, ancient rock bed of the river would sometimes catch the bottom of the boat and, with a horrible grating sound of metal on stone, the canoe would grind to a stop. Joseph would then step into the clear, cold water, trying to keep his footing on the slippery rocks as he dragged them to deeper water.

Sometimes the small rapids felt like a children's ride at a carnival. Joseph made the boys bring their paddles in and sit low, and Noah and Joey gleefully laughed and screamed in feigned fear. Joey kept pressing to paddle, but Joseph would only let him paddle a little because he was afraid they would get turned around or turn over.

Smallmouth bass jumped from the crystal clear water, shimmering in the sunlight. Canada geese and mallards floated in the calmer waters, while bald eagles and turkey buzzards soared above their heads. They passed around a Coke, cheese crackers and a packaged tuna-with-crackers combination they had picked up at the Adventure Raft Company. There was some breeze on the river, but between the tight-fitting life preservers and the afternoon July sun, it got a little hot.

As promised, Joseph used his paddle to splash the boys with the river water, and they shrieked with pleasure and shock from the cold water. Noah and Joey, who both loved to swim, kept pressing their father to let them get into the river.

Finally, they found a shallow place where the current wasn't so fast as to sweep them away.

"Let me lift you out," Joseph instructed, "so we don't capsize the canoe. And stay upstream of the boat, OK?"

The water was cold and exhilarating. The sunlight glistened on the moving clear water. Noah and Joey giggled and played and picked up shells.

Joseph watched his sons, smiling placidly, recollecting Joey's near-miraculous recovery from a life-threatening illness as an infant. *A far cry from the cardiac cripple Joey could have been. Thank you, Lord.*

The canoe shifted in the current on the rocky shelf and Joseph just managed to grab the bow rope. He broadened his stance to steady himself, but his right foot slid into a deep hole. He pivoted back and fell to his left knee, steadying himself. He wedged his boot against a rock and sprang back to his feet. The near miss sobered him. For a moment he recalled his vow. *Malach HaMavet, take my life, not the life of the child. Do what you will to me if it saves the life of our child.*

He looked warily at the boys. *Not now, Lord, please not now while they're standing in the middle of a river.*

The boys watched wide-eyed, mouths agape. Joey held his brother's hand tightly.

"Daddy, you're all wet. Are you OK?"

Joseph steadied his voice. "I am. I just slipped in one of those holes where we fish for the bass."

Then he lifted Noah and Joey back into the canoe and they went through clear deep water where they could see the bottom and weeds and an occasional smallmouth bass dart by. Joseph pointed out red-yellow-and-blue-shelled turtles sunning themselves on rocks.

"Be very quiet and we can drift up to them. Pull your paddles in."

They drifted soundlessly on the momentum of the boat to a calmer area near shore.

"Look," Joseph whispered.

"They're so big!" Joey exclaimed.

"How many do you see, Noah?"

"One, two, three, four, five…"

Joey chimed in, "Six, seven, eight."

The turtles noticed them now and two of the larger ones craned their necks, looking at them. Then they plopped into the water in quick succession.

"Do you think they're snapping turtles?" Joey asked with obvious trepidation.

Noah began to look frightened. "Don't get too close to the turtles, Daddy."

"They look like painted turtles to me," Joseph said, sorry he had worried Noah. "They aren't likely to bite you."

"Look," Joseph said, suddenly pointing to the southwest. "I think it's an eagle."

As the huge bird circled overhead, Joseph said, "See that white head? It looks bald. That's a bald eagle."

The eagle flew lower and circled again for a few minutes before the river current carried them around a bend and the eagle was out of sight.

"Look," Joseph continued. "See those birds on the water?"

Ahead was a mat of large birds with black-and-white heads floating in the water close to one another. "Do you know what they are?"

Joey guessed, "Geese."

"What kind of geese?"

When they drifted close enough to see their black-and-white heads, he responded triumphantly, "Canada geese!"

Very pleased, Joseph responded, "That's right. Let's see if we can drift close enough so that if we were hunting we could get an accurate shot." As they got within around 75 yards of the raft-looking floating flock, a hoarse, honking cry broke out from the closest sentry. It was quickly picked up by the flock into a cacophony as they rose almost as one and flew in a low, careening pattern to the northwest before rising briefly and then descending several river bends to the north.

"That was pretty good," Joseph said. "Maybe we'll float into them again downstream."

"Would we have been close enough to shoot them?" Joey asked.

"Just barely, with a shotgun. They have very thick feathers, like armor, and you have to use something almost like buckshot to get through it."

"Do we want to hunt the geese, Daddy?"

"I don't hunt geese anymore."

"Why?"

"I was hunting once in western Canada with Granddaddy and his buddy Mac Levy. I wounded the lead goose in a small flock. He was able to make a controlled descent to the ground. But what shocked us was that the whole flock went down with him and guarded him when we walked up, making a big ruckus with their honking. We had to shoot the leader because he was hurt bad and couldn't fly anymore, but the others wouldn't leave him, no matter what. They were more loyal than a lot of people, I think. When they marry, they stay loyal to their mate, too."

"I bet that goose had a wife and family he was thinking about," Joey added, thinking.

"Probably so."

"I feel bad for the goose."

"That's good, Joey. Not everybody can step in another person's or creature's shoes and see what it's like to be them. You just have to be able to step out again."

"What do you mean?"

"You want to be able to feel what other people feel in order to be sensitive to them, but you don't want to get so caught up in their experience that you can't step out of their shoes and be yourself again and take care of your own business."

"Is that what you told us a psychiatrist does, Daddy?"

"That's what any good listener does, but it can't be taught."

"Is that empathy, Daddy?"

"Very good, Joey. There are very few 7-year-olds who know that word."

Noah had a precocious sense of direction and seemed to know they were back just before they turned the bend in the river and saw the white placard with "7" marked on it nailed high in a tree. They let the current glide them into the inlet where they had left the car. Joseph got out in knee-deep water, dragged the canoe to the concrete launch and pulled it up until they could exit without getting wet. Then he turned the boat over to drain it, dragged it up the ramp and over to the grass to await its pickup by the raft company. Joseph loaded the car, watching the boys nervously while they frolicked in knee-high water at the end of the launch, collecting shells. Afraid the boys would step into the current and be swept downriver, he made them get out.

They stopped by the Adventure Raft Company to settle their bill. The Raft Company was just a few bends in the river from their summer house. The owners lived nearby and as children had played in the pastures and hills near the Jacobson vacation house.

"Did you ever get an odd feeling walking upriver near our place?" Joseph asked.

"Like someone was going to put a bullet through your head?" asked Lilly, one of the owners.

Noah and Joey hadn't brought dry clothes and were still wet from their swims in the river. Before Joseph could answer, Noah interjected, "Daddy, can we go? We're cold."

Joseph and Lilly spoke in hushed tones for a few moments, then Joseph turned to the other proprietors and told them he hoped he would see them over at the house for dinner or an ATV ride before too long.

After they got in the car, Joey asked, "Daddy, what's the weird place you were talking about?"

"I'm not sure what it is."

"Where is it?"

"Well, it's just a strange place not too far from our house. It must have an odd smell. Actually, Shane led me to it."

At that moment, a deer, almost white in color, leaped from the brush into their lane on the narrow road. Joseph pressed hard on the horn. The boys' attention was turned to the near miss of their swerving car and the thrill of seeing the oddly colored buck.

8

Wild Goose

Page County, Virginia
July 31, 1998

THE ONLY WAY TO GET from the Jacobson house to town or
back to Washington, DC, was by boat or south along Highway
264. On this narrow, curving road, with its constant switchbacks, vehicles going in both directions tended to slide into each other's lanes.
A small miscalculation could send a car careening down the bank
into the river or into a head-on collision with another car or truck.
Joseph played music from Frankie Laine's *Hell Bent for Leather* album
to babysit the boys so he could concentrate on the road:

> My heart knows what the wild goose knows,
> And I must go where the wild goose goes.
> Wild goose, brother goose, which is best?
> A wanderin' fool or a heart at rest?
> Tonight I heard the wild goose cry,
> Wingin' north in the lonely sky.
> Tried to sleep, but it weren't no use,
> 'Cause I am a brother to the old wild goose.

"Daddy, will you please change the song?"

"Why, son? I thought you loved this album."

"I just don't like this song. Can you please skip it?"

"What don't you like about that song?"

"I don't know," Joey said, irritated. "I just don't like it."

"What's your favorite?"

"Wanted Man."

Joey pushed the arrow on the CD player until it reached song 1:

> Bullet in my shoulder,
> And I'm always, always, always on the run.

Noah and Joey sang along happily. The song was from one of two albums that Joseph's mother had played for him and sung to him as a child. Songs like *High Noon, Rawhide* and *Cool Water* by Frankie Laine and *North to Alaska, Sink the Bismarck* and *The Battle of New Orleans* by Johnny Horton. Making her music part of his children's lives was another of the ways he tried to keep his mother's memory alive. It worked. But it was puzzling why *Wild Goose* was one song Joey couldn't stand. It seemed to aggravate and depress him. He could never explain why.

The drive home took the Jacobsons north on a narrow road between Massanutten Mountain and the river. The road was slow going because it was unpaved, bumpy and rough. Joseph was a cautious but aggressive driver. The 13-mile drive from downtown Luray to their house could easily take a half hour. A few hundred yards from the back edge of their property, an oddly shaped building was barely visible through the trees from the road.

"What's that, Daddy?" Joey pointed.

"It's called a mausoleum. It's like a family cemetery in a little building above the ground. Our former neighbor built it for his parents and brought their bodies over from Germany after they died."

"Why would he do that, Daddy?"

"His parents were far away. He probably wanted to feel close to them."

"Even after they died?"

"You don't necessarily stop feeling close to someone you love just because they're dead."

"Do the dead know you still love them?"

"I don't know. If they have a soul that lives in some way they might know."

"What happens to the soul? Can it come back?"

"Some religions think it goes to heaven. Some think it comes back in another form, such as another person or an animal. It's called reincarnation."

"What do we think, Daddy?"

"Officially, we Jews are vague about it. Our religion doesn't promise much that way."

"Were the bodies really stolen from the mausoleum?"

"Where did you hear that?"

"I heard the lady tell you that and that something bad was done to them, and that, later, somebody cut up animals and left them by the grave."

Joseph cut his son off quickly. "I don't know if any of it is true, but if it is, it means there are some very disturbed people involved."

"Is that why the old owner moved?"

"He never said that. He only said that his children wouldn't come out here to visit him anymore. He never said why."

They pulled up to the house and Joseph got out of the car quickly, relieved to end the discussion.

9

The ATV

THE LIGHT OUTSIDE WAS STARTING to flatten and a late-day breeze blew down the mountain through the screened windows when Joseph parked the car on the long, overgrown road that led to the house.

Joey raced into the house first. "Shane, are you OK?" He immediately checked to see if Shane had water and refilled his bowls. Then he gave the stump of a candy bar he had hidden in a napkin.

"Careful about giving the dog chocolate," Joseph said.

"I know. It's just a little."

Joseph answered the ringing phone. It was Rachel.

"Do you want to meet Teddy, Bevy and me here in town for pizza?"

"By the time we get there, you all will be done. Why don't you go ahead and eat there and bring us some take out? It's still very pretty here."

Joey and Noah surfed through satellite TV shows while Joseph cleaned and oiled his pistol. There were no cartoons on. Joseph liked to watch science shows with the kids. They flipped back and forth between a program about a cloned sheep named Dolly that got old before its time and a show about a famous general named MacArthur who started to shake when he got old. Joseph explained everything in as simple language as he could.

Joey felt very concerned for the general. "Whatever happened to him?"

"Old soldiers never die, they just fade away," Joseph said, winking.

Rachel came home with the pizza, tired from a long day of car problems.

"I had to go to three different garages before I could find someone to fix that tire. And each guy seemed more resentful than the one before. I don't know what's wrong with people around here. They don't seem too fond of city slickers."

Joseph, Noah and Joey sat on the flatbed trailer near where they had had target practice that afternoon and voraciously devoured the entire pizza.

Several minutes later, Rachel walked over. "I guess I'll go jogging. What are you going to do?" she asked Joseph.

"When you get back, I thought I might try to hook up the bushwhacker and cut the weeds down in the meadow by the river."

He was anxious to cut the grass because there were so many ticks that it wasn't a question of whether a tick got on the kids, but how many would. His family hadn't worried much about ticks when he was growing up, but he knew that around here they were more dangerous. Many were small and hard to see and can transmit Lyme disease. He thought the ticks would be less likely to get on the kids if the grass weren't so high. When they had shopped for mowers, most of the salesmen advised them that cutting the thick, sturdy weeds in the field would require a heavy machine towed from a tractor called a bushwhacker.

They didn't want a big tractor, so to drag the bushwhacker, they had bought an all-terrain vehicle, which was much larger, heavier and more powerful than the kind people rode for fun.

When Rachel returned from her jog, Joseph was sitting outside, watching the boys battle with sticks. Bevy sat at his side, drawing.

"I think it's too late to mow," Joseph said. "I had a great day with the boys while you had a horrible day fixing the car. Why don't you go for a ride on the ATV and enjoy yourself?"

The brothers were fascinated by everything about the ATV, including the mysterious revving sounds the engine made. Bevy was mortally afraid of it and couldn't stand the sound of the engine.

Bevy suddenly looked uncomfortable as if she felt something in the pit of her stomach. It was still afternoon, but an unexpectedly cool breeze, the kind that usually blew just as the sun dropped over the horizon, shook the leaves of the tulip tree above their heads. In the late-afternoon sunshine, the wind cast a melody of fluttering heart-shaped shadows. The remaining light of the day seemed to be in a tug-of-war between the sunlit, green river meadows teeming with life below them and the dark, unfathomable national forest above them where they always feared getting lost.

Something struck Joseph in a funny way as well. His countenance fell a shade darker. If he had been able to see himself, he would have seen his shoulders rise subtly, his stance widen and his hands rise to his chest as if preparing to defend himself. Then he seemed to catch himself. He looked puzzled for a moment and then turned to Bevy and smiled, trying to recapture the lightness and mirth of the day.

"Daddy, can we can go back to the house and read a story?" Bevy pleaded. Joseph took her hand and they entered the house.

Rachel climbed aboard the ATV and turned the key. The engine roared to life. The boys walked alongside the ATV. When they got to the river, Shane and the children played with their Frisbee and then hide-and-seek in the tall grass of the meadow. A year ago, Joey had used a twig to rouse brightly colored june bugs crawling in the soil near the riverbank while his father made the property owner an offer. Now the bugs were dead.

The riverbank was a wooded cliff dropping steeply to a rocky bottom. The neighbors had warned the Jacobsons not to bring anything heavy too close because the bank sometimes collapsed. Shane sniffed around the animal slides and burrows in the mud, climbing up and down the nearly vertical face, which was held together by tough low shrubs. A fallen oak tree lay just off shore. Shadowy cigar-shaped fish with flat heads lolled in the shallow water around the branches, looking huge.

"Look." Rachel pointed. "I think those are catfish or gar."

"Can we eat them?" Teddy asked.

"Some people eat the catfish. I think the gar are too bony."

Just to the right of their land, a backhoe had cut a more gradual ramp down to the water. It was overgrown but made a gentle descent to the gravelly shore where the boys took off their shoes and stepped into the cold water. A few feet from shore, the current was strong enough to sweep them away. The boys threw big reddish rocks out into the current.

"Boys! Stop that. The more stones you take out of the side of the bank, the weaker it gets. Come here. I'll show you how to skip rocks. I'm a rock-skipping champion, you know."

Rachel gathered some small flat rocks and handed a few to each boy. "You've got to keep your arm parallel to the ground, like this."

Joey imitated her movement, while Teddy and Noah contorted their arms in odd motions. They began wrestling with each other.

"Teddy. Noah. Watch," Rachel said. She flicked a stone across the river and they all watched it bounce, counting each hop. The brothers each got to throw until they too got several bounces.

Along the bank, there were roots and dead tree trunks that looked people-like and spooky in the dimming light. Rachel identified some of the plants as mandrakes. There were remnants of a campfire in the meadow near the bank. Someone had piled up stones there.

"You know," Rachel said, "these rocks may have been put here on purpose. I think it's a cairn. It's part of someone's religion."

The boys looked at her quizzically but were distracted as they passed a nearly 4-foot black snake in a tree on the riverbank. They stopped to look. It looked back at them too. It wasn't afraid but it didn't attack. They passed a very large hole in the ground with big pile of brown dirt in front of it.

"Hey, that's a badger's den, I think. Remember when we saw that badger earlier?" Rachel asked.

"Yeah," Joey chimed in. "Daddy thought it might get Shane."

They came across another gentle ramp dug through the bank that provided easy access to the river. Nearby, the honey locust trees were covered with thorns big enough for them to hang their towels on when they had swam earlier in the summer. On a path freshly trampled down through the weeds leading away from the campfire site, they came across the remains of an otter with a spine and no skin. It had been cut in two across the middle. You could see both halves. The bottom part looked like it was half-alive because it had been left standing on its hind legs.

"Yuck," Noah grimaced.

"What did that, Mommy?" Joey asked.

"I don't know. It could have been an animal, I suppose. I don't know why a person would cut an animal in half like that and leave it. It's kind of creepy." *Probably the same people who cut up those animals at the mausoleum*, she thought.

On the edge of the green meadow where it abutted the woods, a decaying wooden deer stand sagged under the branches of a huge oak tree, with its corrugated metal roof on the forest floor 12 feet below. As they approached, a small flock of wild turkeys, mostly hens and poults, melted into the forest. From the deer stand, a hunter could watch broad expanses of meadow, deer paths leading from the hilly national forest to the river, and a small clearing in the woods that filled with pulpy green horse apples in the fall.

Joey and his father had hunted from that deer stand last Thanksgiving Day, Rachel recalled. Joey had been very frightened of climbing the rickety, half-rotten slats nailed into the tree that made a sort of ladder. They had seen deer creeping down the deer paths at dusk and a white deer gallop across the upper field just at dark. Joseph said that the previous owner had told him that the deer was believed to be a spirit and the hunters had agreed among themselves not to shoot it. Joseph had thought the ticks wouldn't be active on Thanksgiving Day because the temperature hovered around freezing but one got on him anyway. He tried with no success to suffocate it with Vaseline and drown it in whiskey. It wouldn't let go. Finally, he pulled it off, but the jaws stayed in. They looked like little black tubes under the magnifying glass. He had to take them out with tweezers. They were hard, he said, like porcelain.

10

Twilight

THE BOYS WALKED THROUGH THE woods and fields in the clear late-summer twilight, with Rachel and Joey lighting the way with the bright halogen headlight of the ATV. Shane trotted along behind them, dashing off occasionally to chase whatever creature crossed their path. They meandered, laughing and singing *Down by the Bay*, silly and dizzyingly high from sweet chocolate ice cream they ate from cones Rachel had pulled out of a small cooler. They could just make out the glow of fireflies in the treetops as they came out of the woods into the fields.

"Look at that moon!" Rachel exclaimed. "That's the second full moon this month. That's pretty rare. It's called a blue moon when that happens." She began to croon, "Bluuuue moon, I saw you standing alone…"

As they turned the ATV toward home, a gray rabbit with a white tail froze in front of them, staring into the headlights. They stopped, the rabbit tensed. Rachel waited, but the rabbit didn't move.

"Joey, get off for a minute so I can turn around. We don't want to bother that bunny." Rachel laughed. "Boys, stay there."

She backed up and shifted back into neutral. The twins stood by the side. Joey climbed back on, behind his mother. He put his arms around Rachel's belly and held very tight, as he had been told. She stepped on the brake and shifted into forward gear.

Shane's ears pricked up and he sniffed the air, growling softly. Suddenly, the sound of the engine revving became very high pitched, like a racecar about to leave the starting gate. They pitched forward.

Rachel squeezed the brakes. Nothing happened. Unable to stop, Rachel tried to turn onto the dirt road at the bottom of the hill to avoid the steep embankment, but they were going too fast to turn. They sped across the road as if the throttle were stuck and there were no brakes. With no other choice, Rachel did her best to negotiate the shrub-covered embankment with the rugged off-road vehicle speeding out of control. Abruptly, they stopped as if they had hit an invisible brick wall.

The ATV, weighing over a quarter of a ton, turned and flipped 180 degrees in the air. Joey flew through the air over Rachel's head, his arms in front of him.

There was a cry of surprise from Rachel when the ATV left the ground and then a prolonged sound of agony, "aighhhhhh," like all the air was being pressed out of her. She was upside down, with all her weight on her neck and the ATV's weight on top of her. She could speak only with great effort. She couldn't feel her arms or legs. The horrific smell of cooking flesh wafted over as the overheated engine burned a fist-sized hole in her left leg.

Joey was pinned under the ATV, which rested upside down with its fulcrum on Rachel's back a few feet above him and the remainder of its weight concentrated downhill on his back. Face down, with his feet uphill, only his head and neck protruded from the underside of the metal demon.

Noah ran over. "Mommy, are you OK?"

Rachel's voice sounded very faint.

"Go get Daddy. Hurry."

"Joey, are you OK?" Teddy asked, afraid to look at his brother.

"Yes," Joey managed to say in a weak voice.

Noah set out alone, barefoot in the late dusk, to find the house. Rachel worried he would get lost, and they'd often seen bears in the woods, especially after dusk. The route was convoluted. There were forks in the road and potential wrong turns. The house was hidden in the trees and he had never before been alone in the woods.

On the steep hillside, the ATV, unstable, resting on its human cargo, rocked and swiveled as if uncertain how to do the most harm. Ultimately, it settled with most of its 569 pounds concentrated on the 1–inch diameter back rim of the luggage rack squarely across the back of Joey's head where it met his neck. Now, like the fist of the Angel of Death correcting the imprecision of the first blow, the ATV fractured the base of Joey's spine and began to suffocate him from its weight. The machine pressed his face squarely into the matted grassy, fertile black soil, filling his mouth and nostrils with fresh scents of life even as his breath was choked away. The weight of the ATV prevented Joey from turning his head to gasp for air. Just enough air passed through the thick mat of weeds and the soft, deep humus to sustain his life.

"Joey, speak to me," Rachel cried out.

Some minutes later, Joseph arrived, aghast beyond words when he saw Rachel.

"Rachel, my God. Are you all right?"

She answered calmly, "I can't feel below my neck."

"Can you breathe OK?"

"Yes."

"If you can talk, you can breathe, thank God. We need to get you out of here before you go into shock. I'm going to roll this thing off you." *Please, God, give me the strength.*

"First check on Joey."

"Where is he?"

"He's down there, I think."

Joseph's voice suddenly changed tone and rose in great alarm. "Is he OK?"

"I don't think so."

Joseph rushed through the thick shrubs. When he saw the full weight of the four wheeler resting on the back of Joey's neck, he cried out, shock and angst radiating from the depths of his being. His voice echoed through the forest. "Nooo! Noooo! Nooooo!"

It took a few moments, but Joseph regained his composure. He felt the pulse in his son's neck, checked for breathing and touched Joey's skin. "He's still alive!"

Joseph climbed up to Rachel. "I'm not sure I can move the ATV without it rolling back and injuring you or Joey even worse. The cell phones aren't working here. I've got to go to the house to call for help."

I'm a physician. I've dealt with emergencies all my life. Stay calm, one thing at a time. Rachel, thank God, seems stable. Keep them alive until the helicopter gets here. He sprinted the path back to the house and searched desperately for the cordless phone.

"My wife and son have been in an ATV accident. We're at 500 Stampler Farm Lane. They need to be airlifted."

"Sir, please calm down. We'll send an ambulance out. What is their condition?"

"An ATV my wife was driving flipped. It's on top of them and crushing my wife and son."

"All right, sir. We've got your location. We're sending an ambulance."

Clutching the phone, Joseph shouted at the top of his lungs to the 911 operator, "An ambulance will be too late! You've got to get a helicopter out here or a woman and a child are going to die and you'll be responsible for their deaths!"

"Sir, please calm down. An ambulance is on its way."

"We need a helicopter, goddamnit!"

Joseph rushed through the woods back to the accident scene. His heart felt like a hammer trying to smash through his chest. *How am I going to get that thing off them without it rolling back and finishing them off?*

Even upside down, with over 500 pounds resting on her broken neck, Rachel calmly gave advice on how to get the four wheeler off without it rolling back on and causing further injury. "Use the edge as a fulcrum."

If I lift it and it rolls back, they're both dead. He tested the weight of the ATV. It didn't budge.

"Pretend you're home pumping iron," Rachel said in a weak voice.

Joseph could see she was fading. *There's not much time. Now or never. One, two, three, lift!*

Somehow, Joseph lifted it off and rolled it to the side. Rachel was alert and had a strong pulse. He blew a long sigh and nuzzled her cheek. "Everything's going to be OK. The ambulance is on its way from Luray and a helicopter is en route from Charlottesville."

He felt for his son's breath. It was very shallow. Joey's neck lay askew. A straw-colored liquid dripped from the base of his skull. Joseph's eyes widened in horror. He struggled not to panic. He started breathing into Joey's mouth but knew it was not enough. *Joey, Joey, my son, my boy, my love. If only I could give you my life.*

11

Joey

WHEN THE BRAIN IS SHORT of oxygen, the non-essential parts, the so-called higher functions, shut down first in order to preserve the essential parts. The process proceeds from the frontal lobes and cortex down, like peeling an onion, one layer at a time. As consciousness wanes, the brain unleashes the preconscious, then subconscious layers of the mind. Memories come forth and are juxtaposed into elaborate dream-like sequences, marching out as if freed from their dungeons into the light of day. Eventually, only the deeper and more essential parts of the brain remain fueled. Like a broiler oven where the gas (in this case, oxygen) is gradually reduced until all that is left is the tiny blue pilot, capable of relighting the oven when the gas is turned on. As the flame diminishes, the dreams become fragmented and simpler until finally life clings as a dull glow of cerebral activity. The lights can survive and come back on if the fuel is resupplied soon enough, the brain function returning in the reverse order that it turned off.

Joey felt the life draining from his body, a sensation of slowly winding down. His mommy and daddy's voices drifted further and further away. Fluid poured into his sinuses and windpipe from his injuries. The sensation was like drowning. He hovered near consciousness, passed out and woke up again. Far away, as if from the bottom of a well, he heard men with heavy rural Virginia accents shouting to one another. His father's voice, still ringing with the confidence and authority of a physician, gave orders: "Suction him, give him oxygen, hurry!"

He felt something like a vacuum cleaner sucking fluid from his nose. It made a sound like the dentist's office. Then cold oxygen blew in. He felt a burst of energy. He couldn't feel his legs and arms. He tried to move them but they seemed disconnected from his brain. He heard the whirr of a generator. A floodlight switched on. He tried to open his eyes but could not. For a few moments, he felt as if he were floating in an irresistibly delicious somnolence. The EMTs flipped him upright and the clear, red-hued fluid that leaked from his injuries no longer drained. The drowning sensation returned. Then he passed out.

In a dream he awoke to the cacophonous sounds of children frolicking in a swimming pool on a blindingly sunny day. The ropes and buoys that marked off the cobalt blue 12-foot-deep area under the high diving boards had been removed for a drown-proofing course. With a jovial smile, the pleasantly overweight coach, his stomach protruding like a huge gourd over his skimpy swimsuit, explained in the manner of a drill sergeant, "To pass the final exam, you must survive in the deep water for fifteen minutes with both your arms and legs tied. This will simulate staying afloat with a serious injury."

A fawn-like junior high school girl dressed in a white uniform gently bound Joey's hands and feet together with soft, thick plastic-covered wire. The sun was very bright and the glare on the water made Joey squint. Things went OK in the shallow water where he could easily hop pogo stick-like from the floor of the pool back up to the surface. He was intrigued by the contrast between the bright, noisy bedlam above the surface and the smooth, cool, muffled world underneath. But the pool was too crowded for this exercise to occur safely. The next time he broke the surface, he heard someone shout, "Marco!" Several children's voices nearby answered, "Polo!" The Marco sound came closer. Someone bumped him hard from behind. He drifted into deeper water. It seemed to take forever before his bound ankles touched the bottom. He coiled his legs and sprung hard for the surface but fell short of breaking through. He drifted slowly downward. The numbed silence was punctuated only by the occasional muffled crashing or whooshing sound of a diver.

Joey settled to the bottom and crouched, telling himself, *Don't thrash, conserve energy, make the last breath last.* He tried to slip his hands loose. They were bound behind his back. No success. He tried to free his ankles. No luck. He was becoming hungry, very hungry for air. A wave of panic electrified his body. He was determined not to breathe in water. Then he began to feel calm. It dawned on him that he had done everything he could do to save himself. It was out of his hands. Someone would realize he was missing and carry him to the surface. But would it be too late?

Joey pondered how he could conserve energy and increase his chances of survival. His father had once told him that, during meditation, everything in the body slowed down, like being in a refrigerator. He tried to imagine that his father and he were in his room, upstairs, where it was quiet. He imagined that they were sitting on his bed, side by side, their backs propped straight against the wall.

"Will you teach me to meditate, Daddy?"

"You need a mantra."

"What's a mantra?" Joey asked, scooting closer to his father.

"It's a word sometimes taken from ancient languages that helps your mind leave the things you usually think about so your brain and body can rest. Your heart rate and metabolism slow down so you use less energy, almost like hibernation. Your granddaddy, uncle and

I use it so we don't have to take so much blood pressure medicine. Most of the time, you just rest and come out of it feeling refreshed. But sometimes it puts the top of your brain to sleep, I think, so that memories come out just like they were happening again. Other times, you can imagine what your future might be like just as vividly as if it was real. Some religious people think that if they get really good at it, their spirit can get closer to God for a while. Once, when you were a baby and very sick, Mommy and I took you to all the best doctors, but the sickness kept coming back. I'm not very religious, but once I tried to use meditation to help me feel connected to heaven when I prayed for you."

"What happened?"

His father seemed lost in thought for a moment. "You got better much faster than anyone expected. Most people would say that you would have gotten better from the medicines with or without the praying."

Joey looked in his father's eyes. "What do you think, Daddy?"

"I don't know, son," he said, shaking his head.

"Will you teach me to meditate now?"

"Here is your mantra." His father whispered a one-syllable word from another language. Joey didn't know what the word meant, but he liked the sound it made.

"Close your eyes, straighten your back and let your mind settle on this word. If your mind wanders, gently bring it back to the word. Relax your muscles. Listen to your breathing, then let it slow down. Sometimes my breathing stops for a moment when I meditate and I wake up gasping for air. That just means you really slowed down a lot."

"OK, Daddy, I'm going to start now. You meditate too and let me know when it's time to stop."

After a long while, his father spoke. "Son, it's almost dark outside. I think we must have fallen asleep. It's time to get up." His father shook him gently. "Joey, wake up. Son, are you OK?" His father's voice was beginning to show concern. He put his ear to Joey's mouth and nose and listened to his shallow breathing.

Joseph's voice rose in alarm: "Son, are you OK? Joey!"

Joey heard his father's voice in the distance, but he couldn't move or open his eyes. He felt very, very cold.

Far away, he heard his father's voice as he had never heard it. "Nooooo!"

But Joey was already lost in the memory of a happier time. It had been cold then too.

12

Flashback — First Hunt

"DAAAAADDY," HE SAID, DRAWING OUT the A's in the way that always got his father's attention, "I'm cold."

After a long day of hunting pheasant in a blizzard, it was finally bedtime. An icy wind howled outside. Their little cabin at a hunting ranch outside of Pierre, South Dakota, had thin plywood walls with no sign of insulation. The small windows were opaque with frost. The heat from the tiny gas heater's pitiful blue flame was virtually undetectable a few feet away. His flimsy metal-frame bed with its thin mattress was little more than a cot.

"Why are we sleeping in here, Daddy?"

"Well, we get to be by ourselves, and you don't have to hear the TV go all night or the other hunters snore."

Joey had a feeling that some of the other hunters hadn't been too keen about having a 6-year-old around, but he sensed that his father would be happier if he accepted his explanation. So he changed the subject to what was really on his mind.

"What was Mac talking about at supper tonight?"

His father had seemed a little uneasy about the conversation that broke out after the hunters sat down to dinner following several rounds of "very expensive whiskey."

"Do you mean the Klan? The men in white hoods in Mississippi?"

"Yes, Daddy. What made them so mean?"

Joseph looked lost in thought for a moment, as he often did when Joey asked him a question about his childhood. "Your grandmother thought that they were unhappy with their lives and wanted to blame other people."

"Why did they pick on us?" Joey turned off his Game Boy so as not to be distracted.

Joseph sighed. "We were Jews and some of us tried to help black people. So they exploded bombs at our Temple in Jackson and at Aunt Sarah and Aunt Ida's Temple in Meridian and at Rabbi Nussbaum's house to try to scare us."

"Did the police get them?"

Joseph clinched his teeth and shook his head slowly before speaking. "In some cases, they were the police. In other cases, the police were sympathetic to them. If you managed to find a good policeman who would catch them, then the judges or the juries in Mississippi would let them go."

"And Mac Levy fought them?" Joseph asked expectantly, knowing the answer from the earlier dinner conversation.

"Mac and others. He told us one day in Sunday school that when the Klan bombed our synagogue he took it personally, just like someone had bombed his own house. Not everybody at the Temple wanted us to fight back, so he had to explain it. They got up on the synagogue roof with guns and they worked with the FBI to buy informers and set ambushes."

"Did you fight them?" Joey asked, excitedly.

"I was too little, but I slept with a shotgun under my bed after that. I had the bedroom next to the front door and it made me feel better."

"Should I sleep with a gun under my bed?"

64

"No, Joey. There are no men in white hoods where we live now."

"Why does Mac Levy think we need a radiation detector?"

"I thought you were playing with your Game Boy when Mac said that. Mac thinks a different kind of bad man might try to blow up Washington someday. But we live out in McLean. It would take an awful big bomb to get to us. That's the last thing you need to worry about."

His father quickly reached up and turned off the lamp as if to say, "that's enough."

Joey knew Mac had been drinking a lot of whiskey when he said that. Besides, it had been a very long day, so he didn't mind.

"I'm tired now," he said, pulling up the covers. "Will you lay down with me?"

His father pulled off his boots and lay down the best he could on the edge of the narrow cot, sprawling over the edge with one foot on the floor.

"I'm cold," Joey said and shivered.

"I think the heater is as high as it will go. Here's another blanket. I'll stay in bed with you to keep you warm."

"I love you, Daddy," Joey said, drifting toward sleep.

"I love you, Joey. Dream of the Hunt."

The only part of the hunt Joey didn't like was the freezing, cold, dark pit in the mud they called a duck blind. Granddaddy was the best duck caller, and when the spotter saw the ducks, they flipped off the roof, stood up and shot. Of course, Joey didn't have a shotgun, but his daddy let him shoot the BB gun. Mac Levy said the ducks' feathers were like armor, but if it hit just exactly in the right part of his head, the duck might drop. Otherwise, the duck blind was very boring for Joey, even with all of the books and games that his father and grandfather brought to keep him quiet.

Keeping quiet and keeping his head down were the hardest

parts. There was a man from Mississippi with eyes that went in different directions who always blamed Joey if the ducks flew the other way. On the other hand, Granddaddy and Mac Levy were always jovial, told stories and liked to teach things like how to blow a duck call. Joey dreaded the loud sound when the guns went off. Even with the plugs in his ears and muffs, the sharp crack of the shotguns from close-up explosions made him want to cry. His hunting hat, goggles and outside ear protection were too big and were always cockeyed or falling off.

He loved to watch the hunting hounds, especially the black Labradors, leap into the freezing water and swim after the downed birds. The guides seemed to really love their dogs. They talked to them and pampered them as long as the dogs did what they were supposed to. They were very harsh if the dog bit up the bird or went the wrong way.

One morning, a couple of hours after sunup, Joey just couldn't take being quiet in the cold and mud any longer, so he and his father left the blind early. Everyone seemed to understand except the ill-tempered man from Mississippi, who practically said "good riddance." Joseph and Joey walked along the muddy Missouri River, shooting at the wintry remains of big sunflowers with the BB gun and fishing to no avail in a nearly frozen pond.

They had hot soup and sandwiches for lunch. There were no bathtubs, so his father gave him his first shower to clean off the mud and warm up. His father put a rag over Joey's eyes, but the shampoo still stung and made him cry. But the hot shower felt great to Joey and chased away the last chilly memories of the duck blind and the nasty man with the darting eyes.

After they got home, when people saw the pictures, they would say to his father, "Why didn't you buy him some hunting clothes that fit? That vest swallows him!"

"They don't make them for 6-year-olds," his father would say.

13

Night

Page County, Virginia
July 31, 1998

THE SHERIFF TURNED TO JOSEPH. "Were there other chu'llen?" he asked in a booming voice.

Joseph shuttled between Rachel and Joey a few yards apart on the hillside. "Yes. The boys are OK, just shook up. My daughter was with me." Joseph pointed toward the SUV, where Bevy had been left in charge of her brothers. The children peered through the window as the tall, heavy officer, service revolver and billy club hanging from his belt, swaggered toward them. He opened the door abruptly, startling the children.

"You guys OK in there?"

Teddy studied the man's appearance.

"We're OK." His voice was high and shaky.

The officer shined his flashlight in Noah's face. Noah squinted in the light.

"I'm OK too," he piped in.

The sheriff shined the light on Bevy next. "And you were with your daddy?"

Bevy nodded, then turned her head away defiantly.

The lawman's voice softened. "Y'all come out of there and get in my car, OK? I have some candy. These are the ones my daughter likes."

In his hand were various brightly colored hard candies wrapped in cellophane. Noah and Teddy picked their favorite colors, blue and green

"Thank you," they said politely, nearly in unison. The sheriff seemed taken aback for a moment by their manners.

"And you, honey?" He held out the candy toward Bevy.

"No thank you," she said, clenching her jaw, looking down.

"What's your name?" Noah asked.

"Samael," the sheriff answered.

"Do you mean Samuel?" Bevy asked.

"No, it's Samael. S-a-m-a-e-l," he answered.

Samael turned to Joseph. "I need to ask your wife some questions about the accident."

"She has a broken neck and can barely breathe. She may lose her son. She could go into shock at any time. Don't you think your questions can wait?"

The sheriff glared at Joseph, then gave a slight nod.

The police set up floodlights and, after the ambulance arrived, Joseph ordered the emergency workers to give Joey oxygen and suction him nasally. Joey's color then improved. The emergency workers fastened him onto a board and flipped him. They attached EKG leads to his chest. Joseph was certain he saw a regular heart rhythm.

He ran to Rachel. "He's alive!"

The EMTs took Joey into the ambulance, stopped the suctioning and oxygen and shut the door.

Joseph roared, "What on God's earth are you doing?"

He tried the door of the ambulance. The sheriff, his hand on his revolver, blocked his way.

"You need to step back, sir. You can't go into that ambulance. If you don't step back, I'm gonna have to handcuff you."

"For God's sake, I'm his father."

Samael rested his hand ostentatiously on his gun.

"I'm a doctor!"

"I don't know what you are, sir. The EMTs are with your son. You need to step back. I told you already, I'll handcuff you if you try to get into that ambulance again."

Joseph sneaked a glance at the sheriff's gun, calculating whether he could grab it and get to his son. The sheriff noticed and took a step back. Joseph thought to himself, *The others will blow me to pieces and then what will happen to Rachel and the other kids?*

Joseph saw Shane crouched low behind the policeman, body tensed as if ready to spring. *Easy,* he mimed with his hand.

In the ambulance, without oxygen, the rosy color of Joey's skin gave way to ashen gray. Small hemorrhages appeared on his skin and the whites of his eyes like tiny red snowflakes. A few flurries at first, then coalescing as it snowed harder. His heart pumped just enough blood to feed his heart and the unconscious centers of the brain necessary to sustain life and to dream.

"Daddy, can we go to the house now?"

"Not quite yet, son. Soon. It's almost dark."

"I want to go inside where Mommy is."

"Feel the wind, Joey. It's starting to blow. It comes up just at dusk. The temperature just dropped a little. Did you feel it?"

"I'm getting cold, Daddy, very cold. Can we go inside soon? I want to see Mommy and Bevy."

"Look, Joey. Look at the sky. See the colors? What colors do you see?"

"I see pink, purple, white and blue."

"Do you see that trail of white in the sky? Do you know what that's from?"

"An airplane?"

"Good. What kind of airplane?"

"I don't know, Daddy. Can we go inside soon?"

"It's from a jet. It's called a contrail. It contains water vapor from the engine."

There was a huge plop sound in the pond.

Joey, alarmed, whispered, "What was that?"

"Maybe one of those bass jumping."

There was a high-pitched, sweet sound like a small bird. Then another answered, then a third, then a chorus struck up of high-pitched, sweet chirping sounds. The cicadas joined next in a machine-like crescendo. It was hard to tell where it came from.

"Do you know what that's called?"

"Peeper frogs!"

"And the other sound?"

"Cicadas."

"That's right. Do you know why they sing?"

"They're looking for a wife?"

"That's part of it, and, for the cicadas, it scares off the birds. You're a very good listener, Joey."

Now they listened to the honking of two very large birds with black necks and white cheeks.

"What's that bird?"

"Geese!"

"What kind of geese?"

"Canada geese!"

"That's right. And why don't we hunt them?"

"They're more advanced than people!"

"More loyal than some people. Maybe most people." His father smiled.

Two swallows careened through the air over the pond, searching for bugs. The moon rose, a three-quarter orange orb, its tips pointing down, rising over the open field.

"What kind of moon is that?"

"Oh, umm, I know. A dry moon!"

"That's right. Why dry though?"

"Because the water would spill out? It's upside down!"

There were bats that regularly came out and hunted bugs at dusk. His father said they had seen them the night they bought the house. They twisted and turned, coming low at times, almost menacingly, but never close enough to touch them.

"They're good. They catch the bugs?" Joey queried. "They only eat bugs?"

"That's right, but a high enough percent have rabies that you need to stay away from them. They can even pass on rabies from their poop."

The sly-looking, eerie figure of a fox, eyes yellow, squinting, silver hair bristling from his neck and hind quarters, emerged from the edge of the woods a few feet from them. It sniffed the ground, unaware of them. It came unpleasantly close before it noticed them. Then, to Joey's surprise, it sat on its haunches and peered at him silently. Joey thought of Brer Rabbit and Brer Fox. A moment's delight and amusement quickly sobered into fear as he recalled his schoolteacher, Ms. Richard's, warnings of rabies in overly friendly animals.

"Daddy, is it supposed to do that?"

No answer.

"Daddy, why isn't the fox afraid of us?"

No answer.

It was dark now, very dark. Where was the moon? He couldn't see his daddy. Suddenly, he felt terror.

"Daddy, Daddy!" he shouted as loudly as he could. Nothing came out. He tried to leap up and run toward the lights of the house. "Why can't I move?"

Rapidly, the terror of feeling trapped away from his parents and brothers and sister overtook him, rising to panic. The wind was picking up. It was getting colder fast, too fast for a summer evening. Something was definitely wrong. He recalled that, sometimes, as he awoke from a nap, for a few terrifying moments, he would lie half-awake, half in a dream, unable to move any part of his body. It felt like that now, but he wasn't dreaming and it wouldn't go away. It was dark, pitch-black. Where was the moon? He called again for his father. There was no answer. He felt fear growing in him. He tried to stand and run, but he couldn't move. He wanted to scream.

Through the shadows, he saw his father standing over the old campfire site down by the pond at the McLean house. The fire had burned very low. As his father bent over him and cut one of the last glowing embers from the fire, Joey felt a faint pinch on one ear, then the other. Then he saw only black.

Joey felt his grandmother, Nana Beverly, tucking in the sheets under him. He knew it was Nana Beverly from the way his father had described her touch. The sheets were cool and smooth. She tucked them around him meticulously, lovingly drawing it out as only a doting grandmother could. He felt her tears falling on his face. She had not expected to see him so soon. She washed Joey's body carefully with a warm rag and dressed him in white pajamas. It was dark, but Joey thought he could make out her outline in white too.

"Gay schlafen," she said, smiling at him with an expression of infinite love and pity.

A man with a very deep Virginia accent shouted into a satellite phone with the authority of one authorized to make life-and-death decisions, "Get me Pegasus!"

At approximately 9:20 p.m. EDT on July 31, there were no other traumas requesting air transport to Charlottesville.

"We've called a medevac helicopter," the man with the accent old Rachel. "The same one that rescued Christopher Reeve when he had his horse accident. You know, Superman? It's got night vision. Can go 177 miles per hour. You'll be in Charlottesville in no time."

There was a roaring sound. It was the wind. It was very strong. Rachel could feel it on her face. Dust and leaves were blowing. It sounded like the helicopter. Men on the ground and in the aircraft shouted to one another by walkie-talkie. Rachel couldn't feel or move her limbs but knew she was strapped to a long board. Two medics hopped off the helicopter and lifted the gurney into the helicopter.

"We're taking you to University of Virginia Hospital Center," one said gently.

On board, she lay face up, her neck immobilized by a fat do-nut-like collar. "You're headed to the best place," the same medic continued. "They'll give you steroids. Young, healthy people like you have excellent recovery outcomes when they're treated early."

"Some would dispute that I'm young," Rachel quipped.

The medic spoke into the radio. "We have a 39-year-old female with traumatic neck injury at the level of C3. She is conscious and her vital signs are stable."

Rachel's tall, athletic figure seemed to have shrunk. The clear hazel eyes that had shone and laughed under her bangs only hours ago were red now, barely visible through swollen lids. Her shoulder-length brown hair was strewn across her face. *Two hours ago, I was jogging and eating ice cream with happy, bubbly children. Now my oldest son, my treasure, Joey, may be dead, and I may spend the rest of my life a quadriplegic. How can I be a mother like that?* She closed her eyes and tried to squeeze back the tears, but they ran down her cheeks. Then they came in torrents. After a few minutes, she swallowed hard, set her jaw and said to herself firmly, *I still have my mind.*

The sheriff allowed Joseph to board. He gently brushed her hair aside and kissed her tenderly on the lips. "Rachel, my love, my doll,

I'm so sorry." She burst into tears again. He gently dabbed the moisture from her cheeks and took her hand, now cool and limp. "They got here in time. You're going to get better."

In a faint voice, she said, "What about Joey? Is it too late for him?"

Joseph took her hand, put his mouth close to her ear and whispered. Rachel's eyes widened, first in disbelief, then in hope. In the strongest voice she could muster, she said, "May God be with you. Whatever it takes, bring Joey back."

Part

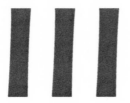

Born Again

14

Can the Soul Be Cloned?

Old Town, Czech Republic
December 31, 1999

IN A SIDEWALK CAFÉ UNDERNEATH the astrological clock in the old quarter of Prague, Joseph and Rachel sat with the brilliant but eccentric Czech scientist.

"You were not chosen because you can get the money. In a situation like this, everyone finds the money somehow. In order to maintain secrecy and quality – and now you know all the problems we have to overcome – we can only take a very few. The money some people are willing to pay is beyond anything you could ever raise or dream of raising. We are not here merely because we're greedy. There are causes we support with the proceeds. But there is another reason that your case was selected. All of us are scientists. One of us is also a rabbi. He became interested in your case because it is his understanding that Joey's death was a mistake, therefore a divine injustice. He thinks that, in this case, the divine may assist in righting the mistake – that is, in producing a perfect embryo despite all the problems, an embryo where the spirit is transferred."

"How did he know about us?"

"Do you remember the mohel who circumcised your son?"

"Yes, of course. We heard from him after the accident."

"He was distraught because he failed in his duty to warn you."

"To warn us about what?"

"There is an old Ashkenazi legend. Some might call it an old wives' tale. Not to name after the living if the name is the same. You and your son were Joseph. The mohel should have warned you that Malach HaMavet, the Angel of Death, might take the wrong Joseph by mistake."

Joseph thought for a moment. His grandmother, Fanny, who had grown up in Russia in a shtetl near Smolensk, had warned him. There had been pogroms. The family had had to hide in the woods many times. Once, great-grandfather had had to ransom Fanny's sister, Aunt Alice, when the Cossacks tied her up and were going to rape her. For safety, Fanny, who was considered a great beauty, was sent to Nashville to live with cousins. She had always been nervous. Joseph had not taken her warning about naming after the living seriously. *The old woman may have been right*, he thought.

Then Joseph recalled that the original plan on the day of the accident had been for him to ride the ATV. Inexplicably, he had changed his mind at the last moment and then, disaster…

"Do you believe this?" he blurted out, torn between wanting to understand what had happened to his son and the horrible realization that maybe he had been responsible for Joey's death. As his son had lain in his arms, he had prayed, pleaded and begged that God would take him instead, to change places with his son. He had placed his hand over his son's heart to symbolically give his son his life energy. But instead he had watched the hemorrhages appear in his son's eyes as he died.

"It doesn't matter whether I believe it or not. To tell you the truth, I rather doubt it. But what is important is that the mohel has a penchant for the metaphysical, or maybe self-flagellation, or both, and he feels guilty for not warning you. It's part of the ritual. You are a medical man. You have your standard operating procedures. He has his and he didn't follow them. There was a very bad outcome. He feels guilty and he used his favor with our rabbi, his former classmate at yeshiva, to jump the queue for you. To clone Joey gives him a chance to right a wrong, reverse his oversight, just as it does for you. So you might say, doctor, as you are a psychiatrist, that you are the benefactor of his ruminations, his obsessive-compulsive disorder, his obsession with what might be and cannot be disproven. We see a lot of it among the ultra-Orthodox. The rituals give the obsessive-compulsive among the Orthodox legitimacy, structure and social acceptance."

"What about the spirit? How does Joey's spirit get into this embryo?"

"Some things have to be left to God, but it would seem that the nucleus of an egg containing his genetic blueprint is as good a place as any. The soul should recognize it, you might say. How it gets from there – wherever 'there' is – to the egg, we have to leave to God. How does it get there the first go 'round? Why should it be any different this time? And if it was not his time – how can it ever be the time for a child? – perhaps it is closer, in reserve in some way, more available. On the other side of the Styx, you might say, like a soul that doesn't have the money for the ferryman. The Greeks believe they can be stuck there for a year or more. The Catholics call it purgatory."

"What does a Jew know of this?" Joseph asked.

"The rabbi, we call him, but he was thrown out of yeshiva for his heretical views. A generous person might call him eclectic, mixing the science from his PhD in molecular biology from MIT and ritualistic magic with orthodox Jewry. In addition to Kabbalistic writings, such as the Sefer Yetzirah, he claims to be inspired by texts many Christians are more familiar with than are Jews. The Kabbalah was often used by the church, sometimes even to prove the existence of Christ. But there was a text reconstructed from bits and pieces scattered around the world called the Clavicula Salomonis, The Key of Solomon the King, and then there was the Lesser Key. The books contain formulas for rituals and they're very complicated. Supposedly passed on from Solomon to his son. But they are so complicated, no one can ever do them exactly right. Hence, once again, they can't be disproven.

But they're an obsessive-compulsive's dream. The relevance to your question is that the magic is designed to summon various levels of divinity. Some would say demons. But you don't have all night. Let me get to the point."

As if on cue, the celestial clock struck again. The saints came out and marched around.

"The point is," the old man continued, "that the cloning process is combined with the ritual in some way. He was inspired by the *Clavicula Salomonis*, among others. You are not a Hebrew scholar, is that correct, doctor?"

"That would be an understatement, a serious one," Joseph said sheepishly, anxious for the man to go on.

"Do you read Greek or Latin then?"

Joseph shook his head. "Not beyond what was needed for the study of medicine."

"I only mention these texts because they are available in English. The rituals symbolically summon the soul. Who knows? I don't believe it myself. I doubt he believes it, but he does it, perhaps as a gesture of respect."

"Respect?"

"Making life and all in a test tube. He doesn't want to be struck down. So in his mind, by inviting God to send the soul, he avoids blasphemy, sidesteps the notion he is creating life by inviting the Almighty to send the soul."

"Where is this done? Can Rachel and I be there when this happens?"

"No, that is forbidden. But I can tell you, as a further gesture of respect, that it is done in a synagogue. In the attic, to be exact. I can't tell you where in the Josefov the laboratory is, only that it is not there by accident. It's a very old synagogue. The legend is that the stones were brought from the second temple. It somehow was never destroyed by the Nazis. There is a legend of life being created there in the ghetto. Do you know the story of the golem? The legend is that Rabbi Loew created a golem, a huge protective being in the attic, to defend the Jews. Of course, this was a symbolic story."

Joseph, a frequent visitor to Prague on business and familiar with its history, briefly shut his eyes as if recalling something. Then his face lit like something had fallen into place in a puzzle. The thought seemed to bring a smile to his lips, which he quickly smothered.

"One last question before we move on to science," the old man said. "Was there a religious funeral?"

"Yes. It was done by an Orthodox rabbi."

"Mrs. Jacobson, I know you were hospitalized for some time."

"Please call me Rachel."

"I understand the body is interred at your home. One of you was physically present at the funeral?"

"I was," Joseph said quietly, looking at the man with quiet curiosity.

"Was there a moment you would describe as a spiritual high point or intensity in the service?"

"It was all intense."

"Of course. It was the death of your son. I didn't mean to imply otherwise, but was there a particular moment you recall that stood out?"

"Well, yes. I've spoken of it to Rachel and some of my friends. There was a moment after the coffin was lowered into the ground. I don't recall what the rabbi was saying or if he was even talking, but there seemed to be a force. Almost a wind, but not a wind, that felt physically like air. More of a force that seemed to flow from the ground and carry my gaze up. It literally seemed to pull my head up toward the sky."

"And after, were there circumstances after when you or other people independently felt the sense of your child's presence?"

"There was a night when the younger of the nannies, who had known Joey well, was in the side yard and had a feeling, strong enough to bring her almost to hysterics, that Joey was present. Before I knew what was happening to her, I had the same feeling and apparently so did the dog, who behaved very strangely, but no one saw or heard anything. She slept in a room that abutted the land where Joey was buried and complained frequently that she sensed what she regarded as Joey's spirit or, in her words, his ghost, although she never saw anything. I believe that was the primary reason she started making her plans to move out."

"And you, did you continue to sense anything?"

"From time to time it would be very strong, a sense he was there."

Rachel interjected, "He would come to me and tell me, 'Rachel, you've got to get up. Joey is here, I can feel it. Let me wheel you outside.'"

"But you never heard or saw anything?"

"Never, just a feeling."

Rachel added, "But once, when you were very upset about Joey and what might be his predicament in the afterlife, you dreamed he said to you, 'I'm OK.'"

"Yes, but I'm enough of a psychiatrist to recognize a classic wish-fulfillment dream."

"Who knows?" the man said without a trace of condescension or transparent attempt to comfort them. "Unlike almost everyone else in the world, we Jews are very vague about the afterlife. No promises, no reassurances, but no disavowals either.

"But the sensation you felt at the funeral, not a physical wind but a sense of a wind, reminds me of the Hebrew word for wind, *ruach*, which also means spirit. A Kabbalist might wonder if that was what you felt forcing your head up and your eyes to the sky at your son's funeral. If your son was taken before his time and his spirit lingers at his grave at your home, as your description of the nanny's behavior seems to imply, then, God willing, if we bring together the dust and the plan, the DNA that made your son what he was to begin with, then the holy spirit will blow his soul, who he was to begin with, back into his body. If your son's spirit resides at home, then after we place the cloned embryo in your wife, the *neshamah*, or breath of God, Holy Spirit willing, will enter his body when you get home."

The man broke eye contact and made some notes, apparently to share with the rabbi. He looked distracted for a moment and tired.

"I need to discuss with you now the science and medicine of what may go right and what may go wrong when we clone your son."

Joseph thought it was clear the man had reached the end of the spiritual pitch he had developed for couples who were skeptical of whether their cloned child would be the same person or just the same body as the original and was ready to get on with business. He wondered if he should give the slightest credence to the man's words on spirituality. He snuck a quick glance at Rachel and sensed the same unease. *It's the best that we can do, the best anyone could do,* he mouthed to her silently.

The man took two copies of an informed consent document from his briefcase. Rachel and Joseph read it hungrily, fearful they would come across a warning that might force them to reconsider the only path for giving their son his life back. In a long list of potential things that could go wrong, "unknown risks" and "accelerated aging" stuck in their minds. But there was no alternative but to go on.

Joseph attempted to quench a bolt of anxiety by finishing his drink, but not to be too obvious about it. He set the empty glass down slowly and wondered how he could order another without calling attention to how much he was drinking. *Could be perceived as weakness,* he thought.

"Crappy bourbon," he said under his breath. "Can't they get something other than Four Roses at a place like this?"

"Doctor, is this going to have a happy ending?" Rachel asked suddenly, her brow wrinkled and eyes squinting.

The old scientist looked her in the eye and seemed to be calculating his answer thoughtfully behind his beard. "Happy enough," he said.

"I need to ask you some technical questions now. How quickly did you obtain the skin from your son's earlobes? How soon after he expired?"

"Almost immediately after he was pronounced dead."

"How was the tissue preserved?" the Czech asked in a business-like voice without missing a beat.

"Liquid nitrogen, -196 centigrade," Joseph answered, searching the man's eyes for confirmation this was sufficient. As an NIMH neuroscientist, Joseph had easy access to the technology.

"Why so cold?" Rachel asked, blinking back tears.

"That temperature effectively stops time for the cells, putting them in suspended animation," the old man explained. "But it has to be done just right, so ice crystals don't form and it doesn't dry up the tissue. You took care of that?"

Joseph nodded several times. "Per protocol."

"Perfect," the Czech responded with a single deep nod, almost a bow. "So, here is what should happen, Mrs. Jacobson, assuming the tissue survives the freezing and defrosting process without too much damage."

"What kind of damage?"

"The blueprint for making the individual, in this case, Joey, is contained in a code made of proteins called DNA. If the freezing and defrosting process occurs too rapidly or too slowly, or without being bathed in the right nutrients and protective chemicals, it can damage the DNA or even break it apart, essentially changing the code or making it unreadable in places. Depending where the breaks occur and how extensive, this can interfere a lot or a little in bringing back your son the way he was. But I'll tell you more about the risks in a few moments. First, let me tell you what will happen if things go right. We will need to harvest some of your egg cells and remove the DNA from their nuclei. Are you still having regular menses?"

"Yes."

"Then you are most likely still ovulating, and judging from how easily you produced your last four children, we assume that your eggs are very healthy and fertile."

"I assume so, unless the accident did something."

"There's nothing in your medical records that would suggest damage to your reproductive capabilities. The challenge is that, although your naturally produced embryos apparently implanted in your uterus very easily, with cloning, in animals at least, it may take a hundred embryos to get one implantation. Each embryo requires a new egg from you."

"What if I run out of eggs?"

"We can use a donor egg, but that would be unfortunate."

"Why? I understand that donor eggs are used all the time in infertile women."

"That's true, but remember you are trying to produce an exact copy of your son."

"We are, of course, but what does the egg have to do it? I thought you removed the DNA from my egg and replaced it with DNA from our son."

"That's true of the nucleus of your egg. We remove the DNA completely and wash out everything we can, especially those substances that tell your DNA how old your body should be."

"Then, if you're getting rid of everything inside the egg, what difference does it make if it's mine or a donor's?"

"Well, that's a very good question. We don't actually want to get rid of everything."

Rachel looked a little skeptical, as if waiting for the punch line.

"Actually, part of the body's blueprint – part of the DNA, that is – lives outside the nucleus in a very interesting cell structure. They call it an organelle, or little organ, called the mitochondria. The mitochondria convert energy to a form the cell can use, but the DNA they contain are actually thought to have evolved from bacteria that our ancient ancestors dined on. The relevance for cloning your son is that if we use a donor's egg instead of yours, the mitochondrial DNA in the new body that Joey has will not be the same as was in his old body."

"What would that affect?"

"We don't know."

"Aren't the DNA in a cell inherited from both parents anyway? Won't Joey be missing his father's mitochondrial DNA?"

"We're lucky on that one. Unlike the DNA in the nucleus, the child's mitochondrial DNA all comes from the mother."

"It's always the mother's fault, isn't it?" Rachel quipped.

"Or in this case, to her credit," the man said with confidence. "We have a much better record of implantation with humans than is reported with the animals, so I doubt that you'll run out of eggs. But I have to tell you of everything that can go wrong. Aside from people who think they can legislate what is moral and immoral, there are medical reasons why cloning isn't yet considered ready for humans. We think we can overcome most of these problems and we have a pretty good record, but we don't know what time bombs are out there."

"Time bombs?" Joseph bristled at the term.

"Yes. I didn't choose that term randomly and you must decide if you wish to take the risk. As I alluded to earlier, we have to wash both Joey's DNA and your egg of all the natural substances that tell a cell how old it is and what kind of cell it is. We need to reprogram everything as if it's a freshly fertilized egg. The reprogramming process isn't perfect, though, and there may be aging factors in the nucleus or cytoplasm of the cell that get left in place simply because we don't know about them. If the fetus thought it was an adult and grew too big, it could endanger you."

"Could I have a Caesarian if that happened?"

"Yes, but you might have to make a choice whether to take the baby out early before it could survive."

Rachel's face dropped and she looked ahead pensively without focusing her eyes on anything.

Sensing he might be losing her, the doctor quickly responded.

"The incidence of this is low in animals and we haven't seen it at all in our work in humans. Remember, ethically, I have to tell you everything that could go wrong, even if very unlikely. Have you ever read the *Physician's Desk Reference*? If you read all the warnings, you would probably never take another aspirin. Did you know that you can bleed to death from aspirin or have an allergic reaction that can close your windpipe? I tell you this only to put risk in context."

Joseph pursed his lips. He didn't want to interrupt the doctor but made a mental note to remind Rachel that the safety analogy between aspirin, which was FDA approved, and human reproductive cloning, which was in its infancy, was ridiculous.

The doctor read Joseph's face and quickly added, "The analogy with aspirin gives you a context for understanding low-probability risks. The real danger with cloning is that, although we think we're at the point now where we can prevent a lot of the early physical problems, we don't know the subtle or late effects. The DNA in the mitochondria, for example, are very vulnerable to damage from stress. Mutations in mitochondrial DNA can cause premature aging. We won't know what these kids are going to look like thirty to forty years from now."

"At the very least, we could give him his childhood back," said Rachel.

"That in and of itself would be enough," Joseph said with finality.

15

The Angel of Death

Washington, District of Columbia
January 4, 2001

I T HAD BEEN AN UNCOMPLICATED labor and delivery at the same hospital. Mother and child were healthy and Joey had immediately latched onto her breast, sucking strongly, just as he had eight years earlier. Joseph felt a strange sense of peace. He likened it to what people sometimes said at the end. *No regrets. Isn't that what cousin Joel had said of Aunt Mildred at her death at 86 years old, when she was ready to be with her husband, Leo?*

Well, it wasn't true that Joseph had no regrets, but he had done everything that he could do to fix things. Joey could never be exactly the same. His place in the family would be different. Joseph knew that birth order mattered in personality development. The child development literature overwhelmingly pointed to that. He would be the youngest, not the eldest. But he might become the leader. *So much of it was in the genes, you know,* he thought.

He hated to think Joey would lose anything that he was entitled to. But he had done the best he could. *Full circle*, he thought, as he stepped under the gazebo where, nearly nine years ago, he had smoked a smuggled Cuban cigar with his friends Ahmed and Steve the night Joey had been born. *Full circle.*

He brushed the snow off the shoulders of his long, cashmere coat, surprised at how much had accumulated there in a few moments. His assistant, Caitlyn, had left a message that her car was hopelessly stuck in the snow and she couldn't come get him. There had been no taxis at the hospital for thirty minutes and no answer from their dispatchers. *Typical of Washington, DC, in a snowstorm*, he thought. *I'm going to have a hell of a time getting home.*

Rachel had gone into labor suddenly and dilated quickly. The babysitter was a neighbor girl who was only 15 years old, albeit a mature 15, and they knew her well. She had been kind enough to babysit with no notice, but she would have school tomorrow and was probably sleeping now. He needed to get home to the kids and relieve her.

He stepped out into the heavy snow and blackness, leaning against a howling wind as he made his way down to the corner of Loughboro and MacArthur Boulevard to try to hail a taxi. He pulled up the collar of his coat to try to protect his exposed ears from the cold. The swirling snow stung his face. *I really must buy a fedora*, he thought, chuckling at how many times he had said that to himself over the years.

Standing at the intersection, he saw a long dark car. He couldn't be sure about its color in this light. It was coming his way down Loughboro, perhaps 200 yards away. There was nothing about it to suggest it was a taxi, so he ignored it and turned his attention to looking up and down MacArthur Boulevard, which was normally a busier artery. The road was deserted and all the businesses dark, which was no surprise, given the late hour and the fury of the storm.

He looked back up Loughboro and saw the car he had noticed before, now no more than 50 yards away. This time, he noticed its yellow taxi roof light flickering in the heavy snow. It already seemed to be slowing to stop for him when he hailed it. The roof and hood were heavily caked with fresh snow, but as he opened the door, he could see that it was a Virginia taxi. *What's it doing up here?* he thought. *Virginia cabs hate coming into the District.*

The driver was a neatly dressed old man with a white goatee, blue-gray eyes, and short-cropped gray hair.

"Good evening." He spoke with an exotic accent that Joseph didn't recognize.

Somewhere from the Mediterranean, Joseph thought.

On the dashboard was an 8-inch tall figurine of a bearded Jesus standing in a robe with a Byzantine-style halo suspended above his head. Hanging from the rearview mirror was a wooden rosary. The car smelled perfumed. Not like the cheap kind the drivers sometimes used to cover up the smell of cigarettes. It was an oily smell but somehow masculine and distinctively old-world. Joseph decided it was coming from the driver.

After Joseph got in and closed the door, the driver started driving without asking where he was going.

"Do you know how to get to McLean?"

"Yes."

"Cedar Lane. It's just off Leigh Mill. Cross the Chain Bridge and then head out toward Great Falls."

"I know the house very well."

That's plausible, thought Joseph. *I call Yellow Cab of Falls Church pretty much every week or two for the airport.*

"That's good," said Joseph. "So you know how to get there, even in a blizzard?"

"But I don't recognize you."

I can't place that accent. Eastern Mediterranean perhaps, Joseph mused. *That's strange he would recall the house but not me.*

"Maybe you picked up my wife there," Joseph said. "Are you sure you're thinking of the right house?"

"I know the house very well. I know the dog."

"How would you describe the dog?"

"A big dog that smiles. But I don't recognize you. Maybe your hair has gotten grayer."

He clearly knows the house if he can describe the dog.

A little unnerved, Joseph instinctively looked at the door lock to see if he could manually open it and get out if necessary. There was no visible latch to open the door. *Odd*, he thought. *Cabs have to take precautions about people jumping out without paying*, he supposed. He tried the window. It wouldn't budge. *Must be frozen*, he thought. *That doesn't mean anything. There had been something odd about the car. It had been long, that was it. A stretch limousine, perhaps. The color was wrong, too. The cabs that came to the house were always Yellow Cabs based in Arlington. They don't normally cruise in DC. On the other hand, if he had started in Virginia and dropped someone off in DC, wouldn't he be allowed to pick up a passenger on the way home? But hadn't this cab stopped before he had hailed it? How would the driver have known he was going to Virginia?*

"Is this a Yellow Cab?" Joseph asked.

"Yes."

The car had looked black when he had hailed it. *But cars always got dirty in the snow, didn't they? Maybe it was just gray in the light.* The usual hacker's license with the driver's name was nowhere to be found. *Why didn't the man have his picture ID showing like all the other cab drivers? That was the law, wasn't it?* He felt a seed of panic springing up and a sense of déjà vu. He couldn't place it. Clearly the man was from the east.

"Where are you from?"

"Greece."

That fits with the Greek Orthodox Christ image, Joseph thought. *He's telling the truth about that.*

"What part of Greece?" Joseph asked, more to see if the man would trip over the details than out of any real feeling of curiosity.

"Thessaly."

"What town?"

The man didn't answer.

"How long have you lived in the United States?"

He looked at the driver carefully. There was definitely something familiar about him. Maybe the driver had grown grayer as well. Without thinking why, he asked, "Have you ever driven an ambulance?"

The man didn't answer.

The view outside the car was almost totally black with darkness except for fleeting white specks of snow dancing in the mostly ineffectual headlights.

"Wouldn't hurt to have halogen bulbs in a storm like this," Joseph said.

"No kidding," said the driver in a tone of friendly agreement. He said "kidding" as if it had three d's in the middle and two g's at the end.

"I think there are a lot of crosswinds on this bridge," said the driver as if preparing Joseph but with no reassurance in his voice. He said "think" like "tink," leaving out the blend.

"The surface will be icy, so be careful." Joseph's alarm was slightly tempered by the assumption of confidence one has in a professional driver, especially one who had lived to the age of this one. He looked again for the man's cab license, trying to reassure himself that hopefully the man had been doing this for a very long time. Disquieted further when he couldn't find it, Joseph tried to ask disarmingly, "By the way, what did you say your name was?"

After a pause, the driver said, "You didn't ask, I didn't say."

Unsure whether the driver was trying to be humorous or evasive, Joseph feigned not having understood his reply. "I'm sorry, I couldn't hear. Could you say your name again?"

It sounded like "Kharon." When the driver turned around to say his name, Joseph got a somewhat different impression of him, as the retinas of his eyes briefly reflected the scattered light from the snow in a momentary flash of brilliant red. Before Joseph could ask how he spelled his name, there was a rushing sound of gusty air on the left side of the car and simultaneous lateral movement to the right as if the car were being blown.

"Whoa," Joseph said, peering out the frost covered window into the inky blackness as if through a huge cataract lens. He wondered how wide the shoulder of the road was and what kind of barrier protected them from going over. Before he could finish the thought, there was another gust, louder than the first. It dealt the car a sharp blow from the right. The car felt almost lifted into the center of the road.

"It's a good thing there aren't any cars coming from the other direction."

"Never," the driver said.

"What? What do you mean?"

The driver was hunched up over the steering wheel, squinting into the blackness. The headlights seemed weaker than ever, vaguely yellow, impotent against the darkness and swirling snow, like little white stars twinkling and winking in the dark.

I had better let him concentrate, Joseph thought. But the kernel of anxiety was growing. Something indefinable was wrong. *Dead wrong*, he thought. Straining to see ahead through the windshield and beginning to lose his cool, he said, "This is an awful long bridge. What river is this?"

Before the driver could answer, Joseph saw through the dim yellow headlights, perhaps 70 yards ahead of them, what looked like a homeless man dressed in outsized long pajamas with the sleeves hanging out over his hands, his face obscured by a hood.

"Watch out!" Joseph yelled.

The driver slammed on the brakes. Ineffective on the slippery surface to begin with, the front wheels locked as the rear wheels spun, causing the car to flip, back end over front. It slid into the 3-foot concrete barrier on the side of the bridge, easily clearing it. Joseph felt the end-over-end motion as the car left the ground and tumbled through space toward the river. Held in place by the seat belt and shoulder strap, Joseph thought of how Joey, the good boy, the obedient child, had flipped through the air on the back of the ATV, holding tightly to his mother's waist. He had had the trust and love and indefatigable confidence of a child who knew and had never had any reason to doubt that, if he did what he was told by adults, everything would be all right.

The fall seemed to take a very long time. Perhaps he lost track of the time from the motion and he wondered if Joey had lost consciousness as soon as he hit the ground. He hoped so. If so, his last experience might have been like a ride at the state fairs he had loved so much. *No, Teddy had said he was conscious. He had spoken afterward. If he could talk, he could breathe and feel pain. Something had cut off his air after he hit the ground.*

The car, upside down, rear flipped over front, hit the ice-covered river. With the impact, he felt something in his back crack along with the ice on the surface. He heard himself exhale loudly, "Aighhhh!"

Out, he thought. *Got to get out.* But he could not make his hands work to release the seat belt and shoulder strap. He heard the muffled sloshing of water. It reminded him of being in the bilge of the houseboat they had ploughed the Pearl River Reservoir in as a child. The driver didn't seem to be in the car. *How on earth could he have gotten out?* he wondered. The thought was interrupted by the frigid water sloshing in through the heating ducts and the cracked windshield. He recalled there were no manual door locks to pull, even if he had been able to use his hands. He choked on frigid water and coughed violently, expelling it. He gasped reflexively, partially filling his lungs with cold water again. This time his cough was but a sputter, and then nothing. His bronchi had spasmed closed against the onslaught. He felt a pressure in his chest as if it would burst and then that, too, passed. As even the dark turned to gray, he felt the car spiraling downward.

How can it take this long? he thought as the numbness from the cold water and the lack of oxygen spread upward over his extremities like a balm. There was a photograph of the family before the accident he always kept in a pocket over his heart. He thought of it now. It had been taken only weeks before Rachel and Joey's accident and was one of those rare shots where the whole family seemed to stare into the camera with a carefree zest, as if embarking on a long happy vacation.

He felt a dull blow on the back of his head as the car hit a truck-sized boulder at the bottom of the bottom of the riverbed. Memory fragments danced out of his unconscious. "So the baby will be named Joseph Jacobson just like you if it's a boy?" the obstetrician had asked.

Joseph had replied, "My grandmother always said it was bad luck to name after the living. Dangerous, in fact. She said that, when it's time for the father to die, the Angel of Death – she called it Malach HaMavet – could take the younger person by mistake. She said he could take many forms."

Then he recalled stepping off the ATV and offering it to Rachel the night Joey was killed. "Why don't you go for a ride with the boys and enjoy yourself?" he had said. He recalled that, in the darkest hours of Joey's battle with Kawasaki disease, he had offered his life as a sacrifice if Joey recovered. *That vow came due in Luray. The ATV accident was meant for me. The Angel of Death took Joey by mistake. The cloning was successful. Joey was born again, but now I have to die to keep my vow as the price for Joey to live.*

In the fast-moving current, the car slammed into the rock wall of a canyon. The light of Joseph's imagination scattered into a few tiny, darting meteors of light. Just before it flickered out, he connected the dots into a picture one last time. He recalled Joey sitting in the big therapist's chair in his psychiatry office, posing for a photograph, smiling broadly. After Joseph took the picture and set the camera down, he recalled Joey smiling even more broadly so he knew he had really been happy.

16

The Second Circumcision

McLean, Virginia
January 11, 2001

T HE MOHEL SAID, "I'D LIKE for both of the child's grand-fathers to hold him during the ceremony."

"I thought after Rachel had the twins, we were done with this sort of thing," Don, Rachel's father, quipped with feigned lightness.

"I never got used to doing circumcisions," Ralph, Joseph's father, responded. "In the old days, if they couldn't get a mohel to come to the little Southern towns, they would have a Jewish doctor do them if they could find one. I must have done a dozen of them, but I never got comfortable with it."

The mohel pulled two chairs together and signaled Don and Ralph to sit and jointly hold their 8-day-old grandchild. Then the mohel soaked a napkin in red wine and put it in the child's mouth to blunt the coming pain. The baby seemed to taste it thoughtfully, then sucked it robustly, as if with pleasure. The mohel had chosen a sweet fortified kosher wine.

"Why do we do this?" asked Bevy.

"The Torah is clear: you can't be a member of the Hebrew tribe without it," Rachel said firmly.

Elisabeth, who had worked for Bevy's father and had attended all the major Jacobson developmental gatherings, attempted to reassure Bevy further as she wiped away a tear. "The wine will make him drunk and he won't remember a thing. An infant's nervous system is really not developed enough to feel pain anyway."

She forced a reassuring smile for Bevy. Her tears streaked the over-application of rouge she had applied that morning to conceal the deep mourning she felt for Joseph, who had mentored her for nearly twelve years and had helped establish her career.

Caitlyn blew her nose quietly. "He looks an awful lot like his daddy." She whispered to Elisabeth, "This is our fourth Jacobson bris. Remember how proud Joseph was at the first one? Now he and the first one are in the ground and they're circumcising his namesake again. Did they ever find the driver's body?"

"Not a trace," answered Elisabeth, shaking her head with an exaggerated, perplexed expression. "Odd. The newspapers said the driver's door was jammed and the window shut. They can't see how anyone could have gotten out of that car."

"Maybe he crawled out through the back," mused Caitlyn. "If he did, with the flood from the snowmelt, the body could be anywhere. Maybe in the top of a tree. Maybe eaten by an animal."

"Maybe at the bottom of the river."

"Maybe."

"Shhhh," Elisabeth said, "they're starting."

The mohel slathered the child's penis with a clear, heavy ointment, wiped his hands with a thick ornamental white and blue tasseled towel, and said, "Praised be Thou, O Lord our God, King of the Universe, who hast sanctified us with Thy commandments, and commanded us concerning the rite of circumcision."

This time he used what appeared to be an ancient, stone-hewn knife with a Star of David emblazoned on it.

"That's more like we used to do it," Ralph drawled. "But with a stainless steel scalpel. None of those fancy machines like he used with the other boys."

"The results have a lot more character this way," quipped Elisabeth.

"It seems awful big for a little baby," whispered Bevy to Rachel. "Is it supposed to be like that? Is that what they look like before they cut them?"

The mohel cut away the foreskin in several short strokes as if they were brushes of an artist's paint on a palate. The child's expression was compliant, almost curious at first. Then he began to cry. His cries grew to a wail. The mohel gave him a fresh cloth covered with sweet wine to suck and he soon quieted.

The grandfathers were prompted by the mohel to recite together, but remained just a bit out of step. "Praised be Thou, O Lord our God, King of the Universe, who hast sanctified us with Thy commandments, and hast bidden us to make him enter into the covenant of Abraham, our father."

The Jews in the room responded, "As he has entered into the covenant, so may he be introduced to the study of Torah, good deeds, and long life."

The mohel's strangely triumphant look contrasted sharply with the agonized looks of the crowd.

"It was the strangest look," Susan said to Don later. "As if he was proud of this, as if he created it somehow."

The mohel said, "Creator of the universe, in Thy abundant mercy, through Thy holy angels, give a pure and holy heart to Joey Jacobson, the son of Joseph and Rachel Jacobson, who was just now circumcised in honor of Thy great Name."

After the crowd had left, Shane limped painfully over to Joey's crib, where he slept, and sniffed thoughtfully. He made loud snuffling sounds and looked puzzled. Uncharacteristically, he began to bark at the child excitedly, not menacingly. Finally, Rachel put Shane outside.

When the mohel walked to his car, Shane approached him curiously, smiling. The mohel drew back warily, unsure if the showing of teeth was prelude to attack.

17

Après-Family Life Class

"HOW EXACTLY DO YOU MAKE a baby?"

"These days there are a lot of ways," Rachel replied nervously.

"Does the man just put his ding dong in the VJ?" Joey asked with a sheepish grin, followed by a self-conscious giggle.

Rachel hesitated, lost in thought for a moment. "Yes," she replied, seeking closure.

"But how does he do it?"

"He puts the ding dong in the VJ," Rachel said matter-of-factly, as if that was all there was to it. Her face registered a mixture of amusement and discomfort.

"But how does it happen?"

Rachel answered as vaguely as she could. "When two people are married, they decide to make a baby."

"But how do you ask?" Joey's brow was wrinkled.

"What do you mean?"

"How do you ask about doing it?"

"You say, hey, do you want to make a baby?" Rachel said lightly, enjoying herself now.

"No, really, how do you ask?" Joey looked irritable.

"One parent says, 'Do you want to make a baby?' And the other one says, 'I've got to take the garbage out. I've got a headache. I need to play another game of computer poker, or I'm watching TV.'" Rachel laughed.

Joey looked curious, then caught on to the joke and broke into a broad smile. "Come on, really, how do you ask?"

A little too amused with herself but relieved with the facetious turn the conversation had taken, Rachel sang, "Birds do it, bees do it, even educated fleas do it, let's do it, let's fall in love."

"Come on!" Joey snapped.

"Well, the man and the woman start kissing, and one thing leads to another, and then he puts the ding dong into the VJ."

"When do they get naked?"

For a moment, Rachel considered what she wanted to convey in her answer. "Sometime after the kissing starts."

"How do they get naked?"

"It just happens! That's enough for now. Why don't you go out to the backyard and play with Shane awhile."

She heard the back door open and close as Joey whistled and Shane excitedly barked. Safely alone, she began to sob quietly, thinking of her husband and how he would have laughed at her feeble efforts at sex-ed. This was supposed to be his job, having a "man-to-man" talk with his son.

She walked over to the bar and rummaged through the liquor cabinet until she found a dusty bottle of tequila with a handwritten label. A tiny smile came to her lips. She and Joseph had brought the tequila back from Mexico after a long weekend getaway without the kids, mere weeks before the accident. She dusted off the bottle with the tail of her blouse, swirled the remaining few ounces of caramel-colored liquid around several times, and poured an ounce into a souvenir shot glass labeled "Tepoztlan." She swallowed it quickly, winced, closed her eyes, and savored the burning feeling in her stomach. "Like old times." She felt a blush come over her face and chest, poured another ounce and sipped it, enjoying the oily taste. She made her way unsteadily across the den to Joseph's favorite chair, a black leather recliner. She and Joseph used to lie in the recliner together, reading and chatting, sometimes sharing a nightcap after the kids had been put to bed.

She finished the tequila and recalled the trip to Tepoztlan. It had been fun but short. With four young children, they could never get away for long. She stretched out on the recliner, closed her eyes and remembered the heady euphoria of their lives the summer before the accident. They had four healthy, happy kids and an idyllic summer home in the mountains. Then she grimaced. The accident flashed through her mind. She wished she had brought another bottle over to Joseph's chair.

Life had changed so fast. Although devastated after the accident, she and Joseph never indulged in despair. They both believed there was always a way forward. They shared a mission to give their family the life they would have had. Through grueling physical therapy, she had fought millimeter by millimeter to restore her mobility and was able to walk unassisted with a brace within six months of the accident. They had managed to clone their son, for God's sake. Then, on the night he was born, her husband was killed in an accident.

She reached for the glass to take a sip, forgetting it was empty, then shook her head silently and let the glass drop to the floor.

The grandfathers had carried on for Joseph the best they could. The kids were expert marksmen and hunters under the tutelage of Ralph. Don had inoculated the children with his enthusiasm for the Torah. They had just completed the Five Books of Moses and had dived into the Prophets.

But she had nagging worries about health problems from the cloning. "Time bombs," the doctor had warned. For the time being,

Joey was healthy, vivacious, in fact. They would live every day to the fullest, just as they had after the first Joey's recovery from Kawasaki disease. The first Joey.

Had they succeeded in their mission to give the Joey his life back? If so, the soul of the first Joey must be in the body of the boy playing in the backyard. Did the two Joeys share the same soul? Did it matter? Yes, it mattered. The first Joey deserved his life back, to grow up, to love, to grow old. It was Joseph's and her duty to literally give him his life back, to put his soul back in his body. If the first Joey's soul hadn't returned to the cloned body, then they had created an identical twin of sorts –same name, same face, same voice – but had not recreated the first Joey. How could she ever know?

The cloned Joey seemed to have more of her lightheartedness and wit and less of Joseph's seriousness than the first Joey. Perhaps that was to be expected from the change in birth order, from oldest to youngest. Strangely, though, he sometimes acted like the leader and was already peace-maker when the twins quarreled. That was more like the original Joey.

Try as she might, she couldn't shake the question of whether the first Joey's soul had passed to the new Joey. She started to feel drowsy from the tequila. She closed her eyes and pictured Joseph reclining next to her, reading and chatting like they used to. "Joseph, can you help me?"

In her imagination, he nodded in his reassuring way. "What do you feel when you look into his eyes?" he asked.

Don took Rachel and the grandchildren to the Shakespeare Theater in DC from time to time. She searched her mind for the relevant quote from King Richard III. *"To thee I do commend my watchful soul, Ere I let fall the windows of mine eyes." Joseph would tell me the eyes are the window to the soul.*

She dozed for a moment, woke with a start and glanced at her watch. *Time for Joey's lunch.* She let her weight fall on her stronger leg, pulled herself to her feet and made her way to the coffee maker. She stuck in a capsule of Starbucks and drank it black. Rachel felt her energy return quickly. She opened the refrigerator. Her eyes lit up as they fell on a pair of California rolls, a favorite food of both Joeys. She put her hands over her eyes, relishing memories of times at a sushi bar with the first Joey.

She sighed deeply and hobbled onto the back deck where she spied Joey and Shane playing in the backyard near the first Joey's grave. She yanked the little rope cord on the dinner bell she had salvaged from the now neglected house in Luray. Joey and Shane looked up from their game. "Lunch time," she shouted.

Joey and Shane bounded up the stairs from the yard, nearly knocking Rachel over.

Shane sniffed the air and made a beeline for the sushi Rachel had laid out on the picnic table on the deck.

"Down, you idiot!" Rachel shouted just as Shane stood up on two legs at the table. Shane twisted in mid-air and scurried under the table for safety from Rachel's feigned wrath.

"No counter surfing!" Rachel shouted, wagging her finger. Shane smiled back obsequiously.

"Do you know what Shane did?" Joey asked.

"Nothing would surprise me from that beast." Rachel laughed.

"James came over from next door and we were playing keep-away from Shane. Shane finally got the ball, then he ran all the way over to the pond, swam out into the middle and dropped it."

"That's a smart dog. He had a winning strategy. Keep him outside until he's dry or we'll be cleaning up dried mud all day."

Joey climbed onto the picnic bench, sitting on the backs of his legs to reach the table.

"Would you like milk?" Rachel asked.

"Yes, please."

She poured into his cup from a glass bottle of grass-fed milk.

"Look what I got you," Rachel said, unwrapping the California rolls.

"Sushi!" In between bites Joey hummed, "Mmm."

The first Joey hummed like that when he ate his favorite foods. When he was done, she asked, "Are you still hungry?"

"A little."

She returned to the refrigerator and brought out a bowl of cold pasta sprinkled a little parmesan cheese on top. Joey dug in, paused and looked up at his mom. "More parmesan cheese!"

That's exactly what the first Joey used to say. She ladled it on.

Her eyes twinkled. "I'll be right back."

She opened the sliding door that led from the porch to the den and limped over to the mantle above the fireplace. First her eyes fell on a picture of her husband – long hair, a little rakish, triumphant with a fat Cuban cigar in his mouth – and his friends Ahmed and Steve standing nearby. *The night the first Joey was born.* Then her eyes fell on a picture of Joseph and the first Joey on a pheasant hunt, young Joey so proud in front of his father. She smiled, looking at how the blazing orange hunting vest swallowed him. *They don't make hunting clothes for boys that age.* She focused on young Joey's eyes. *So mirthful, like life was a bowl of delights waiting to be eaten.*

She glanced outside on the porch and saw Joey slip Shane a taste of pasta. She smiled, opened the freezer, removed a tub of chocolate ice cream, spooned it into a bowl and added a generous portion of multi-colored sprinkles. *The first Joey's favorite. Our last snack together.* She limped back onto the porch and set it in front of Joey, watching his eyes. Her mind flipped from the pictures on the mantle to the boy presently enjoying his ice cream and back again. She felt a rushing feeling, and a weight seemed to lift from her shoulders. *It's him.* She hugged Joey a lot harder than usual.

"Mommy, are you OK?"

"I'm just so happy."

Joey smiled broadly and shoveled more ice cream into his mouth. "Mmm," he hummed.

Rachel looked up at the sky, glanced back into Joey's eyes, then back up at the sky. "Thank you, Joseph," she said.

18

The Boy Under the Surface

THE HUNTERS, INCLUDING THE THREE Jacobson boys, Granddaddy and Granddaddy's best friend, Mac, flew to Tegucigalpa, Honduras. Carlos met them at the airport and put money in several men's hands in succession to get their shotguns through customs. Then they were driven through the country to Choluteca in a very old but sturdy school bus. As they got closer to the Nicaraguan border, there were army checkpoints. Sometimes the soldiers searched the bus, but Carlos paid the tolls and knew how to get through. There were lots of old cars on the road. One of Joey's teachers used to say that old cars never died, they just went south of the border. Now he knew what she meant.

The hunting camp was a very primitive, ramshackle affair consisting of a mud-brick oven, a few old plastic chairs and two rotting wooden shacks that looked like they might slide down the mud into the lagoon at any minute. Before departing on the hunt, they sat around a bonfire, warming themselves, drinking thick black coffee and hot chocolate out of tin cups, and choking down gooey cheese quesadillas that turned to stone after they cooled.

To pass the time, Joseph's father, whom Joey called Granddaddy, told about his adventures hunting moose, Kodiak bears and reindeer in Alaska and the Northwest Territories. He also related funny stories about his first hunts with his daddy when he was just barely potty trained.

"Your great-granddaddy wanted the hunt to get in my blood," he said.

Granddaddy and Mac helped the boys squeeze into their rubber hip waders and they climbed into the least dilapidated of the three ramshackle makeshift airboats. The airboats were necessary because their draft had to be shallow enough to get by in the most areas of the grassy swamp. The propellers roared to life and the boat skimmed over the black water of the canals and lagoon, frightening hundreds of black, duck-like birds from their watery roosts. That got the boys to thinking how much was ahead in the hunt.

"No," said Granddaddy. "See how long their necks are? And how their feet pull back at that funny angle? I think these are cormorants, boys. We don't want to shoot them. They're fish eaters, they're not edible."

The boats were primitive, essentially metal platforms with unanchored plastic chairs for seats. An unprotected propeller protruded at a perpendicular angle from a rusty gasoline engine crudely bolted to the deck. It received fuel through a naked clear plastic tube directly attached to a rusty portable gasoline can on deck. The engine made an enormous noise like an airplane and emitted showers of sparks. They had to wear hearing protection. At face value, this seemed dangerous and it was. Indeed, on the very first day before they got to the duck blind, an engine caught on fire and they all had to hop off into the swamp in the dark for fear the gasoline can would explode. The pilot salvaged a walkie-talkie and eventually they were picked up by airboat number two, but the sun was high in the sky by then and the morning hunt was lost. By the time they were picked up out of the mud and water, they were hungry enough that the soggy quesadillas in their pockets had started to seem tempting.

They had lunch back at camp and spent the middle of the day playing poker while Grand-daddy and Mac napped. Carlos told them that, to make up for the morning's debacle, he had a special treat in mind. Just before dusk, he would take them to hunt a relatively slow-flying duck called a peachy willow that was characteristic of the area. There were no blinds. They drove out in the vans to an outcropping on a hillside.

At dusk, several small groups of large, black-bellied, long-legged ducks whirred past just out of range, flying low in the heavily overcast sky. A few moments later, Joey turned toward a strange whistling sound and was startled by a pair of ducks close enough for him to hear the beating of their wings. He had grown out of his little hand-me-down .410 and had a much better chance of downing a duck with his father's old 20-gauge pump that shot the pellets over a much wider area. He waited for them to cross like Granddaddy had taught him, then swung just past them and pulled the trigger.

To his utter amazement, they both dropped.

"Dos muertos!" cried the bird boy, excitedly, his face beaming. They were big, slow-flying ducks, but it did wonders for his confidence.

The bird boys had no sooner picked up the birds than it started to rain heavily. They returned to the cars and the drivers of both vehicles ground the tires into the mud up to the rims. They all got out and pushed to no avail. They tried to dig out by putting branches under the tires, but the rims were hopelessly deep in the mud. They ended up soaked from the rain without accomplishing anything.

Finally, one of the younger Honduran boys was sent out to find a farm and returned several hours later with a rusty tractor so small it looked like a toy. But it had hugely disproportionate wheels that were deeply treaded. It was driven by a gnarled old man, an apparent veteran of many muddy fields, who succeeded in pulling out the trucks one by one. Whatever Carlos paid him made him smile broadly under his bushy gray mustache and wide-brimmed rain hat.

The hunters arrived back at the hotel very late and got a call very early in the morning telling them to dress for hunting white-winged dove. They would be picked up in an hour.

Normally, the tropical swamp was honeycombed with richly soiled islands, lushly cultivated with corn and sorghum, and grazed by free-ranging cattle. The two primary hunting attractions were the paloma, mostly white-winged doves who feasted on the crops, and patos of all kinds who wintered in the relatively temperate tropical marsh. The farmers considered the paloma to be pests who stole their crops and were glad for the hunters.

This winter, an unusual succession of tropical depressions had stagnated on their way east from the Pacific, leading to sustained torrential flooding. Most of the islands were underwater. So this morning, the old bus drove east into the hills and stopped near fields of millet and corn.

Granddaddy spread them out along a fence line and under trees. He said the birds had to have landmarks to fly by. He warned the boys not to shoot the parrots, which were larger and more vividly colored than the doves. The farmers were glad to have the hunters assist their scarecrows in protecting their crops. The dove seemed annoyed by their presence and determined to come in to feed. Unlike in the United States, there are no bag limits in Honduras, so they shot until their arms ached. Carlos assured them that the local people, who generally were impoverished and mostly lived without running water or electricity, would not waste one ounce of the meat.

The birds flew very quickly. Granddaddy seemed to down a bird with almost every shot. He had taken his grandsons to practice on the skeet range many times before the hunt and it paid off. The brothers knew how to shoot when the birds were flying straight at them and when they were flying past. They were told to shoot the slow-flying blue and green pigeons as well. The farmers called them paloma magna and said they were the worst thieves of their crops.

Joey took a shot that was too long at one particularly slow-flying green pigeon. It seemed to almost float in the air and then whirred slowly to earth like a damaged helicopter. The bird boy ran to pick it up. He stared at it as if confused.

Joey knew something was really wrong when he didn't put it into the bag with the other birds that hung from his vest pouch.

"Pájaro!" the boy said, holding out a very young, wounded parrot.

Joey's heart sank. Its wing was injured, but there were no other wounds on its body. At first, it scolded and pecked at them. The boy giggled and tried to talk to it in reassuring tones. Eventually, it quieted down, watching them warily.

Granddaddy put his arm around Joey's shoulder. "It's OK. You didn't mean to shoot it. I'll buy you a cage if you want to take it home. You'll have to be very lucky to get it past customs, but if you can get it to eat at home, it may survive and make a nice pet. Your father wanted to breed parrots when he was your age, but we never got around to it."

When the sun was almost directly overhead and they were baking in the heat of the field, Carlos drove them to a grassy hilltop overlooking the valley. They ate barbecued dove and pigeon. Granddaddy and Mac drank a local, very young red wine that was just good enough. Everyone napped and then got back in the bus for a ride back to the lagoon for late-afternoon duck hunting.

When they passed the field where they had hunted, they saw a large crowd of local people queued up. There were mothers holding babies, children of all ages, and even elderly couples. They had come for the birds. Joey had been embarrassed at how many he had shot and felt sad for the birds. But the thin, hungry people changed all that. Noah and Teddy reminded Joey that their father had always said they were "meat hunters" and distinguished that from "trophy hunters," whom Joseph looked down on.

Carlos kept just enough birds to bribe the soldiers and get the hunters through each checkpoint along the way. Except for having wounded a parrot, it had been a very good day so far. They napped on the bus and the drive back to the duck-hunting camp went quickly.

At the camp, Carlos persuaded the parrot to eat a piece of fruit and everyone applauded. Granddaddy sent one of the boys into town with money to buy a cage so Joey could take the bird home with him when the hunt ended.

The two remaining airboats divided up, with granddaddy and Mac in one, and Noah, Teddy and Joey in the other, along with a young boy of 9 years or so without waders who was assigned the job of picking up any birds they might manage to bring down. The boats were crewed by local boys in their early teens.

The reputable international outfitter had nearly canceled the season's hunting after reading the weather reports. Granddaddy and Mac had come because the local contractor, Carlos, had convinced them that the floodwaters had crested, and that the hunting was better than ever because the ducks in the northern reaches of the province had been driven south by even worse weather. In fact, the water levels had continued to rise several inches that afternoon.

Due to the flooding, it took the airboat a good hour and a half to find a suitable area to hunt from. The usual metal hunting platforms were submerged. It was late afternoon when they clambered over the side of the airboat into the water and tried to find solid footing in the deep, sticky, black mud. They were told they would be picked up before dark. Carlos pushed a large burlap sack of decoys over the side of the airboat, and the Honduran boys set them out one by one and motioned for the brothers to stand in a large pod of reeds that matched their camouflage clothing almost perfectly.

In the heat of the day, with the sun still relatively high in the sky, there were no ducks flying. Only a few confused doves flew back and forth over the submerged crops that normally sustained them. They sometimes lit on the tops of the trees that they had apparently frequented when the area had been dry. The group managed to bring down a few as they flew by and the bird boy, despite their worry, didn't seem to mind wading to pick them up. The hunters never knew what direction the birds would fly from, and it was somewhat hard to maneuver in the water.

The swamp was like a theater set, where the curtain closed and then reopened in a different scene at dusk. As if on cue, when the sun hovered a few degrees over the horizon, the wind came up abruptly, the temperature dropped several palpable degrees, the hue of the sky darkened and the ducks began to fly like crazy.

Noah saw them first, five or six dots in the sky flying straight toward the boys from the east. "Joey, Teddy, get ready. Nine o'clock. Keep your head down."

They bowed their heads toward the birds, presenting a view of their camouflaged caps instead of their faces. The glare of the day's last sunlight, scattered prism-like over the swamp from the low trajectory of the sun, helped hide them from the ducks.

The older of the bird boys blew on a simple duck call composed of a reed in a wooden bamboo cylinder. The sound was perfect.

"Now!" Noah called.

The three boys shot almost simultaneously. One duck fell, another changed its trajectory slightly and began to lose altitude, wounded. Teddy re-sighted great-granddaddy's old Remington Model 58 and fired again at the wounded duck, this time dropping it.

"Muerto!" the older bird boy shouted as he and his younger sibling began to slog off through the mud to pick up the birds.

"Wait," Noah called.

The other birds had flared after the first shots but now had turned and were flying back in the brothers' direction. They made one pass, well out of the hunters' range. The older bird boy raised the duck call to his lips to try to call them back, but before he could blow, the birds turned on their own and flew straight toward them. Noah saw Joey stiffen.

"Not yet," he said, sensing Joey's excitement. "Keep your head down. Wait, wait. Now!"

They emptied their shotguns, bringing down one more. A second managed to land and then swam in little circles slowly before succumbing. They worried that the bird boys might drown as they set out after them. The swamp was pockmarked with holes. But they returned safely with all four. They were gadwalls, medium-sized ducks with gray backs and white undersides.

Joey felt bad for the ducks but didn't want to acknowledge that to the twins, who were squabbling over who had brought down which duck. Long before that controversy could be settled, the teal began to fly. Cinnamon colored, blue-green, smaller than the gadwalls by half, they careened through the sky, twisting, turning evasively like fighter planes. The boys had to turn and twist in the deep mud to track these fast-flying acrobatic birds while their boots often stuck as if in concrete. The birds came in so fast and so thick, they couldn't load fast enough. The lever on great-granddaddy's old Model 58 came off in Teddy's hand. The birds practically landed on him after that, so close they didn't dare to shoot for fear of hitting one another. From time to time, the birds would cross in the sky. Joey scored a one-shot double and three two-shot doubles. Now they really understood why hunters traveled across the world to hunt in Honduras and Argentina.

Just before dark, the bird boy pointed at two small dots on the horizon flying out of the last remnants of the sun as it sank below the horizon.

"Put your head down," whispered Teddy. "They should only see the top of your cap."

They peered up and ahead, standing like statues as the two points in the sky came closer, taking shape.

"Canada geese," whispered Teddy.

Joey pumped a shell into the chamber of his 20-gauge and waited. The birds started to turn north. The older Honduran boy blew a series of mournful honking sounds.

"Sounds like Saba blowing the shofar on Rosh Hashanah," whispered Teddy, giggling impishly.

The birds started to turn back north, taking a look at the decoys. The boys kept their heads down. The geese flew past, still out of range. The Honduran boy blew again, this time several blasts, much more robustly.

"Now that was sexy," Teddy quipped.

Noah didn't say a word. He had a faraway look on his face. Not his usual ebullient self on the hunt with birds approaching.

Joey wrinkled his brow, wondering what was bothering Noah, and waited for instructions. He had never shot at geese.

"Shhh," the boy scolded them. "Keep your head down. Que van a venir!"

The pair was flying straight toward the decoys. Teddy and Joey released the safeties from their shotguns simultaneously, looking up under their caps but keeping their heads down. Noah didn't move.

"Get ready," the boy whispered, his body coiled in tension, his face laced with excitement and anticipation. The geese were gliding. They raised their wings in the set position and seemed to float in midair almost straight above the decoys.

Something was clearly wrong with Noah. His face had a pained expression. Joey lowered his gun and studied him.

"Now!" the boy cried. "Shoot!"

"No!" Noah cried before Teddy could sight his gun.

Teddy lowered his gun.

The geese beat their wings furiously, making a sound like a helicopter, reversed their descent and gained altitude. They looked down and assessed the situation and flew vigorously away into the last rays of sunset, honking first with alarm, then annoyingly, then defiantly.

Joey looked at Noah with amazement. Teddy was furious. The Honduran boy looked astonished. The words seemed to be coming into Noah's head faster than he could say them as he tried to explain himself.

"Dad told us about the geese. On the day of the accident, we were canoeing. He was hunting with Granddaddy when he was little. One went down and the others were loyal and stuck by him. He said they're more principled than a lot of people. He wouldn't want us to shoot them."

"Are you sure Dad said that, Noah?" asked Teddy.

"I was there, Teddy," Noah said in the voice that was typical of an argument between the twins.

Joey vaguely remembered hearing the same thing himself and decided to try to make peace.

115

"Then Dad would be proud of us," Joey said, looking deeply into Teddy's eyes and nodding softly and reassuringly at Noah.

No one seemed to have anything else to say on the matter and they were quiet for a moment before they unloaded. It was dark. There would be no more shooting at birds today. There was nothing to do but wait for the airboat to take them back. Surely it would be along any minute. They were surprised that they would navigate after dark, with the mud flats and stumps to dodge.

Dark brought not the airboat they expected, but instead clouds of hungry mosquitoes. Now the wind had died down. They found themselves prey, literally covered with clouds of humming, hungry insects only partially deterred by their 95 percent DEET insect repellant. They were grateful that Granddaddy had been adamant that they take their antimalarial pills. They had grudgingly swallowed the bitter-tasting pills as prescribed.

They were supposed to be picked up just before sundown. No one came. As the sun went down, the wind picked up again. The air felt electrified as one band of thunderstorms after another crackled around them like high-powered rifle shots, illuminating the landscape time after time with vivid white, jagged bolts of lightning arising from the earth like some primeval theater. They were the highest thing in the swamp and had no place to lay away the metal barrels of their guns.

After several waves of storms, they were soaked to the bone and the bird boy began to cry. The rock-like quesadillas they had complained about were now mush. Joey had a couple of packs of cellophane-wrapped peanut butter crackers that had stayed dry. He opened one and offered it to the sobbing young Honduran boy who, before the storms, had excitedly set out so many times to retrieve their birds. Joey felt generous despite the uncertainty of their next source of food. The water, already in flood stage, and which had forced them to stand immersed in water above their ankles on what should have been dry dove-hunting ground, was rising fast.

Standing in the poncho he always carried folded up in his pocket for hunting trips, Joey said, "I'll be damned, Teddy, but I think it's rising faster."

"Yep," said Teddy, trying not to sound alarmed. "The water table must already be saturated. This marsh we're standing in drains the runoff from the mountains and funnels it down into the lagoon and sea."

The water now lapped at his knees. If it got much higher, he would have to take off his hip waders to keep them from filling with water and pulling him under. "You sound awful calm. I may start to get a little nervous when the water starts to fill up these waders," Joey said with an anxious chuckle. His brow furrowed just enough to convey, despite his attempts at levity, the growing gravity he perceived in the situation. Turning away from Teddy, he shook his head slightly and rolled his eyes, saying just under his breath, "Holy Shit."

"Where the hell is the boat?" growled Teddy, trying to sound more pissed off than worried.

"I hate to think about being on that metal boat in a lightning storm," Joey sighed.

"Jesus," Teddy added, turning toward Joey, "not to mention all that gasoline."

Noah had just returned with the bird boy from a several-hundred-yard scouting expedition testing the depth of the water and stability of the bottom of a green area they had spied through their binoculars in the distance. They were looking for higher ground if the water kept rising.

"No luck. It's just weeds," Noah reported, out of breath from his slog through the mud. "It gets deeper out there."

"Do you hear those cows lowing out there somewhere?" Joey asked. "They have to be on land. If we had to, we could swim in the direction of that mooing. Eventually we would have to hit the shore, or at least an island in the flood."

"Sound carries a long way over the water," Noah said dubiously. "That may be a very long swim."

They watched the sky. A line of thunderheads passed to the west, giving a temporary respite from the soaking tropical downpours. They told old jokes, reminisced, and fretted about Granddad and Mac.

"Granddad's diabetic, you know. He needs to eat or he'll get low," Teddy said a little guiltily as he munched on a dry peanut butter cracker.

"He can't go too long without insulin either," Noah said, his face falling glumly.

"Carlos knows that. If there's trouble, and apparently there is, he'll get the old guys out first," Joey said reassuringly.

"If he can," added Noah.

"Carlos could always call a helicopter to pick Granddad up," Teddy put in, attempting to keep his voice steady, but sounding a little wooden, as if he were parroting a false reassurance with the best of intentions.

"Where would they get it and where would it land?" Noah quizzed Teddy.

Another broader line of thunderstorms appeared in the west. This time there would be no escaping it. They watched the approaching sheets of gray stringy rain reaching from the clouds to the earth. They re-donned their ponchos. The first clear drops struck the surface of the coffee-like swamp water and were obliterated. The sound of the rain drops bouncing off the surface made a deep thudding roar in the distance and became more high-pitched, like a million steamy shower spigots, just before it enveloped them.

There was nothing to be done during the downpour but to look at one another and laugh. Then, just as quickly, the storm was gone. The air cooled several degrees with each squall that came through. Mercifully, the swamp water retained the day's heat. The boys had the sensation of the upper parts of their bodies being cold while the lower parts were immersed in a warm bath.

After the last storm moved on to the west, the clouds parted and a huge white moon seemed to fill the sky. Its brilliant light shimmered over the swamp. Out of nowhere, a cacophony of birds began to sing, an orchestra to the left answered by a symphony to the right and then behind them. The bird songs were astonishingly loud. Flocks of white swans landed a stone's throw away, unafraid, as if cognizant the night belonged to them.

Suddenly illuminated and teeming with song, the swamp felt magical, wondrous, hospitable. The feeling was one of extreme delight, of nature revealing its heavenly secrets, its choruses of angels as it only could late at night when man was not supposed to be present. The bird symphonies died down. Another squall came through. The moon was obscured and the dark broken by flashes of lightning and crackling thunder.

"The water's over my knees," Joey said softly. He was still confident that, before the night was over, they would be warmly ensconced in their beds at the hotel talking about this misadventure after a hot shower. But an alarming thought crossed his mind. *In addition to diabetes, Granddad's got terrible high blood pressure. If he stops his beta-blocker suddenly, he could get a heart attack. We've got to be sure we get him out of here. I wonder if they picked up the older guys first. Maybe something happened and they had to take them to the hospital?*

Joey knew that the boys' genes were loaded for early-onset hypertension, but only he had developed high blood pressure thus far. He too took a beta-blocker. He would miss the evening dose. He decided to say nothing, as he knew Teddy and Noah were drawing some of their strength from him.

"I wouldn't want Granddad in one of these hospitals," Teddy said, his brow knitted.

"We would fly him home," Noah said.

"Mom could do something to get him out of here," Teddy added.

"If she knew," Noah added skeptically.

They fell silent for a half hour.

"This water is still rising, you know," Joey said at last, pointing above his knee. "We don't have forever."

"Do you think they remember where we are? Or worse, do you think they can find us in the dark?" asked Teddy.

"Maybe they decided to wait until tomorrow morning," said Noah.

119

"We won't be above water tomorrow morning at this rate," said Joey.

"It won't hurt to shoot every fifteen minutes or so. That way they can locate us by the sound" suggested Noah.

"Maybe Granddaddy and Mac will answer with a shot," Teddy added.

"Cover your ears," warned Noah.

Teddy mimed covering his ears for the young Honduran boy, who spoke little English. Noah turned off his safety, pumped a 12-gauge shell into the chamber, and pulled the trigger. The crack of the explosion sounded like an artillery piece in the darkness, immediately silencing the choruses of birds, rhythmic humming of the insects, and the seductive high-pitched singing of the frogs. They heard the beating of wings as hundreds of birds on every side of them took to flight and countless plunking sounds as frogs, turtles and other creatures dove into the safety of the water. But there was no answering shot.

After a while, Teddy broke the silence. His voice was a little shaky. "What lives in this swamp, anyway?"

Noah immediately picked up on his twin's anxiety. "You mean besides jaguars, alligators, crocodiles and fer-de-lance?"

"Would you rather die drowning or at least serve as a meal for something?" Teddy asked dryly, his face twisted into a self-conscious smile.

"If an alligator gets us, we could die both ways at the same time. They take their prey alive down to the bottom and stick it under a log to cure for a while before they eat it," retorted Noah.

"You know, shooting that gun from time to time is sounding like a very good idea," Joey added with a wry smile. "Nothing that would eat us is going to get anywhere near here after they hear that."

A second shot crackled from Noah's 12-gauge, fire spewing from the carbon buildup in the barrel. The sound quickly died out. There was no echo to be heard in the immense flat swamp because there was nothing tall enough to bounce the sound back. This time, there was no beating of wings or plopping of swamp beasts diving to safety. As Joey had predicted, every above-water creature that could get away had fled. Joey silently worried about what might be prowling under the surface but decided not to further up the ante of his siblings' anxieties for the moment.

Around midnight, they saw two Honduran boys, one 11 years old or so and the other in his mid-teens, wading through the water hauling an airboat by a rope. The young guide was exuberantly relieved to see his brothers. In one another's company, the Honduran boys quickly recovered their spirit and sense of humor. "Un gran baño," one said, referring to all the trash, sewage and debris that had been washed into the swamp by the floodwaters.

"What happened to our grandfather and Mac?" Noah asked.

"The radio stop," the elder Honduran boy began. "They in broken boat. I think still in water. Pero, radio no work. No estoy seguro."

A fourth, even older air boat that had been previously mothballed had been brought back into service, but the engine had been patched up many times and the boys were not confident that it would run for long. Moreover, the Honduran boys did not have a GPS system and were unable to give clear directions. The swamp was huge and dark, and they felt that if the group were found that night, it would be by sheer luck alone.

Noah, Teddy and Joey felt they could look out for themselves overnight if they had to. But their spirits were dampened when it started raining again. It was colder than they had expected for a Honduran swamp and they were soaked to the bone. They slogged through the swamp together for a couple of hours, unsure what direction they were traveling in.

"Trépate a un árbol," one of the older boys would say to the younger about every half hour to try to see land.

Each time, the boy would shimmy down the tree and say, "Nada. Sólo agua."

"¿Qué hora es?"

"Dos…"

The older cousins were looking tired and anxious. Their slogging had become more labored. Suddenly, the older boy's body disappeared

121

in the water up to his chest. He struggled forward and up, remerging with a pale, pained look on his face.

"Hell, you stepped into a hole! Your waders filled up!" cried Noah.

"We have to stop now. He can't walk with his waders full and he must be cold," said Teddy sympathetically.

"Let's anchor for tonight," suggested Noah.

They all climbed into the boat and huddled together for warmth in a circle with their arms around one another's shoulders.

"Tengo que levantarme," the older boy said. He slid over the side, his waders hitting the bottom suddenly. Foul-looking silt swirled into the water and released its odor on the surface.

Joey could not suppress his urge to gag, followed by Noah and Teddy. They tried to suppress their laughter, but it seemed to flow out involuntarily, like the contagious, naughty laughter of children in class. One of the younger bird boys exclaimed something unintelligible in Spanish, and they started to laugh too.

The cold rain continued and no one slept.

At dawn, they were all still awake, barely rested and miserable, but glad to see the sun.

"Let's get going!" said Noah.

"Which way?" asked Teddy.

"This time of day, toward the sun is east, and east is toward the coast and toward camp," Joey observed. He went over the side first and immediately commented with alarm, "The water rose through the night! It's up to my waist!"

"Thank goodness we have the boat," Noah said. "We won't drown, but the higher the water gets, the harder to slog through this crap and drag the boat. Soon we'll be swimming and dragging it behind us."

Joey felt a thumping in his chest and took his pulse: 96 beats per minute. *I'm probably dehydrated*, he thought, *so that would elevate my heart rate. But I'm probably also not beta-blocked.*

The front that had brought the storm of the previous day had passed, and the sun rose higher into a bright, clear blue sky. Their upper bodies dried off. It was hot and there was no fresh water to drink.

"Well," mused Joey, "which was worse? Being soaked to the bone in a cold rain or frying in a warm bath of stinking swamp water?"

Teddy, now in a reasonably good mood and not perceiving any real threat, chanted the old proverb, "Water, water everywhere and not a drop to drink."

For the next six hours, they slogged slowly through the mud and waist-deep water, experiencing the irony of parched throats and soaked bodies. The going was arduous as they dragged the boat, now their home, and fought the mud to lift their feet.

Joey wore scuba boots instead of the much heavier boots worn by the others and found it much easier to maneuver. He said to his brothers, "Geographically, if we continue east, we have to hit land."

The older Honduran boy remarked that it was easy to find east when the sun was low, but the higher the sun rose, the more uncertain the direction.

"Does someone want to climb a tree and look for land?" Noah asked.

But no one seemed to have the energy. They slogged on. The sun began to sink in the sky and they realized they would be spending another night in the swamp.

"How long do you think it takes to organize an air search?" Teddy asked as if he was certain one was already underway.

"Depends on the resources around here. It would be expensive," Noah said. "You could probably hire a crop duster, but they might require cash. I doubt Carlos has it."

"How motivated do you think Carlos is to get the money?" Joey asked innocently.

"He ought to be damned motivated if he ever wants to see another hunter down here," Noah added.

They were all worried about Granddaddy, but no one wanted to talk about it now. The horizon was a mixture of gray and blood red when the sun set. They climbed into the boat to wait. The night was very still and the sky overcast. The darkness was broken periodically by flashes of heat lightning in the distance. There were no magical-sounding symphonies of birds tonight. Their lack of sleep, food and water had begun to take its toll. They were exhausted and slept. Around 9:00, the older Honduran boy stirred.

"He oído algo!"

"He heard something," Joey translated.

With his binoculars hanging from his neck, the boy climbed over the edge of the boat, slogged through the water and climbed to a perch on a high branch of a cypress tree. He shouted down to the boys.

"Una luz! Tres disparos!"

"A light," Joey said with great relief.

The boys whooped and leaped the best they could in the deep muck, smacking their hands together in high fives.

"Our saviors!" Noah shouted.

Teddy put in his earplugs, slipped three shells into the chamber of his shotgun, pumped, clicked off the safety and fired. The sound tore through the swamp and ricocheted back from the northeast.

"We're closer to land than we thought," Noah said.

Teddy fired twice more. Then they waited.

The Honduran boy watched the small dot of the boat's searchlight from the tree. It turned toward their direction, spraying a small jet of white over the water. The boat was moving very slowly and cautiously in the dark water. The boy waited until he was sure the light was growing larger and brighter. But the light began to veer. The boat was going to miss them.

"Fuego de nuevo," he said.

Teddy reloaded and fired again, this time spacing the shots by several seconds to help the searchers triangulate their position. The boat corrected its course, the searchlight turning this way, then that way, before settling on a course directly toward them. The boat moved surprisingly fast. Before long, the roar of the exposed steel propeller was upon them. The pilot cut the engine and glided toward them. They scrambled aboard and swilled fresh water from plastic milk jugs.

The engine quickly roared back and they glided over the dark water to continue the search for Granddaddy and Mac.

The wind came up quickly, giving them only a few moments warning before they were lashed by blowing hail and blinding sheets of cold rain. There was no roof on the boat and they were completely exposed. A boy no older than a teenager sat stoically in the elevated pilot's chair, turning the bow into the wind to keep from capsizing. Bolts of jagged, brilliantly white lightning illuminated the murky gray darkness. It crackled like artillery, first in the west, then from every direction as the squall engulfed the boat.

Terrified, each boy recognized their vulnerability on the ungrounded steel boat in the midst of a thunderstorm. But somehow the earth's electricity chose the taller mangrove trees that honeycombed the shallow edges of the lagoon, exploding them spectacularly, one by one.

Suddenly, the boat listed violently like a dog trying to shake off water. Joey lost his footing on the wet deck. Then the wind shifted suddenly and the boat lunged forward. Joey felt a surge of panic as he felt himself falling backward over the stern. In the howling wind and crackling thunder, no one heard the muffled thud from the collision between the back of Joey's head and the edge of boat's metal hull. His lungs sputtered, then he coughed violently as his head jerked above the surface. He expelled a jet of dark lagoon water and gasped for air. He found his footing in the shallow water over the sandbar that had destabilized the airboat and stumbled toward the shadowy outline of the mangrove forest that marked land.

The atmosphere had a warm tropical feel that he found comforting. The rain fell gently but steadily. *Like a warm shower,* he thought. He was solidly on land now. *Perhaps I could rest just for a moment. I'll lie down and close my eyes and then I'll get a second wind and figure out what to do.*

There was something wet trickling down his neck. He couldn't tell whether it was from his ears or the jagged tear in his scalp. He recalled that he had crawled onto a sandbar near the shore and wondered whether he had hit his head on a rock or on the boat. The open wound worried him. He knew the lagoon water could be filthy from untreated sewage. *What happened to Teddy and Noah and the Honduran boys?* He thought. *Had the boat sunk or been hit by lightning? Or did I fall overboard in the confusion of the storm?*

The full moon and stars appeared tenuously through the broken, wind-blown clouds. The temperature had dropped at least 10 degrees. A vigorous freshwater stream traversing a bed of smooth rock fed into the lagoon near where Joey had stumbled ashore. He had a terrible thirst. The stream descended quickly over a gravely bottom and was cold. He judged that, if the water came from an underground spring nearby, it could be pure and safe to drink. If it had somehow meandered from the distant hills, there would have been many opportunities for it to be polluted. It was probably safe. But he was really too thirsty to care much.

The torrent of clear, cold water parted the dark, warm swamp water, creating a transparent pool amid the inky blackness. The rippled surface glowed, transilluminated by moonlight, shifting constantly in hues of gray and white as windswept clouds raced across the sky.

Joey found himself standing near the shore in the pleasingly cool water, transfixed by the silvery rippling motion of the reflected light. He thought he saw something under the surface obscured by deeper water. He tried to step out to get a better look. The sandbar sloped gradually at first but dropped off quickly where he was looking. He stepped back, unsure of his footing but determined, drawn somehow to see underneath. The wind broke for a moment before changing direction but permitted him a glance into the depths unobscured by windy turbulence.

There was a body under the surface. It appeared to be a child. The breeze briefly shifted southerly and the view was obscured, but something had been there. He stood transfixed, watching patiently for fleeting glimpses of the body. The water was too deep and the edge of the sandbar too unstable for him to reach the body. But when the wind died momentarily, his view was clear. He thought the child looked strangely like him. The body appeared to be undecayed. He

ould not be sure of the age. The water distorted his view. He felt an
ffinity for the child he could not understand and fought a desire
lmost like the pull of a magnet to lie down under the water with the
orpse. He found himself testing the unstable drop-off of the sandbar.
Perhaps he could get closer. He stepped forward and sank to his waist
s the unstable bank collapsed. But then there was a sound he knew, a
nan-made mechanical sound. He listened. It was from the sky. There
vas a bright star low in the sky in the direction of the noise. He had
1ot noticed it earlier, but the night had been cloudy. It seemed to be
getting brighter. *It must be an airplane*, he thought.

The airboat had been within the most intense area of the thun-
lerstorm for almost ten minutes before the wind and rain cleared
ufficiently for the boat pilot to realize Joey had been lost. He took
1 compass reading in an attempt to retrace his steps. But he soon
ealized that he had no idea what direction he had come from in the
torm and made a call to base requesting assistance in finding Joey.

Granddad and Mac had been located and were back at base.
Granddad was alarmed but kept his head. He remembered Steven,
1 close friend of the family who had been a ranger in the U.S. Army
oefore working with the Drug Enforcement Agency and had reput-
:dly been active in "hunting" smugglers near the Nicaraguan border
of Honduras. He called Steven by satellite phone, and in less than
:hree hours, a former "hunting" buddy of Steven's, Jose Rodriguez,
1ad commandeered an agency helicopter and was searching for Joey
oy air.

Rodriguez flew rapidly toward the compass readings taken by
:he airboat pilot after he realized that Joey had been swept overboard.
Compared to GPS, a compass reading was a very blunt instrument
for finding a place, but it was a start. Rodriguez had worked as a
guide and part-time bounty hunter for the DEA and he knew the
wamp like the back of his hand. He worked on the theory that, if

Joey had survived, he would have made it to the shoreline. Although the swamp was filled with caimans and poisonous snakes, he figured the worst threat to Joey, if he had not drowned, would be confusion and exhaustion from exposure to the elements.

The helicopter was a stealth model, designed to fly at night and in bad weather with reduced propeller noise. It could fly at nearly 200 miles per hour and then hover a few feet over the marsh. Rodriguez reached the compass coordinates from the boat pilot, descended to 50 feet, deactivated the noise-cancellation system, switched on the powerful searchlight and began to methodically illuminate the shoreline.

When the helicopter hovered a few inches above the ground near Joey, he was confused by the powerful beacon of light and initially mistook the elderly man who rushed out and embraced him to be his father. *It can't be, my father's dead,* Joey reasoned to himself.

A moment later, he realized it was his grandfather. As the helicopter reached a safe altitude to gain speed, Joey suddenly remembered the boy under the water and pleaded with his grandfather to return to recover the body.

Granddaddy explained to the pilot the best he could in broken Spanish. The pilot seemed skeptical but Granddaddy was persistent, and so the pilot returned to the sandbar, hovering a few feet above the water and searching underneath with the powerful light. The turbulence from the rotor stirred the sand and water and nothing could be discerned below the now opaque surface. The pilot waited patiently while Joey and Granddaddy peered down in futility.

As they flew back toward the landing pad, Joey sobbed softly, describing in vivid detail the image of boy under the surface. Then, exhausted, he quickly fell asleep.

When he was sure that Joey could not hear, the pilot said to Granddaddy in a sympathetic tone that lacked his usual bravado, "Fue su reflejo, señor."

19

Spin the Bottle

Nashville, Tennessee
March 30, 2024

MADELEINE, VALEDICTORIAN OF VANDERBILT MEDICAL School's senior class, was a shapely beauty at 5' 9". Tonight she would be escorted to the Cadaver Ball, the school's graduation party, by her classmate and long-time chum, Joey.

Elisabeth, Madeleine's mother, was a Vanderbilt alumna and close friend of the Jacobson family. She had been present at all the Jacobson children's brises. The last few years of Madeleine's life had been shaped by her mother's cancer. During the latter stages, Madeleine had flown home every weekend. Elisabeth had maintained her equanimity and sense of humor to the end. She had imparted to Madeleine that, although she was disappointed that her life would be short, she was happy with the way she had lived and wanted her wake to celebrate her life. The best thing that Madeleine could do for her in the long run, she said, was to live life to its fullest. She wasn't sure whether there was a heaven, but her idea of eternity was that her spirit would live on through Madeleine and ultimately through Madeleine's children.

After her mother's death, Madeleine became determined to become a cancer specialist and buried herself in her work. On her oncology rotation, she found herself dating a distinguished visiting cancer researcher and jumped into a committed relationship. He was based on the West Coast, worlds away from Nashville. He was rumored to have other girlfriends and some said he regularly preyed on medical students. Madeleine was having serious doubts about whether to carry on the relationship but hadn't told him. She had called him several times that weekend but only reached his answering service. Earlier in the evening, she described the relationship to a girlfriend as like dry tinder that only needed a spark to go up in smoke.

Madeleine and Joey had drinks with friends at Tootsie's Orchard Lounge and dinner at the Hermitage Hotel. By the time they arrived at the ball, most of the students had begun to drift off to smaller parties. A group of upperclassmen had rented the capacious presidential suite. A live band covered Neil Young & Crazy Horse. There was a very large hot tub and talk of skinny-dipping at midnight. As the night wore on, many of the couples drifted into various semi-private areas of the suite. When someone organized a game of spin the bottle, Joey tried to slip away. Madeleine giggled and yanked on the sleeve of his sport coat.

"Where are you going?"

Joey's eyes fell on the subtle pink of Madeline's lips. He shook his head almost imperceptibly.

"Unh, uh, nowhere," he said under his breath. *We've been friends a long time, I don't want to screw that up,* he thought. *Besides, there's the boyfriend situation.*

He looked up into the eyes of his friend. "Do you think this is a good idea?"

She took a long drink from her wine glass. "Aw, come on. It's only a game," she said playfully.

"Only a game," he muttered.

The first spin paired a married couple. They gave each other a little peck.

Someone hissed. Another voice taunted good-naturedly, "You can do better than that!"

They kissed again, this time with tongue, and everyone clapped.

The bottle spun again and matched a couple who were dating. They locked their mouths together passionately, clearly enjoying it. Several people whooped and clapped. Everyone was having a good time now.

Finally someone said, "OK, OK, that's enough!"

The bottle spun again and missed everyone.

Joey reached over and spun the bottle hard. It went round and around and pointed directly back at Madeleine. There was silence. Some looked on quizzically, others with big smiles.

Joey laughed. "Really, folks, we're just friends."

He reached for the bottle to spin it again. Madeleine caught his hand in midair, leaned over and pressed her lips to his. Joey pulled away, stunned, and tried to compose himself. When he looked up, Madeleine's lips were directly in front of his. He lost himself in the moment and kissed her lightly, closing his eyes. She closed her eyes too. Then he made an exaggerated smacking sound and broke away. Their friends clapped and whistled, and the whole effect was that of a light joke as he had hoped. He quickly pushed the bottle to the next reveler and the party's mirth turned to someone else. He leaned back and let out a long sigh. It felt like his temperature had risen a hundred degrees.

The bar closed and the noise of the band started to get old around 1 a.m.

"Want to check out the minibar downstairs?" Madeleine asked. "There's a balcony with a view of the city and we can take a break from this noise."

Joey walked her to the room. She lit a cigarette on the balcony and Joey coughed from the smoke.

"You don't have a cold, do you?" she asked gently. Then, with a tease in her voice, she added, "You don't want to get anyone sick."

Joey nodded in complicity. "It's the smoke," he quipped, feeling energized. Then his countenance turned serious. "Why the hell do you smoke? You're almost a doctor. You know better!"

"It was the one thing my mother could control that would give her pleasure when she was dying. I wanted to share it with her and then I couldn't stop."

"Jesus, I'm sorry, but you've got to quit. For your own good."

She took a long draw from her cigarette and blew the smoke out very slowly. "Get me a drink, please." She stubbed out her cigarette and followed Joey inside.

Joey began to poke in the refrigerator minibar.

"I'll have whatever you have," she said as she closed the door to the bathroom.

Joey found little bottles of wine and Jack Daniel's in the refrigerator and presented them to her as she walked out of the bathroom. "My great-grandfather, the original Joseph, drank a shot of Jack Daniel's every night when he got home from his store."

"Do you want me to drink a shot with you?"

"Are you game?"

She gave a big nod and smiled.

Joey poured the whiskey from two bottles into glasses. "Cheers!"

"Wait," she said, and she intertwined their arms as they raised their glasses to their lips.

"To your namesake!" she said.

Joey's shot burned the back of his throat, all the way down to his stomach. He smothered an urge to cough, thinking it unmanly. Then a very pleasant warm feeling seemed to spread from his chest. He noticed Madeleine hadn't drunk her shot.

"Here," she said, "this time we'll really do it together."

She opened another bottle and poured the whiskey into Joey's glass. She re-hooked her lean, soft arm through Joey's arm and raised her glass. Joey did the same.

"To graduation!" she said.

This time, they both drank their shots in one swallow. She winced, made a funny face and smiled. She looked at his lips, still wet with Jack Daniel's. He looked at hers. The first hints of a warm flush on Madeleine's chest had begun to appear. She wore a light white blouse that hung on the edges of her shoulders with a low round neckline that became lacy just above the subtle swell of her breasts. She rubbed the back of her neck nervously and he was sure she was waiting for him to kiss her.

But he wasn't ready to risk their friendship with a kiss. He chose a diversion.

"Your neck looks tense. Can I work on it?"

"I slept funny last night. I didn't have my pillow."

"Where does it bother you most?"

She pointed to an area just below her neck between her shoulder blades. "It gets all knotted up."

Joey took this as an invitation to apply his nascent therapeutic skills. He looked at her back. Her neck was crooked to one side and her shoulders hunched.

"Wow, you *are* tense," he said softly. He used brush strokes at first, getting her used to his touch, then gently worked the old knots between her shoulder blades. He applied broad, firm pressure to her trapezoids in a kneading motion. "Am I doing this right?"

"It's wonderful," she whispered, eyes closed. "Where did you learn to do that?"

"Just instinct, I think."

He was struck by the warmth and softness of her skin. His touch became more like a caress, she noticed, as she switched off the lamp. "When you get a massage, they always dim the lights," she said innocuously.

Joey was not soothed. *We're not going to cross the line.* But before he knew it, she began to lean back on him, gradually letting him support more of her weight. He found himself broadening the field of massage down her arm and over her shoulder.

In a matter-of-fact tone, she said, "Let me get this out of the way a little." She brought the strap of her blouse down over her shoulder, uncovering the top of her lacey lightweight bra and the subtle swellings underneath.

Joey felt an overwhelming urge to kiss her. To defeat it, he stood up and turned on the light. "We need to talk, my friend!"

Madeleine nodded as if she had expected this. She grabbed her purse and took out a cigarette and her lighter. Joey pointed at the smoke detectors on the ceiling. She nodded, stood up and walked to the glass door of the balcony, opened it a few inches and stuck her head out. She lit her cigarette, took a few deep puffs, stubbed it out and returned to the couch, taking Joey's hand and pulling him down beside her. She held onto his hand and looked into his eyes with a knowing smile.

"You're worried about screwing up our friendship."

Joey nodded and smiled. "Not to mention you have a boyfriend."

"I wouldn't be here if it was right with him."

"I thought you loved him?"

"I don't know, Joey. I think he lies to me. How can I love someone I don't trust? I got involved with him so quickly without really knowing him. Mom was dying and dad left. It was so hard for me then. I had to have somebody. He was there for me then. But it hasn't been right in a long time."

Joey nodded several times. "And he was about the same age as your dad?"

"It wasn't rocket science to figure out what was going on, but that doesn't always help."

"What are you going to do?"

"I'm going to break up with him."

"OK, that's one piece of it. But what about us? We've been friends forever. Do we want to screw that up?"

"Are you asking me to choose between being your friend or lover?"

"We have to decide or the night will decide for us."

"I want us to be both," she said earnestly, her eyes pleading. The edges of her mouth rose in a hopeful smile.

"Yes," he said after a slight pause.

She looked up and parted her lips slightly. He kissed her lightly at first, and then tested a deeper kiss, then a French kiss. In every case she responded in kind. He began to caress her breast through her blouse. Her body answered and he began to unbutton her blouse from the top, one button at a time.

"I don't want you to be disappointed," she said as he unsnapped her bra.

"It's the total package," he said. "I won't be."

Periodically, Joey hesitated. "Are you sure this is a good idea? Are you sure you're ready for this?"

She would answer, "I want to," and they would go on, only for Joey to raise the matter again as each milestone was passed, except one. He dug his heels in at the end.

"Not until you break up with up with him," he said, slipping back into his underclothes.

Around 4 a.m., he took Madeleine home, smitten, happy, unsettled. He woke up late to his clock radio the next morning. The station was on a sentimental, early '70s set. Joey smiled as Neil Young sang of the girl of his dreams in *Cowgirl in the Sand*.

20

Love in the Ruins

Nashville, Tennessee
June 27, 2025

MADELEINE AND JOEY WERE NEARING the end of their first year of post-medical school internships. They had worked side by side on the hospital wards and slept in the same on-call bunkrooms for nearly a year. She had held a live human heart in her hand while he had sewn on new coronary blood vessels and he had done the same for her. Her hand shook so hard the first time, she almost dropped it.

"Hold it like a hamburger," Joey had whispered, his eyes sparkling over his surgical mask. She had thanked him afterward and bought him breakfast later that night when the hospital cafeteria reopened at 2 a.m. They were famished and had just sat down to a steaming platter of fried eggs, bacon and buttered toast when the stat call came overhead.

"Code team to Ward 3B."

"Here we go!" Joey said. "That's one of ours." And they sprinted out of the cafeteria, up three flights of stairs and across the ward into the patient's room. A lone nursing student stood at the patient's side.

"Where's the code team?" Madeleine asked.

"There was a big accident out on I-40. Everyone's tied up in the ER."

Madeleine and Joey worked together seamlessly. She pierced the vein and established intravenous access while he checked vital signs and stuck on the heart monitor. The patient's heart was working, but he struggled loudly for breath, his face blue.

Madeleine looked at Joey for confirmation. "I think we've got a respiratory problem here. We'd better get a trachea tube into him."

"Agreed," Joey said, nodding, and pulled the patient's head back while Madeleine attempted to work the tube in. Joey waited for Madeleine to finish so he could tape the tube in place and connect the oxygen hose. It was taking too long. Something was wrong. He glanced at the oxygen monitor. The level was falling.

"Qué pasa?" he asked in an intentionally soothing tone. Madeleine looked up at Joey, wide-eyed, her normally rosy complexion white.

"It won't go!"

"Maybe there's something in the way. May I?" Joey removed the tube and placed his hand in the patient's mouth, feeling down the throat toward the trachea with his fingers. "There's something there. I can't get to it but it's soft."

The nurse asked, "Do you want calipers?"

"Not yet!" Joey said.

The patient was a large, obese man. Joey pulled him to the side of the bed, lifted his trunk upright and circled him with his arms, clasping his hands together just below his sternum. He squeezed hard. Nothing happened. He squeezed again, harder. He thought he heard a very faint hiss of air escape from the man's trachea. He quickly glanced at Madeleine. She shot him a smile. She had heard it too. He was on the right track. There was something in the man's trachea blocking his breath. He just needed to squeeze harder. But before

138

he could, the man collapsed onto the bed, pulling Joey with him. Madeleine and the nurses rushed to set the man upright again.

"Wait!" Joey said. He took a deep breath and squeezed his locked wrists into the man's abdomen upward toward his ribs, exhaling as if he were in the gym lifting barbells. A 3-inch section of hot dog exploded out of the man's throat. The man quickly stabilized and began to breathe on his own. Stroke patients who had difficulty swallowing were only supposed to receive soft food.

Madeleine rewrote the intern's diet orders. They got back to the on-call bunkroom with an hour to nap before morning rounds. Joey was almost asleep before his head hit the pillow, but his last waking thought was the radiant expression on Madeleine's face after the patient had breathed.

Generally, they labored thirty-six hours on call, twelve hours off, for stretches of fifteen weeks at a time. Late one Christmas Eve at one of the city hospitals, she nearly panicked while performing a C-section. After making her incision, she noticed the womb was stuck to the bladder from scarring. Joey had just settled into the on-call room bunkroom when the alarm on his beeper went off. He had set the alarm to Jingle Bells for the holidays, and when it rang he thought he was dreaming. Then a loud voice mixed with static came over the intercom.

"Dr. Jacobson, please come to OB surgical suite III, stat."

He sat up suddenly, bumping his head. "Ouch!"

A woman's sleepy voice above him said, "You all right down there?"

He had hit the springs of the bunk above him, which gave way, cushioning the blow. Joey chuckled good-naturedly.

"Just my head. Nothing important."

"Are you sure you're OK?" she asked sympathetically.

He was already out the door. He trotted down the stairs to avoid waiting for the elevator, burst through the double doors of the surgical suite, scrubbed his hands with Betadine three times, donned his gloves, and was by Madeleine's side within six minutes of being paged. Her normally smooth brow had furrowed into deep trenches. Her incandescent blue eyes immediately riveted his gaze to hers.

"The baby needs to come out right away," she said through her mask.

"What's the obstacle?" he asked as calmly as he could.

She motioned toward the surgical field. Between the retractors was a mass of tangled scar tissue the size of a football. He nodded. There were so many adhesions between the bladder and womb that it was impossible to know where to make the incision. They had to figure out what was bladder and what was womb.

He turned to the scrub nurse. "Give me a syringe, 20 cc of blue dye, please." He gently squirted the colorful liquid into the catheter that was inserted into the woman's bladder, inflating it until it was clearly demarcated from the womb.

He turned to Madeleine. "Cut the womb slowly. As long as you don't see blue dye, you'll know you haven't cut the bladder."

Madeleine carefully applied her scalpel to the uterus. After the baby was safely out and the mother's wound sewed closed, she turned to Joey. "Now get out of here," she said playfully, grinning broadly from the edge of her surgical mask to the corner of her eyes.

Joey smiled back and nodded. "Service is my business."

She laughed and her eyes danced below her hairnet. For a moment, it felt to him like his brown eyes were swimming in the blue sea inside hers. Suddenly, he was conscious of the anesthesiologist and surgical nurses still in the room and unlocked his gaze from Madeleine's. As he stepped through the double doors of the operating room, he felt a deep pang of longing. It was a bittersweet feeling that somehow reminded him of the passing of summer to fall. They had dated and lived together for a year, but this was the moment when he conceived the notion of asking her to marry him.

21

Hard Rock

Stowe, Vermont
December 22, 2025

WIND-DRIVEN SNOW SWIRLED OVER THE mountain road, making it difficult to discern the yellow dividing line from the edges of the pavement. Joey peered warily through the frosty windshield, craning his neck, his back bent forward like an old man straining to see on a moonless night. The halogen lights of the shiny red Ford Explorer they had rented at Logan airport projected bravely into the blowing curtains of snow, only to dissipate a few feet later. He could just make out the yellow reflectors mounted on the top of poles marking the edge of the road as they caught his headlights, winked, and disappeared into the swirling torrent. The wind seemed to blow the car from side to side on the road at intervals. Nevertheless, from time to time, he dared to take a hand off the wheel to fondle the solitaire diamond ring in his pocket. He felt more certain than ever that he wanted to be with Madeleine for the rest of his life.

By his side, Madeleine followed their progress on the GPS map with her iPhone. It never occurred to either of them that there could be a situation they couldn't handle when they were together. Thus, as the engine whined and strained to pull the heavy SUV up the steep mountain road in a blinding blizzard, neither of them was afraid. Just as the GPS signal flickered out, they came around a bend and were met by the cheerful lights of the Stowe, Vermont, ski resort's inn.

A blast of warm air from a blazing fieldstone fireplace big enough for a moose to stand in met them upon opening the heavy oaken door. The lobby bustled with guests gazing at the storm through the expansive picture windows or waiting to be seated in the dining room. Joey took off his gloves and gave Madeleine a little kiss. She squeezed his hand, her face shining in anticipation of their holiday. They checked in, left their bags with the porter, and headed straight for the bar.

Joey looked at the bottles of bourbon whiskey on display and was pleasantly surprised. "Pretty good for a Yankee joint," he said under his breath to Madeleine. He ordered a shot of Booker's on the rocks and she a Kir Royale.

The bartender explained that the Cedrus lounge was named after the lightning-felled Cedar tree from which its bar had been carved. They took their drinks and found a quiet corner of the lounge.

"Ah, that feels good," Joey said as Madeleine and he sank into an overstuffed couch in front of a small crackling fire.

Madeleine spooned a plump raspberry from the bottom of her Kir Royale, rolled it over and over with her tongue as if to taste it from every angle, then silently mouthed "mmm," looking up at Joey.

Joey met her gaze and drained the last of the still dark Booker's from his glass, ice cubes clinking. His stomach burned for a moment. Then he felt pleasantly warm. He looked at her ring finger and took her hand in his, savoring its warmth. He noticed her lips were lightly frosted with pink lipstick and he suddenly felt very restless. He kissed her lightly but savored it, closing his eyes. She closed her eyes too, but then opened them as if suddenly conscious of where they were. She squeezed his hand sharply.

"Later," she said, sitting upright. They both sighed and drained the last of their drinks.

"We depended on each other a lot this year," Joey said, taking her hand again.

"I don't know what I would have done without you, Joey. I always knew you had my back."

"And you had mine. A toast. To a great year," he said, lifting his glass. "I think we need new drinks."

Madeleine stood up, walked to the bar and ordered.

Joey touched the ring in his pocket and drained the last few drops of whiskey from his glass. The bartender didn't recognize the drink at first, so she wrote out the name for him. The dessert and Viennese coffee they had ordered came before the drinks. It was a puffy soufflé shaped like a mushroom for her and apfelstrudel topped with stiffly whipped cream for him. She spooned the top of the soufflé onto a plate. The outside was golden brown and the inside sugary white. She poured in the accompanying little pitcher of sauvignon sauce and replaced the top. Then she dug the little spoon in deep and tasted it. Her eyes seemed to glaze over for a moment.

"Wow," she said, looking at Joey. "It's amazing. Would you like to try it?"

"How could I resist?" he asked.

She handed him her spoon. "Be sure you go all the way down to the sauce."

Before he could respond to the double entendre, the bartender appeared at their table, smiling triumphantly under his gnarly beard.

"You nearly stumped me. I had to google it." He set out clean cocktail glasses and measured clear, golden and dark brown liquid from three separate bottles into a gold-plated shaker. Using silver tongs, he extracted several ice cubes from a bucket, screwed on the top and shook the canister vigorously. He poured half the frothy, amber liquid into each glass before departing with a warm smile and a little bow.

"Are you game?" she asked.

To Joey, her eyes seemed to sparkle and dance in anticipation. He picked up his glass. "Sounds like a dare."

She nodded. "You first."

He raised the glass to his lips as if to say, *I'm game*, and took a big swallow.

Wrinkling his forehead, he grimaced, suppressed a cough and swallowed. It tasted cold, sweet, and oily all at once. It burned going down. He felt a jolt and then a rush. *It's like jumping from a sauna into the snow*, he thought. He composed himself. "What the heck was that?"

She picked up her glass, swirled the liquid around the ice to remix the layers and tasted it thoughtfully, running her tongue over her lips. "It's called a Napoleon cocktail. It's a celebration drink."

"What's in it?" he stammered.

"Two parts gin and one half-part each Courvoisier and Grand Marnier, shook on ice."

"No wonder it had such a kick."

She raised her glass and Joey raised his. "To the end of internship," she said. Their glasses clinked gently when they touched. They sipped and raised their glasses again. "To the Joey and Madeleine team," she whispered. This time they clinked harder and held their glasses together for several seconds before drinking. They each drank a gulp. It took a moment for them to recover their composure from the strong liquor. Joey was beginning to feel a little lightheaded.

They were still a little breathless when Joey said, "To the future! To us."

"To us," she said without missing a beat.

Now or never, Joey thought. He bit his lip and took a deep breath. "I love you, Madeleine."

"I love you, too," she said, as if they were in perfect tune.

"It worked very well for us, living together this year." Madeleine looked at him as if they were playing chess and it was still his move. "I've never been so happy, or even thought I could be so happy."

"We feel the same, Joey. You know we feel the same."

"What I wanted to say is that I want it to continue."

"Of course it will continue. I love you, Joey."

He stammered, "I mean for the rest of our lives."

He saw a blush and a big smile break out on Madeleine's face and spread down her neck to her cleavage. But she remained silent, waiting.

"Will you marry me?"

The smile broke into a big toothy grin. "I do," she said, "I mean, yes, I love you, Joey!"

He took the ring from his pocket. She held out her hand and he slipped it on her finger. It fit perfectly. The light reflected from the white diamond into her eyes and he saw they were wet. They held each other's hands tightly for a moment.

"I want to be alone with you now," she whispered.

"One last toast," he said. Their glasses clinked a little too hard and Madeleine's fractured. They both noticed and, in an abundance of caution, shared Joey's drink before signaling the waiter for the check.

Holding hands, they navigated many twists, turns and small staircases en route to their room at the end of a long corridor on the fifth floor. Joey fumbled the long key into the lock, turned the shank and pushed open the heavy creaking door. The concierge had prepared the room exactly per Joey's instructions. A gas fireplace illuminated dozens of freshly cut red and white rose stems laid out on an antique oaken desk and matching armoire. A dusty old bottle of Blaufränkisch and two Bordeaux-style glasses sat on the night table.

Madeleine looked into his eyes for a moment, smiling through the tears. "Joey," was all she said before kissing him deeply and leading him by his hand to the leather chaise lounge next to the fire. She wiped the neck of the wine bottle clean, carefully removed the cork, poured them each a substantial amount, and twirled the glass in the firelight.

"To us," Joey said, kissing her lightly.

Madeleine took a sip and ran her tongue over his lips.

"Spicy," he said. She closed her eyes in a dreamy way and pressed her lips to his.

Afterward, Joey held her in his arms, her breasts gently against his chest and her head buried in his shoulder. Neither of them was sleepy. He sat up, resting his back on the walnut headboard, and pulled the sheet up over his waist. Madeleine had propped herself up on one elbow and was staring into her ring as if the facets held some deep secret. He wanted to make love again, but she seemed distracted. He sensed they should talk.

"What are you staring at?"

"I never actually looked into a diamond before. There's, like, a zillion lights in there."

"You're not having buyer's remorse, are you?"

"I've never felt better about anything. It's just all those years Mom was sick…" Her voice trailed off.

Joey brushed his lips softly against hers. She shut her eyes, seemed to inhale his breath, then pulled away and looked into his eyes.

"I think every minute I was trying to squeeze in as much life with Mom as I could, knowing it would end."

"Do you realize what a gift you were to her, just your being there?"

"At the end, she just wanted to know that I would be happy. But now I am happy and I wish she could have been part of my life with you. She would have been such a doting grandmother to our children."

Our children? Joey sat up with a start. "No surprises, I hope?"

Madeleine laughed. "Well, the label on the condom box claims they're 98 percent effective when used correctly, so I think we're safe for now." She rolled over. "I want to smoke a cigarette."

Joey rolled his eyes. "It's going to be the death of you."

"I only smoke on *very* special occasions," she said. "I think this qualifies."

Smiling now, Joey raised an eyebrow and pointed to the smoke detector on the ceiling.

Madeleine nodded. "Want to check out the balcony?" she asked, slipping her parka over her shoulders. She pulled the cord that parted the heavy draperies and opened the frosty double-paned glass door.

She took a lighter out of her pocket, ignited her cigarette and stepped just far enough out for the smoke to be carried away by the wind.

"It's like standing on a cliff. Come out here."

Joey grabbed his coat and stepped outside. The wind whistled around them and they huddled together for warmth. The storm had broken and the sky was like an immense bowl of sparkling lights. A faint smudge of orange marked the horizon to the east. She was very chatty after smoking and they talked for an hour before they fell asleep again, but not before using the calendars on their iPhones. They were able to agree on a late-July wedding. The honeymoon would be in the south of France.

Just before they fell asleep, she put both arms around Joey's neck. "I don't want us to ever be apart," she said.

"That's the one thing we don't have to worry about."

22

Honeymoon

Nice, France
July 3, 2026

JOEY AND MADELEINE WERE FINALLY alone on their honeymoon on the French Riviera near Nice. The wedding had been very small, immediate family only, with Noah and Teddy serving as co-best men and Bevy as maid of honor. A big party was planned for friends and relatives in Washington upon their return.

They awoke from an afternoon nap, still naked and pleasantly drunk. Dusk was falling. Their balcony looked out over a palm tree-lined, brown-and-white sand beach some 20 to 40 yards wide, curving along the Mediterranean. Small waves broke on the shore, leaving a pause of white foam for a few seconds before the next wave picked up the remains and turned it over. The sea was like an undulating blue fabric with white seams. The light was the soft early November light of 5 p.m. A ship steamed by, illuminated in the golden sunshine. A woman in a black chador huddled by a jetty of boulders. Next to her was her daughter, dressed the same, and her small son. Their eyes seemed fixed to the southwest toward Africa. To the east, a peninsula, marked by a series of ever lower hills, gradually fell off into the sea. Near the shore, a couple clad in a speedo and string bikini folded their umbrella while their towheaded toddler shoveled sand.

The narrow light of a lighthouse shone in a quick cycle of brightening intensity, fading quickly to pause and return. Seagulls with 3-foot wingspans flew along the shore and occasionally back over the hotel, soaring upward, wings beating as if struggling. On the peninsula, the twinkling yellow and white lights of the hotels by the shore slowly became visible as the bluish-white horizon to the east darkened into purple and the washed-out orange to the west faded, framed by the graying ocean below.

A 50-foot, low white boat with a pointed bow, looking very battered, approached. It had a vertical cabin two-thirds of the way back, like a guard shack, wider on top than bottom. The boat lolled out on the low waves and then turned west. People moved about on board. It stopped at a lighted buoy, then continued on steadily west, parallel to the shore.

One after another, huge jets with massive wings and engines floated from the nearby airport out into the sky. Joey imagined the bittersweetness of the passengers' thoughts as they took a last regretful glance at the palate of sky and ocean while savoring their memories.

"You'd better put on a rubber. We don't want babies yet," Madeleine said in tones more seductive than worried.

Joey sighed. "You're right." He pulled away and fumbled in a drawer by the bed.

"Hurry," she said.

Surprised but half proud at having gone through the box already, Joey said, "Looks like we're out."

"I think they sell them in the gift shop," Madeleine replied.

Joey rolled out of bed and slipped into a pair of shorts. Before he reached the closet to pick out a shirt, she said, "I'll go. I want to smoke a cigarette anyway."

"Hurry," he said, and gave a good-natured smile.

As the door closed behind her, he pulled open the thick sliding glass door and stepped onto the balcony. He leaned over the rail, gazing out to sea into the fine night. He returned to the room and pulled a mostly empty bottle of Pouilly-Fumé from an ice bucket, where it floated among a few diminished ice cubes. He poured the last glass and stepped back onto the balcony in time to see a small skiff embark from a larger, peculiar-shaped white boat that was moored to a buoy.

The skiff beached on shore in front of the hotel and the woman in the chador and her two children boarded. Just as the skiff left the shore, the woman removed her chador and hoisted a black and white flag.

Odd, that looks like a man, thought Joey just before a huge explosion obliterated the front of the building where Madeleine, holding a small package in her hand, had been smoking a cigarette and eagerly anticipating her return to her husband.

23

Katharina

Austrian Airlines Flight 72
July 1, 2028

TWO YEARS HAD PASSED SINCE he had finished his internship. The terrorists who had blown up the hotel had never been captured. Joey was OK when he was busy at work. The hardest times were when he was alone. Some nights he awoke in a sweat, heart thumping, gasping for air as if he were back in Nice, searching through the choking black smoke, digging through the burning rubble and calling for her.

"Madeleine, Maadeleine, Maaadeleine!"

Then the frantic failed attempts to revive her. He thought of all the lives Madeleine and he had saved together as interns. But it had been too late for her. The memories ran through his head like a tape with no end. He would meditate in the morning before work. After the accident, Bevy had somehow found the teacher who had initiated their father. The teacher gave Joey the same mantra.

After breakfast and a shot of espresso, he would sit in the loft, look out at the treetops and let the mantra come into his head – slowly at first, and then a crescendo and then he would be with Madeleine in his head. Sometimes he would just nuzzle her, his cheek pressed on hers, his eyes closed in a repose of deep relief. He envisioned her well. He liked to imagine her pregnant, smiling, his ear pressed to her belly, listening to the heartbeats within. If they had twins, they would call them Maddy and Joey.

Each morning, he would come out of this refreshed and ready to work. He had done well in his residency despite it all. Now, as chief resident, he had elected to spend his last year of training overseas on a fellowship in global drug development. Bevy had suggested a change of scene might be therapeutic and he had agreed.

Joey climbed the staircase of the 747 jet and took his aisle seat upstairs in the business section. He tested the incline of the box-like seat and was pleased when it reclined to a flat position. *Maybe I'll sleep tonight*, he thought.

A petite, attractive blond in tight-fitting slacks caught his eye in the aisle. She was meticulously but not ostentatiously groomed. Her hair was neatly pinned above her head under a black beret. She stretched and arched her body above him to stow her bag, exposing a trim, milky white midriff.

"Excuse me," she said.

Before Joey could clear a path for her through the pile of news-papers and blankets at his feet, she squeezed past to the window seat and sat down. Joey gave her a reserved smile and returned his atten-tion to his book, *The Solitude of Prime Numbers* by Paolo Giordano.

She spoke in perfect German to the Austrian Airlines stewardess.

I guess there won't be much conversation with me, he thought. He studied her. She had taken care to tend to the roots of her hair, which were only incrementally darker than the tips. She was elegantly dressed in well-fitting clothes but not with unnecessary expense.

"Excuse me, I have to get up for a second," she said with only a trace of a German accent and nimbly stepped out, dismissing his offers to move his things out of the way.

He was struck by the polite manners of such an attractive woman who must be accustomed, he thought, to being accommodated. He tried not to stare when she squeezed past him back into her seat. She ordered leg of lamb for dinner and a dark red wine.

When the meal arrived, he discovered she spoke English quite well. They made small talk about airplane food and she invited Joey to taste her wine. The wine reminded him of a Blaufränkisch he had shared with Madeleine. In a split second, the lens through which he saw the world shifted from rose-colored to gray. His brow wrinkled subtly. He tried not to think about Madeleine.

She seemed to notice Joey was lost in thought, pensive. She turned and offered her hand and in a warm tone said, "Hi, I'm Katharina."

Joey was determined to bring himself back to the present.

"I like that name. It was my wife's middle name as well. My name's Joey. Where are you headed?"

Katharina glanced at his bare ring finger. "My family is in Vienna, but I live in Georgetown."

"Where?"

"Near the French embassy."

"What do you do in DC?"

"I'm a lawyer in international relations, but I don't actually practice law."

Joey was curious why but did not want to put her on the spot. *It would be hard for someone from Vienna to pass the bar in DC*, he thought.

She drained her first glass of wine. In German, she summoned the stewardess in an authoritative but patient tone and arranged a refill. The stewardess parked a cart of wines and liquors in the aisle next to Joey and Katharina. Katharina asked, "Are you having wine?"

155

"I'll have bourbon."

Joey turned toward the stewardess. "What kind of whiskey do you have?"

"Chivas Regal."

"Is that it?" Joey asked, trying to mute his disappointment but visibly wincing. "No bourbon?" He looked directly into the eyes of the stewardess to make sure she understood, knowing from experience that many European waitresses did not understand the distinctions among whiskeys.

The stewardess looked carefully at the bottles of liquor on the tray. "No, I'm sorry," she said, sounding sincere.

"It's a decent Scotch blend. It'll do in a pinch," he said to Katharina, having decided to make the best of it.

"What's the difference between Scotch and bourbon?"

"A lot of the taste is the barrel it's aged in. Peat for Scotch and burned oak for bourbon. The lowland Scotches have more peat taste."

"I like bourbon," she said, stroking the long stem of her wine glass thoughtfully. Joey thought she was trying to bond with him but doubted her sincerity. Trying to hide his skepticism, he asked, "Which one?"

"Four Roses," she answered without hesitation.

"Four Roses." He nodded at her and smiled gently. He believed her. The name brought back many memories from his European travels. He drank Four Roses as a last resort when it was the only bourbon whiskey he could find on his world travels. There were good brands of Four Roses available but restaurants rarely carried them. He rarely saw Four Roses on the menu back in the States.

Katharina countered, "It's not bad. It's just mellow."

"You can do much better, though," Joey added, feeling invigorated from the apparent interest of this extraordinarily attractive and apparently intelligent woman. "There are two very good ones I wish I could share with you. Pappy Van Winkles Family Reserve, 23 years old. It's the smoothest. No bite. Then there's Bookers, which is one of the strongest. It's 126-and-change proof. You have to let a little of the ice melt to smooth out that one."

Joey realized he was taking a chance with the "I wish I could share with you." It was a little early for that but he had been sincere. Katharina seemed pleased. It was as if they had turned a corner. She smiled, shifted her position in her seat directly toward Joey, caught his eye, and held his glance, her eyes sparkling now.

"What do you do?" she asked, as if it might matter.

"I'm a psychiatrist."

"Do you like it?"

"I love seeing patients but managed care has ruined psychiatry."

She looked puzzled. Joey wasn't sure she knew what managed care was, so he explained. He felt pleasantly disinhibited by the Scotch. Although he kept his voice low and discreet, his eyes privately conveyed the passion of his views to Katharina.

"Managed care controls the resources doctors need to diagnose and treat their patients. Someone else, who either doesn't know medicine or is only motivated by money, decides what the patient needs. It's not so much managed care as managed cost. They pay big bonuses to so-called doctors, some might call them hired guns or prostitutes, to deny care to patients. That way their bosses can keep the money that should have gone into taking care of the patients who paid insurance premiums all their lives. They use crappy research to justify it, studies designed in advance to show that more intense or sophisticated care or more advanced drugs don't make a difference. It's partially the fault of shady doctors and pharmaceutical companies that exploited the system to make money. But, in trying to fix those past abuses, it looks like the pendulum has swung too far the other way."

Joey paused, trying to gauge her response from her expression. She had squinted her eyes, listening intently while he spoke. Now she smiled broadly as if pleased.

"What are you thinking?" he asked curiously.

"I like the sound of your voice," she said, her tone more self-conscious than seductive, running her well-manicured finger thoughtfully around the lip of her wine glass. The friction of her finger on the moist glass made a faint humming sound. For a moment, Joey was afraid she would tip her glass over. She seemed to be gathering her thoughts. Her tone reminded him of someone making a minor confession.

He concluded with a faint smile, figuring that she probably wasn't interested in discussing public policy. But she was interesting herself. He waited to see what she would say next.

"Did you study psychology?" she asked.

"Of course."

"Isn't psychiatry more about medicine and psychology about human relations?" she asked a little skeptically.

He nodded. "Psychiatry is about both."

"How do they train you to do psychotherapy?" She took a small sip of wine without removing her gaze from his eyes.

Joey held her gaze. He thought of Madeleine's blue eyes and for a moment was lost in memories. He took a long sip of Scotch and stifled a sigh behind the cover of the glass held to his lips. He would put those thoughts away for now. As a psychiatrist, he had learned to keep a poker face that could obscure his reaction to the patient and inner deliberations.

"The essence pretty much of all psychotherapy, or for that matter, really connecting with any person, is to be able to get into their shoes and experience what it's like to be them. Then what a good psychiatrist does is step out of their shoes and put together a formulation for the person's problem. That is, the psychiatrist helps them see, with the advantage of objectivity and distance, how the patient got where they are and a path to get where they want to go."

She was listening attentively, sipping her wine. She nodded to him to continue.

"You have to be choosy, though. The field is very uneven in quality and it's hard to root out the bad shrinks. The books can give you a framework, but you either understand people or you don't. The lousy shrinks either try to stick you into a formula they read somewhere or stick you into their own experience because they really don't know how to understand another person or they can't imagine that someone could experience the world much differently from themselves. In the old days, all shrinks were expected to undergo psychoanalysis and to tay in supervision with another shrink to control that sort of thing."

Katharina's second glass of wine was nearly empty. She summoned the stewardess in German and ordered a refill. Then she turned to Joey.

"Are you having another Scotch?"

"I get woozy when I drink on a plane," confessed Joey, slowly shaking his head no.

"What do you have to do tomorrow?" she persisted.

"Sit around for six hours waiting for a flight. Then fly to Addis Ababa," Joey said. Before Katharina could speak again, he realized he had just weakened his case.

"You have the whole day to recover. Have another so we can toast," Katharina said, turning a charmingly soft variant of her German assertiveness toward Joey for the first time.

"It does feel pretty good," he admitted, nodding a little cautiously but actually feeling pleased.

She leaned over him and spoke to the stewardess. With her body stretched in front of him, from her light blouse he detected a subtle scent. *Opium perfume,* he said to himself. It had been a favorite of Madeleine's. There was something seductive, almost irresistible about it. Madeleine had worn it in Nice.

Katharina retrieved two miniature bottles of whiskey, unscrewed the caps and poured them into his glass. Stirred, ordered more ice, and stirred again.

Joey fought off another pang of sadness. He tried not to think of Madeleine. After her death, he hadn't dated. He wasn't sure he ever would. He knew she would have wanted him to remarry and that the Western mode for healthy grief was to move on. But he hadn't been able to convince himself that love and commitment were so transient as to end at death. Wasn't it geese that remained monogamous for life even when they lost their mates? Tonight was the closest to fun he had had with the opposite sex since Madeleine's death. Without fanfare, he downed the contents of the little bottles, mixed with melted ice, in one easy gulp. He didn't think she had noticed his momentary pensiveness.

"Do you think people are happy?" she asked. Suddenly, her expression was serious.

"What do you mean?" He had understood that it most likely applied to herself. He was back in step with her.

"Do you think they're ever really satisfied?" she asked almost plaintively. "In a relationship?"

"You find the ideal person," he said, "and while you're in love and passionate, you put the ideal qualities on that person, and as long as the relationship is either insecure or new, they look perfect. Then, when you're secure and some of the newness wears off, you begin to see what they really are and you weigh everything and decide if the balance is best. It's usually a compromise."

"You're extremely good at understanding people," she said sincerely.

"Maybe. The first step is to make people feel understood. That's good for them in and of itself. Actually understanding them is another matter altogether. There are so many layers when you peel the onion."

She hesitated only a moment as if she knew what she wanted to say but was searching for the best language. "Well, it seems like once you get close, then things get boring or they stay up in the air."

"It's more exciting if you think you might lose the person, so it's always more like celebrating something new. You're so grateful to have the person back, you don't really have time to weigh who they really are. The most exciting ones are often these tumultuous ones where you're never really secure. Some people get uncomfortable whenever they get too close and create a disturbance that distances them. Then they panic and it goes around and around with high highs and low lows until they can't stand it anymore or something happens that is so noxious, it shocks them out of it."

"That's what you learn as a psychiatrist?"

"There are some really good books on it," Joey said modestly. "We all have a few 'borderline-like' personality traits in us." *Especially in youth*, he thought.

"Borderline-like?"

He decided not to focus on this aspect. "It's a medical term. It's not important. Please go on."

"How do you make a relationship work for the long term?" she asked, her eyes suddenly a little sad.

"As in marriage?"

She smiled faintly, blushing softly, but didn't answer.

"You build something together."

He had already noticed that she didn't wear a wedding ring. But one graceful finger had an exquisite platinum ring studded tastefully with small, clear diamonds, emeralds and rubies. Around her neck hung a pear-shaped, white solitary diamond that Joey estimated at two carats plus. He guessed it had been an engagement ring once.

"Divorced?" he asked, intentionally keeping his eyes on hers rather than looking at her ring hand.

"You're very intuitive. It's clear you're able to see the truth very quickly."

If not for the physical impediment of the massive immovable armrest that was part of the molded shell of the seat, their bodies would have been touching. As it was, just their arms pressed together on the rest, neither explicit enough to be held accountable for it, but both aware.

Joey saw her eyes focused on his lower abdomen. They locked eyes for a moment and she smiled comfortably.

His glass contained nothing but ice and she said, "We can't toast unless you have another."

She paused and waited. It was clear she wanted Joey to pour the whiskey himself this time. He felt manipulated, but in a pleasing, seductive way. He wondered to himself whether this was how she routinely passed the time on a flight.

She seemed to read his mind. "Usually, you try to make as little eye contact as you can and avoid getting drawn into conversation," she said, as if to emphasize the uniqueness of the encounter. "You and I are the only ones talking."

She scanned the business class cabin and again summoned the

stewardess. She ordered more wine for herself and a fresh glass of ice for Joey in the harsh German accent that contrasted so sharply with her soft, congenial English. She poured Joey's whiskey without the faintest expression of defeat. "What will we toast?" she asked, holding her glass aloft. Drifting from the broadly open sleeve of her blouse, Joey absorbed her perfume mixed with fresh feminine perspiration. It had an edge that made him restless. It was late at night and almost cold in the airplane cabin. *Why is she sweating?* he mused. He wanted to take a drink, a big one. He usually got sleepy when he had alcohol on an airplane. He was wide awake tonight.

"A toast to our friendship," he answered, clinking glasses with her and tasting the bite of the straight whiskey. The ice had not had time to melt. He drank the remainder like a shot. It burned his throat and reminded him of the happy shots of liquor he had shared with Madeleine. He closed his eyes briefly, recalling the taste of the liquors and wines he tasted on Madeleine's lips during their many kisses in Nice. He quickly opened his eyes, trying not to look rattled. He noticed that Katharina was putting on shiny lip gloss.

Halfway into the next glass of wine, she said playfully, "Tell me something really secret about yourself."

"This sounds like a drinking-game version of peel the onion," he said.

"Or a mind version of strip poker," she said, sensing his retreat and trying to unnerve him.

Joey was used to deflecting personal questions. "You first," he replied.

"I married very young," she confessed.

Joey guessed that she viewed this as the moral justification of the divorce or whatever had led up to it.

"That's a shoe. No, maybe a stocking," he said, egging her on. "Here's a shoe from me."

He whispered in her ear. She seemed satisfied. "Your turn."

She seemed to struggle within herself for a moment, then said with the faintest sadness in her eyes, "I'm very insecure."

Joey felt the ring of truth and was sympathetic. He thought she might really tell him something about herself now.

"That's only an unbuckled belt," she said with a look that seemed to promise more. She was ready with her next disclosure. "Does the passion last after you're married?"

Joey gathered that the passion hadn't lasted in her marriage but didn't question her further about it. He wanted to keep the atmosphere light.

"Is that an unbuttoned blouse?" he asked in a nonchalant voice. She read the irony in his expression and they both laughed.

"More than that!" She feigned a pout. "It's at least a bra off," she countered.

"Now you have to tell me what you're insecure about, what you feel vulnerable about, and we'll count it as your bra coming off because it's underneath."

"I don't usually wear a bra. It's just that the plane is usually cold and it makes your nipples hard."

"That could be very attractive," Joey said, smiling. "A matter of perspective." He couldn't help glancing at her breasts.

She seemed not only to expect it but looked pleased at his glance and added, "But a bra is so aggravating on a long trip."

"You're wearing one now?" he asked, aware that they both had become comfortable with his looking at her breasts.

"Yes, but I don't usually. I don't need it." She winked. "They stay up all by themselves."

Joey had no trouble imagining how well her breasts were outlined under her blouse and thin tight-fitting bra. His eyes fell on the faint pink line running down her sternum. *She had heart surgery a long time ago.*

Her eyes followed his. "It's from when I was a baby. I scar badly."

"It's called a keloid, it's harmless," he said reassuringly.

"There was a hole in my heart when I was a baby. Before we moved to Vienna, my mother was a nurse at Harvard. She knew the surgeon, dated him, in fact, before she met my father."

"My older brother was treated at Harvard for a heart problem when he was a baby too. They helped him. My mom showed me a cute picture of him in his crib there, grasping the hand of a little baby girl. Wouldn't it be a trip if that little girl was you?"

"That really would be fate," she said, laughing.

"To kismet." Joey lifted his glass.

"Cheers," she said and they both drank.

"Where were we in our game? We were just getting to the good stuff."

She whispered in his ear and he watched a deep red blush spread from her cheeks down to her upper chest.

"That's unsnapping the pants," he said dryly, as if unimpressed.

She touched a perfectly manicured finger with its clear nail polish to her still well-glossed lips, then sucked it thoughtfully before saying, "If I'm going to take my pants off, I hope they're going to turn the lights lower."

Joey decided to call her bluff. "There's only one couple up," he said, emphasizing "up."

"As it were," she quipped. They both laughed. Each took a sip from their respective glasses and they looked at each other for a moment, comfortable with the silence.

He wanted to take her hand and kiss her. She had drawn him momentarily out of the infinity of his mourning over Madeleine. He was amused and impressed by Katharina tonight, but he was still in love with his wife, dead or alive, and assumed he always would be.

The cabin was dark now except for a few faint reading lights. Most of the passengers around them slept, some snoring loudly. They continued to chat, and Joey finally began to feel the soporific effect of liquor on an overseas flight. On the other hand, Katharina showed no signs of getting sleepy.

Just before he dozed off, she asked if she could borrow his laptop to get some work done for tomorrow morning. Hers had crashed. Joey didn't object. The last thing he recalled before he slept was that she plugged in her phone. Shivering slightly from the cold, she had borrowed his sports jacket. He took it as flirtatious, a form of bonding

Chapter 23 … Katharina

As he slept, she looked him over from head to toe, her eyes lingering on his midsection and then his face. She sighed deeply. He was sleeping fitfully, but his eyes were closed and he shifted uncomfortably in the narrow seat and turned away from her.

She booted his computer, activating the software that would copy his hard drive to her phone. Then she took a small but very sharp pair of FTA compliant nail clippers out of her bag. She cut a hole through the seam near the lowest button on his coat, inserted a small microphone, transmitter and battery, and closed the hole with liquid fabric. She quietly asked the stewardess for a glass of vodka, drank it in one shot without flinching, and gently placed Joey's coat in his lap and computer back in its case. She checked once more to see if he was sleeping. Then she slept.

24

The Search Committee

Langley, Virginia
August 19, 2028

T HE SEARCH COMMITTEE MET IN a soundproof conference room in Langley, Virginia, headquarters of the Central Intelligence Agency.

"Next file, please," said the platinum blonde, bespectacled, middle-aged chairwoman who had a master's degree in nursing.

"We have Dr. Joey Jacobson," said the younger mid-level administrator. He was pudgy around the middle but well groomed.

"Could you present him please?" the chairwoman said in an officious tone.

"I'll take this one," said Dr. McAllister, the senior executive head of Medical Affairs for the entire agency. "This is a promising young psychiatrist who is regarded as brilliant and savvy by his colleagues. He already has a legitimate cover for international travel. We have reason to think he may have personal reasons for sacrificing some of his career to work for his country. He's not afraid to take risks, but he's a careful chess player. He has a collaborative style that has earned him no enemies. Interpersonally, he's considered charming but not in a sociopathic way. People experience him as sincere and genuinely interested in others. People who are about as different as night and day feel like he understands them, that he can put himself in their shoes, that it's safe to confide in him."

The chairwoman wrinkled her brow. "Why would a guy like this want to take a huge salary hit to work for the government? Is he recruitable?" she asked.

"That's the $50,000 question, of course," acknowledged McAllister.

"What's his lifestyle like?" another board member asked.

"He's done very well, apparently without trying too hard," McAllister responded. "But he's not ostentatious. The pharmaceutical companies are trying to recruit him and offer him a lead position on a new compound. We'd have to offer him senior executive service to get a shot at him. It would still be a huge financial sacrifice for him."

"What about keeping him outside?" a third man asked.

"Better, really. Easier to maintain his cover outside," McAllister answered. "If he's outside, we don't have to bring our people into Langley to see him, which might blow their cover. Our internal and external assets, anyone with a high security clearance, could blend into his practice."

The chairwoman, who by nature enjoyed extinguishing other people's enthusiasm, probed for weaknesses in the nomination. "Does Dr. Jacobson have any security issues of his own?"

The research analyst spoke up. "We checked out his family back three generations, neighbors, employers, employees, medical records, bank accounts, the usual."

"Any concerns?" asked the chairwoman.

"Joey's father was an occasional consultant for us. No issues there. The one concern about Joey was lots of overseas travel. But it checked out as part of his work," the analyst replied.

"Anything operational? Was a stress test done?" asked the older, husky male voice.

"We had, uh, what's her name this month?" asked the analyst.

"Katharina," answered the chairwoman.

"Yeah," answered the analyst. "Katharina managed to have a few drinks with him on an overnight airplane trip. He held his liquor and behaved himself. No loose lips, didn't spill his guts to her."

"Was she provocative?" asked McAllister.

"Here's what she looks like," said the analyst, holding up Katharina's photo from a file and trying to mask his smile. "Charming too. You can imagine the reaction she would elicit from most men. She did her best on an airplane. He's a normal guy, but he was appropriately cautious. 'Good instincts,' she said." He paused as if unsure whether to go on.

McAllister read his expression and encouraged him to continue. "Anything else?"

The analyst continued. "Katharina said she doesn't normally get attached in these things, of course. Actually finds them unpleasant. But she said this guy was different. She would have dated him, she thinks, if she met him on her own. A sensitive, smart guy and not weird like the other shrinks she's worked with."

"Did she pick up any tangibles?" the chairwoman asked.

"She got a copy of his hard drive off his computer while he slept. We sent it for analysis. It backs up his stated reasons for travel. Otherwise, it was clean. Certainly nothing that would suggest a security risk or that he could be vulnerable to blackmail. We also got seventy-two hours of audio surveillance from a microtransmitter. The guy is as clean as an Eagle Scout."

"Is there anything else of note in his history that we should be aware of?" asked McAllister.

"Yeah, one thing. A big thing, actually. His wife was killed in France two years ago by an explosion."

"What kind of explosion?" asked the chairwoman.

"A terrorist bomb, actually. The dossier says that Joey and his spouse, Madeleine, were on their honeymoon at a hotel on the French Riviera. The hotel was owned by an Israeli syndicate, and that made it of ostensible interest to the Islamic State. Their initial claim of responsibility, however, was later found to have been forged by a right wing, xenophobic French group who actually committed the bombing."

"Xenophobic as in anti-Semitic?" asked McAllister.

"Jews, Muslims, they hated them equally. Probably hate Hindus and Buddhists as well."

"So," said the older male voice as if summing up, "the bottom line, the reason this is relevant to recruitment is that, given that this shrink," he paused and looked at the dossier, "Dr. Jacobson, lost his wife to a terrorist group, he may feel motivated to work with us?"

"Exactly," said the chairwoman.

25

The Road to Butajira

**Rift Valley, Ethiopia
February 21, 2030**

TWO AMERICAN CIA OPERATIVES AND an Israeli Mossad agent of Ethiopian descent drove down the twisting, pothole-riddled road from Addis Ababa to Butajira.

Yefet's skin was the color of a darkly roasted Yirgachefe coffee bean. He had high cheekbones and a gray, scraggly beard. "Before Emperor Haile Selassie was overthrown in 1974, my dad owned a little antique store for tourists in Addis. He made a decent living. After the Communist revolution, the only tourists were Russians, and they didn't buy much."

"Was your family able to get by?" asked Joey.

"We lost the store. The economy tanked, there wasn't any work, and people in our neighborhood were starving. Somehow we always had a little food though."

A moment too late, Joey swerved to avoid a giant square pothole. The Chevy Tahoe's suspension bottomed out. "Ouch," cried Katharina from the back seat.

Joey glanced in the rearview mirror. "Are you OK?"

"It feels like we're back on the roads in DC," she quipped from behind oversized Chanel photochromic sunglasses. "Sorry, Yefet. Please continue."

"The Israeli government made a secret deal with the Ethiopian government, known as the Derg, to trade weapons for letting the Beta Israel—the Ethiopian Jews—emigrate. But news of the deal leaked, relations between Ethiopia and Israel got very bad, and Jews who had applied to immigrate were seen as traitors."

"Did the Derg turn on your family?" asked Joey.

Yefet's eyes took on a glazed look. "One night, the neighborhood watch broke down our door and shouted at my father, 'Spy.' They hit him over and over with sticks until he couldn't stand. Sometimes when I'm alone, I can still hear my mother screaming. It was like, every time they hit him, she felt it. The next day, soldiers came and dragged my father away. A couple of months later, the Derg sent us a bill for the bullet they used to execute him."

Joey winced.

Katharina said to Joey, "That was the Derg's signature insult to the families of dissidents." She took off her sunglasses and rested her hand on Yefet's shoulder. "Was your father a spy? Is that why your family had food when everyone else was starving?"

"If he was, he never told us. Maybe to protect us. Eventually, we did hear from the Mossad though."

"Did they help you get out?" asked Katharina.

"The Mossad operated an underground railroad of sorts for the Beta Israel. They shepherded us to a refugee camp in Sudan. We never could have made it without them."

"They protected you from the bandits? The *shifta*?" Joey asked.

Yefet closed his eyes and shook his head as if trying to ward off demons. "Without them, we'd have been lost a hundred times over, especially in the camps in Sudan. Finally, they took us to Khartoum and flew my mother, sisters and me to Israel."

In the back seat, they heard the "Blue Danube" ringtone of

Katharina's satellite phone. "Sorry to interrupt, guys, the station chief just pinged a warning of possible IEDs and insurgent activity on Route 51 near Melka Kunture." She hoisted the bag concealing her carbine from the cargo area to the back seat and nervously stroked the barrel.

"Too bad," said Joey. "I'd hoped we could exit at Melka Kunture and see where they excavated Lucy. She's one of the world's oldest hominid fossils, you know."

As their SUV labored up the switchbacks, and the verdant Rift Valley unfolded below, Yefet's deep voice boomed over the car sounds. "Here we are in the cradle of civilization. What an irony that the rebels want to turn the clock back a thousand years to the days of the caliphates."

Katharina sat forward, resting her arms on the back of the front seat as she spoke to Joey and Yefet, "Every day ISIS is tightening the noose around the capital."

"Well supplied with arms and money from Sudan and Somalia," Joey added.

Yefet gesticulated as he said, "Most Ethiopians don't want to fight for their government. The regime is seen as a mafia controlled by the wealthy oligarchs. The people see nothing to lose from the government falling. The average annual income is barely $900 per year. In the villages, you're considered wealthy if you live in a hut with an oil lamp and a curtain to separate you from your livestock."

Katharina leaned forward, pressed her cheek next to Joey's and spoke in his ear to overcome the road noise. "Joey, the one institution in Ethiopia that Yefet's government and our government believe has legitimacy to rule, that could potentially unite the country to defeat ISIS, is the monarchy."

At her touch, Joey lost his concentration for a moment. He was back in Nice. "I'll be right back," Madeleine had said. The road to Butajira curved, Joey didn't make the correction, and the Tahoe's tires skirted the shoulder, making a loud grating sound.

"Joey! Wake up!" shouted Yefet. Joey's eyes widened, his head jerked up, he tightened his grip on the steering wheel and corrected their course.

"Sorry, I must have dozed for a moment. I didn't get much sleep on the flight from Cairo to Addis. Let's stop for coffee."

The roadside café where they pulled over a few minutes later was a two-room shack illuminated by a single naked light bulb and decorated with a wall Coca-Cola clock. The waitress was a tall, slim young woman with a high forehead, straight nose and mocha-colored skin. The groaning tray she carried held a black clay jebena filled with steaming coffee, a silver pitcher filled with warm cream and three porcelain cups.

"We invented coffee, you know," said Yefet.

Katharina poured black coffee into her cup, blew on it to cool it, drank it quickly and poured another. Yefet poured a generous amount of cream in his cup, filled the remainder with the coffee and sipped it thoughtfully.

Joey sniffed at the liquid in his cup, frowned, and set it down.

"You don't like it?" asked Yefet.

"It's a little perfumey for me," Joey answered. "I'll drink it when it cools a bit." His eyes drifted back and forth from Yefet to Katharina and back again, eyebrows raised in a question. "So, why are we here?"

Yefet's eyes scanned the room to see if anyone seemed interested in their conversation. His eyes fixed for a moment on the waitress standing at attention in the corner. He lowered his voice. "Sorry to keep you in the dark, Joey. I'm sure you'll understand why there's been so much secrecy." He glanced at the waitress again. She averted her eyes. "The royal family's put forth a candidate for a new emperor. Needless to say, both the central government and ISIS would be threatened by the return of the monarchy. If word got out that a candidate to the throne was speaking to agents of the U.S. or Israeli governments, they would be assassinated in no time. The whole royal family would be in danger."

"What about the army? Where do they stand?" asked Joey.

"We think the generals will acquiesce, as an alternative to being beheaded by ISIS and in return for keeping their jobs. In addition,

ur governments have prepared certain incentives." Yefet winked at
oey.

Katharina put her mouth close to Joey's ear. "Tomorrow at dawn
t the rock-hewn church near Adadi Mariam, we meet the candidate,
he royal family's choice for a successor to Emperor Haile Selassie.
efet and I will present him with terms our governments require in
eturn for supporting the coup d'etat that will install him."

"Jesus," Joey said. "I thought that sort of thing went out with
he Cold War."

Yefet set down his coffee cup. "We're in a new world war, Joey.
his time the object of the domino theory is ISIS, not the commu-
ists. The Russians support the coup. They'll be one of the first to
ecognize the new government."

Joey no longer felt drowsy. He felt pumped up now. "What's my
ole?" he asked.

Yefet explained, "As part of our countries' due diligence before
utting this guy on the throne, his genetic pedigree and mental health
ave to be evaluated. Surreptitiously, of course. Royal families tend to
nterbreed and get eccentric. What's his personality pattern? What are
is vulnerabilities? Does he have any loose screws? He smokes quite a
it of the local herbal stimulant, khat. Has it damaged his judgment?
Does he have manic or paranoid tendencies?"

"OK, I get that, but how do you plan to get tissue for a genetic
nalysis to confirm his royal lineage?" Joey asked.

"That's the easy part. When he signs the agreement, we toast
vith a bottle of Gout de Diamants. When he drinks, it will leave cells
rom his mucus membrane on the glass. As you know, doctor, each
ell contains his full genetic code. Your job is to protect and preserve
hose cells until we can get them back to your embassy."

"Good tactic. Who could refuse a toast from a bottle of Gout de
Diamants?" Joey mused. "Is it genuine?"

Yefet answered, "If it were genuine it would be a small price to
ay to end a war and restore an empire. But we couldn't quite get our
ands on the real thing. It's not exactly a fake, either. You might call
t a less expensive variation."

"Part of the value of that Champagne is in the bottle itself, isn' it?" asked Joey.

"Yes, and the candidate's quite a wine connoisseur, so the win has to be good. Very few people in the world have tasted the rea thing," answered Yefet.

Katharina pointed at her wristwatch. "We'd better hit the roa unless we want to find our hotel near Adadi Mariam in the dark."

The motel consisted of scattered mud-walled, grass-roofed hut on the bank of a river. By the light of an oil lamp, Joey read th briefing book the Agency had prepared for the mission.

In the *History of the Jews in Ethiopia* section he read:

> Many historians believe that the Beta Israel (Ethiopian Jews) are descendants of Menelik, son of King Solomon and the Queen of Sheba. It is commonly believed in Ethiopia that Menelik brought the Ark of the Covenant with him from Jerusalem and hid it in Axum. In acknowledgement of that belief, many Ethiopian churches contain imitations of the ark.

> However, there are competing theories of the origin of the Beta Israel, including descending from the Tribe of Dan or migrating from Egypt. The Chief Rabbinate in Israel didn't recognize the Beta Israel as Jews until 1975.

In the *Dissolution of the Empire* section he read:

> Most Ethiopian people are open to the notion that the Solomonic dynasty persisted more or less unbroken for nearly 3,000 years. However, the empire ended ignominiously. In the early 1970s, the country was ripe for revolution. Emperor Haile Selassie was old and ineffectual.

In the context of the Cold War, in 1974, Marxist rebels abducted the emperor and by the next summer he was dead. The militantly socialist Derg initially had strong popular support for land reform. However, the economy deteriorated and a severe famine ensued, worse than the one under the emperor. Intense political suppression, including systematic murder of dissidents, was dubbed "The Red Terror." The regime became widely and immensely unpopular and was overthrown in 1991.

Joey recalled the political metaphor of George Orwell's Animal Farm that had impressed him in high school: "The liberators become the oppressors in an endless cycle."

In the *Concerns and Vulnerabilities* section he read:

The candidate for successor to the emperor's throne regularly chews the local herbal stimulant, khat. Khat produces an effect similar to amphetamine and has the potential to induce euphoria and impair judgment. In addition, second-degree relatives of the candidate occasionally participate in the Zar cult, involving beliefs in spirit possession. The Agency has insufficient information to conclude the extent to which this represents a normal cultural phenomenon versus a family propensity towards psychosis.

Joey started to download an electronic version of Fuller Torrey's *The Zar Cult in Ethiopia* onto his phone when it chimed Atlanta Rhythm Section's *Spooky*.

Katharina. I wondered when I'd hear from her.

"Will you come over?" Katharina asked.

That's a come-hither voice. Joey looked out the window at Katharina's hut. "You had to bounce a call off a satellite to ask me that?"

She laughed. "Well?"

"You're my handler, is this sexual harassment?" Joey asked face-iously. *The answer's yes.*

There was a short pause. "This is business," she said, sounding unshaken.

"Wouldn't it be more secure to talk business on a walk than in your room?" Joey asked.

"I swept the room for bugs. Besides, it's not safe to walk at night. Did you hear that leopard growling?"

"There were some God awful spitting and snarling sounds toward the river an hour or so ago."

"I rest my case. Get your butt over here."

When he entered her hut, she was sitting on her bed sipping vodka out of a chipped glass. She motioned to Joey to take a seat on the spartan wooden chair next to the bed. "Did you read the briefing book?" she asked.

"Most of it."

"Well?"

"The new emperor likes women and drugs, fancy cars, not much different than a rich playboy in our country."

There was a long pause. The only sounds were the mosquitoes and beetles buzzing around the oil lamp. Joey asked, "What's really on your mind?"

"I just have this feeling that someone has eyes and ears on us," she said with gravity.

"Are you worried about Yefet?" asked Joey, the lines in his forehead bending into a V between his eyes.

She shook her head. "No, not the Mossad. I think the biggest risk of our mission is the possibility that the royal family is under surveillance by ISIS, the Ethiopian government or both."

Joey chewed his thumbnail. "In which case, we could be headed into an ambush tomorrow."

Katharina looked at him a little wide-eyed and nodded.

"We're not equipped for that. Is backup available?" asked Joey calmly.

Katharina shook her head. "Not in time from our station."

"What about from the Mossad?"

"Yefet sent a request for a drone. He doesn't expect an answer before morning."

Joey glanced out the window at Yefet's hut. "His light's off," Joey said.

"Welcome to my world," Katharina replied.

Joey could see Katharina was very worried. "How do you cope with the uncertainty?" he asked.

"That each day could be my last?" She picked up the bottle of Monopolowa vodka from her night table. "With a little help from my friend," she said. "Will you join me?"

"Vodka's not really my drink. But tonight, your friend is my friend," he said.

"Maybe a little toast?" she asked.

"Sure," Joey said. They raised their glasses.

"To life," she said.

"L'chaim," Joey said.

"If we make it back to Washington, I want you to take me to dinner at Plume at the Jefferson Hotel."

"Not if you order that 1988 Speri Amarone della Valpolicella again. I'll never forget the look on the assistant director's face."

"It was worth every penny."

"I'm sure the taxpayers wouldn't feel that way."

"Hah."

"If I'm taking you to dinner at a hotel, it's just for dinner, right?"

"Don't flatter yourself." She sat on the bed, her back supported against the wall by a pillow. She pulled out the pillow and threw it at him.

He caught it and placed it behind him in the hard chair. "Thanks, I can use that."

She feigned a frown, gave him a big smile and held out the vodka bottle. "More?"

"Just a little or you'll have to carry me back to my room. How are you holding up?"

"I'm still buzzed from the coffee this afternoon." She seemed to look inward, thoughtfully, for a moment. "Joey, that night I met you on the plane, our conversation was so one-sided. You didn't tell me any secrets about yourself."

"I didn't have to. You and the Agency already knew everything about me."

"Only your background, not what's in your head."

"After they recruited me they tried to get that too, with the polygraph."

"You've never talked to me about any *feelings*," she said.

Joey took a hard swallow of vodka. "The Agency shared with you what happened on my honeymoon?"

"Of course, Joey. I'm so sorry, I couldn't bring it up until you did."

"Thank you, Katharina. What you need to know is that I'm still in love with my wife."

She answered hastily as if that had been what she expected him to say, "I can see that Joey. I respect that. Is that why you've kept your distance from me?"

"I do have feelings for you, Katharina. It's just complicated for me."

"She would want you to be happy, Joey. She would want you to have a life."

"I don't know," Joey said. "I'm not ready to start again. I don't know if I'll ever be ready." He stood up and stepped toward the door.

"Don't leave yet," she said hurriedly. "I have a secret too. A real secret. You're not the only one who has pain, Joey. I have anguish too."

"I didn't mean to imply," he said.

She interrupted, "Even the Agency doesn't know. I'm a hemophilia carrier. They don't test for it."

Joey returned to the chair and sat down. "Are you serious? What if you got shot? You wouldn't be able to stop the bleeding. You shouldn't be in a potential combat situation. You shouldn't be in operations at all."

"This job is my life, Joey. It's my love, my only love. If I die, I'll die doing what I want to do."

"It would only take one bullet, one piece of shrapnel. In the field, no one could stop the bleeding."

"That's my choice. But the worst part is, I'll never have children."

"Because you don't want to pass on hemophilia?"

"There's a 25% chance any children I have would not just be carriers, but have the full deal-hemophilia. Do you know what that's like? I saw my brother go through hell with it. I could never bring a child into the world with a future like that."

"They can test for hemophilia in utero now. You could terminate the pregnancy if necessary. "

"My dream was a big family. I'm Catholic. Not a goody-goody Catholic, you can see that, but I would never have an abortion. My husband refused to adopt. Not having children was a big factor in my divorce." Katharina was crying now.

Joey suppressed an impulse to take her in his arms and comfort her. Instead, he stayed in his chair and said in as soothing a voice as he could, "If you've lost your dreams, you have to make new ones."

She nodded, dabbed the tears from her cheek and composed herself. She poured herself another drink. "That goes for you too, Joey. You can't live in the past forever. You need a new dream."

"I still love my wife. I mean it."

"Doctor, heal thyself," she said, smiling again. She held out the bottle to refill Joey's glass.

I should go, but she just poured her heart out to me. I could stay a little longer. That would be the decent thing to do.

He held out his glass. She refilled it.

They sipped their drinks. He from the chair, she from the bed. The only sound was the humming of the mosquitoes and buzzing of the beetles.

She seemed pleased by an idea that came into her head. "The light's attracting the damn bugs," she said. She twisted the dial on the lamp until the wick shrank away and the room was lit by the faintest of blue flames.

"Joey, this district is infested with anopheline mosquitoes. And you're not taking antimalarials, are you?"

"There wasn't time."

She patted the mattress beside her. "Come here, I'll lower the mosquito net."

181

"We have an early start tomorrow. I should leave," Joey said. He tested his legs. They felt wobbly from the jet lag and vodka.

"It's so hot in this room. And we can't even open the window because of the bugs."

She lifted her blouse over her head. Underneath was a sheer beige camisole.

The subtle smell of Opium perfume mixed with Katharina's perspiration wafted toward Joey. Madeleine had worn Opium, and it had always made him feel restless and flushed. He felt that happening now.

Katharina slipped the lacey camisole off her shoulders.

"Will you hold me?" she asked.

The next morning, in their respective quarters, Joey, Katharina and Yefet were awoken by the same message on their satellite phones. "Candidate killed by coordinated IED explosion and ambush on Highway 51 near Melka Kunture. Enemy offensive advancing from the west. Return to station immediately."

26

Top Secret Clearance

McLean, Virginia
October 8, 2031

JOEY'S PSYCHIATRIC OFFICE WAS IN a secure building with a non-descript façade near Langley, Virginia. As the morning's first appointment began, the sun reached the level in the east where the first shrouds of direct sunlight penetrated the twin skylights and appeared on the wall behind the patient, General Jeremiah Westfield. The general had been awesome to behold once, tall, proud, magnificent in his military bearing. Now he sat bent, tremulous, expressionless.

A pair of ghost-like Ethiopian wedding costumes hung on the wall behind the patient, a symbol to Joey of his eternal commitment to Madeleine. As the day progressed, the action of the direct sunlight on the centuries-old cowhide, dust and human sweat in the material would release a subtle feral scent, peaking around 2 p.m., then gradually waning as the sun illuminated the opposite side of the room behind Joey.

Under the skylights, in a clay pot painted with dreamy Gauguin-like images of nude savages, a mature datura stretched its canopy upward, reaching for the light. It had been a gift from a highly traveled colleague in the Agency. An elaborate birdcage constructed from sugar cane hung from a sturdy limb of the datura. There the blue and green parrot, rescued decades earlier from the hunting fields in Honduras, still slept. Life-size classical marble busts of Freud and Kraepelin eyed each other uncertainly across the room. The granite pedestals holding the busts were a gift from a shadowy friend of Joey's father who lived in Prague and claimed they were hewn from stone rubble of the second temple and spirited away to Europe for safe keeping. Patients sometimes commented that they saw the faces of the busts when they closed their eyes. Their free associations speculating on the emotions portrayed by the figures and how they related to each other conveniently served as a window for Joey into the patient's secret inner emotional life.

At dusk, and sometimes even on very cloudy days, the datura opened its blossoms, releasing a sweet fragrance, subtle at times, powerful and soporific at others. According to the literature, to the vulnerable brain, Joey recalled, the scent was capable of inducing a hypnotic state. Many of the patients remarked that the atmosphere in the room was a catalyst for a dimension of spiritual and emotional existence beyond their mundane day-to-day lives.

Joey and Jeremiah sat in comfortable chairs. The psychiatrist's chair by tradition was always larger, plusher, symbolic of wisdom and authority. He had given much thought to the placement of the chairs. The patient's and doctor's chairs were oriented at forty-five degrees so that direct eye contact, a two-edged sword like most things in psychiatry, could be assumed or avoided with subtlety by either party as needed. Eye-to-eye communication was critical in conveying trust, understanding from the doctor, and for reading the patient's emotions. On the other hand, Joey knew that in the primate world and in the psychotic human world, direct eye contact could be a precursor to attack. Thus, the angle of the chairs helped Joey avoid the head-on, challenging, sometimes leering stare of the general without appearing submissive. Poker faced, Joey searched Jeremiah's eyes for signs of paranoia. Carefully steadying his voice, he summarized what Jeremiah had told him.

"You maintain that there was intelligence that elements supported by the Islamic State under the code name Babylon II were covertly moving components of Hiroshima or greater-sized nuclear weapons into U.S. and Israeli cities, and their plan was to explode one to obtain credibility and then call for removal of all foreign troops from the Middle East and south Asia, cessation of economic and military aid to Israel, and establishment of a Palestinian state."

Jeremiah looked uncomfortable. He paused, looked serious and said, "They told me you have top secret clearance?"

"That's correct, top secret clearance."

"Can you show me?"

Joey showed him.

"And the help? The secretary, the cleaning people? Have they been cleared?"

He's not paranoid, thought Joey. *These are appropriate questions given the subject matter.*

"Of course," Joey said. *He's a bit concerned because this is a civilian facility.*

"How often are you swept for bugs?"

"That's classified," Joey answered.

"And the windows. Are they coated?"

Joey felt a little insulted but maintained his poker face. These types of quizzes were common from the higher brass. Jeremiah was asking if the windows had been treated to deter eavesdropping. A window vibrates from the sound of a voice just like an eardrum, and a moderately sophisticated eavesdropping device on the outside could decode the vibrations back into the original sound.

"Yes, to most current available sensitivity," he said.

"OK," said Jeremiah, nodding. "That's consistent with the information I was given."

The general sounded ready to talk, so Joey asked, "Don't you get rumors like that all the time?"

"This time it was credible."

"What made it credible?"

"They checked the beltway radiation detectors and it corresponded to the intelligence, date for date."

Joey was well aware of the defense systems ringing Washington but wanted to hear how Jeremiah expressed his thoughts. "What do you mean?"

"The beltway around Washington, DC, and in a similar fashion in a ring around other major cities, is surrounded by radiation detectors to prevent or at least give us a heads-up to this kind of thing. So, if a terrorist or foreign government tried to sneak in a nuclear bomb, we would know."

"That wouldn't prevent it? You would just know?"

"That's correct. Initially, after 9/11, there was around the clock monitoring, but with budget cuts and all…"

"So, sometime after this happened, somebody reviewed the data and there was a signal of something big radioactive coming in?"

"They're not exactly stupid. They probably have unemployed former Iraqi or Syrian military advising them. So it was well shielded in lead."

"But there would still be a signal?"

"Yes. But as I said, they're not stupid and they took pains to disguise it."

"How?"

"In each case they brought in an authorized shipment of stolen nuclear waste at the same time, so it blurred the signal. And since it was announced in advance under the name of a real company, we didn't look that hard at the time."

"But when you went back and looked?"

"The first look is with a blunt device. It's just a screening instrument. But when we went back and analyzed the film further, in each case there were two images superimposed on each other. One was in fact radioactive trash but the other was compatible with plutonium-239 encased in lead."

Without unlocking his eyes from Jeremiah's, Joey tried to recall the briefing he had received on the general. Muscle stiffness and tremor from Parkinson's disease. Substance-induced psychosis from L-dopa, it had said. Systematized paranoid delusions and hallucinations. *L-dopa can't be stopped because his muscles will freeze up. His thoughts are well organized,* Joey thought. *The ideas are plausible. But the government says he is completely out to lunch.*

"That all sounds plausible the way you tell it," Joey said, striving to be truthful but without buying into the general's delusion – if it were one.

Jeremiah's face seemed torn between the opposing emotions of relief that his doctor found his story potentially credible and aggravation at Joey's subtle expression of skepticism. Joey decided to probe further for signs of a systematized delusion. If the patient were psychotic, there might be a wild network of delusional explanations under the surface.

"What in your view would be the government's motivation for discrediting your story?" Before the words were out of his mouth, Joey realized his question was simpleminded.

Jeremiah looked at him hard as if he had just won a hand of poker and was surprised at the dealer's vulnerability. "Can you imagine what would happen to the economy and public order if this got out?"

Joey, of course, could well imagine, but he had wanted to draw out the general. For a moment, he considered nodding candidly and saying "of course." That might cement some kind of rapport with his patient, but it would be counterproductive toward his goal of drawing the high-ranking officer out to see if there were hidden kernels of psychosis.

"I really wanted to hear your thoughts on it," Joey said.

"The value of the dollar would plummet to virtually zero overnight. The government would have to pay usurious interest rates to borrow money. Prices for goods would skyrocket into triple- or quadruple-digit inflation, or even worse. The Treasury would print truckloads of worthless currency that no one would accept. The economy would come to a standstill, and we would essentially be thrown back to the barter system."

Evidently feeling encouraged, the general went on. "Of course, that's just the purely economic piece. With the threat of nuclear annihilation, millions would panic and flee the threatened cities. With no economy and mass chaos, the social fabric might decay into widespread anarchy. Military rule may or may not hold for a while. The country would be humiliated and ungovernable. Depending on who was selected as the scapegoat, you might see a nuclear exchange or a turn to a false messiah or an antichrist like in the Weimar Republic."

Joey listened, spellbound, but then interrupted. "These are worst-case scenarios, all resting on the credibility of the intelligence you cited." He knew that a hallmark of psychotic delusion was that the patient would be fixed on their idea and unwilling to consider alternate explanations. "Do you think you could be wrong?"

"I would love to be wrong."

"Have you considered that the enemy may have planted the information as a bluff?"

"That was our hope, but everything was independently vetted, triangulated and confirmed by multiple agencies. They would have to be awfully good to fool all of us."

Joey noted the faint vibration in the back of his chair signaling him that it was fifteen minutes before the hour. He would receive successively stronger signals at five minute intervals warning him that the session was nearly over and allowing him to wind up the session tactfully without appearing to be "watching the clock."

Jeremiah did not sound psychotic, he concluded, *but maybe he was just having a good day*

Part

IV

Joey

27

Kilotons or Megatons

McLean, Virginia
October 15, 2031

A WEEK LATER AT THEIR NEXT meeting, Jeremiah sat on the edge of his seat and spoke in a measured yet authoritative tone. His facial expression would have appeared earnest had it not been hidden under the mask of parkinsonism. Joey realized he was listening from the edge of his chair, shoulders hunched up, leaning toward the general with his mouth slightly agape in surprise. He slowly sat back in his chair, placing his hands on the silk fabric of the wooden arms. He wanted to appear dispassionate but not affectedly so as he listened to his patient.

"Presumably, ground zero would be the White House and Congress for the symbolic value," the general said.

Wiping out the seat of government and first tiers of leaders, Joey thought.

"It wouldn't take much more to hit the Pentagon, of course," the General continued. "And then if you extended out to the Defense

Intelligence Agency and then the Central Intelligence Agency just down the road from here in Langley, you would have decapitated the government, military and intelligence capabilities. Of course, plans have been made for sufficient decentralization and redundancy to preserve a central government and military infrastructure. They'll announce that, unless we immediately meet their demands, other U.S. cities where bombs have been hidden will meet the same fate and no one will know if they're bluffing. Residents of our major urban areas will flee in panic. The U.S. economy will collapse. They'll make the same threat about London and Tel Aviv or Haifa. It won't matter whether they have the bombs or not."

Joey noticed that Jeremiah had looked at him pointedly when he said "just down the road from here." *Was the General trying to give me a warning or was he blowing smoke to intimidate me?*

In an instant, without taking his eyes off Jeremiah's, Joey tried to analyze the transference, the feelings that Jeremiah brought from his past that might be transposed onto the therapist. *Jeremiah couldn't save his own father*, thought Joey. *Maybe part of his corrective experience would be to save me. Gosh knows he said I reminded him of his father.*

Joey recalled that the general's dad had been in his 30s when he had died. *Is it ethical for me to use this information to get my family out? A childish thought, sophomoric*, he chastised himself. *How could I not protect my family if I knew? I could get in trouble with the medical board. What am I thinking? If the general were right, there would be no medical board.*

Jeremiah added, "We're working on the assumption they'll put all their eggs, hopefully kilotons not megatons, in one basket to make a convincing statement. Others think they'll divide it in two to hit DC and New York City like they did back in 2001. New York City is the financial center, you know, but it will depopulate anyway if they hit DC convincingly, and there won't be any need for Wall Street."

Joey silently calculated the distances from the White House to his office, his nephews' and niece's schools, and their homes further west. *Were they within the lethal range of the bomb?*

Jeremiah continued, "The biggest danger would be a pointless

taliatory strike, or even worse, a doomsday scenario where every-
ing gets shot at once. The end of the world. But we've taken steps
prevent that. Nobody will say how much yield they've got. It's
assified above me. And then the lethal distance from ground zero
ill depend on whether it's a ground or an air blast. It would fit in a
rivate plane. If they want distance, they'll use air. If they want more
llout, they'll use a ground blast. We think they will do air if they can
make a bigger statement.

"The best way to gauge where you need to be is by where they
ut the emergency supplies. If you see them moving medical sup-
lies and other assets to secure buildings out here, you're safe, at least
ased on intelligence. If they put it distal to you, it means you're in
he danger zone. The winds usually blow from west to east, south
north, but that's unpredictable. I'm sending my family back to
Mississippi. Near where I grew up. On a houseboat, actually, far from
he teeming masses."

Without thinking, Joey started to ask *When?* In less than the
ime it took for his lips to pucker and then stretch to complete the
yllable, he stopped himself. *Had counterintelligence bugged his office?
With all the concern about the general's loose lips, it was possible. I could
ose my clearance if I'm seen as milking the patient for information for
ersonal use. There was something about that new cleaning woman. She
eemed to have ears for things. Could she be a spy?*

Without missing a beat in the conversation, he let his eyes ask,
When?"

Jeremiah nodded subtly.

He's playing ball with me, Joey thought. *It is a good transference
fter all.*

But then, without saying a word, Jeremiah, reached for his walker
nd with a great deal of pressing on the handles managed to rise.

Joey assumed a blank expression. *Let the General set the tone*, he
hought, painfully aware he was thinking of himself and his family
ow, not the patient. Watching Jeremiah shuffle toward the door,
ands on his walker, Joey felt an emptiness in the pit of his stomach
nd something like shame.

193

Before he shut the door, Jeremiah's eyes caught Joey's one last time. "Tisha B'Av," he said, exaggerating the lip movements without making a sound. "Tisha B'Av."

What more fitting a day? Joey thought to himself glumly. Tisha B'Av was the anniversary of numerous major disasters that have befallen the Jewish people including, the destruction of the First and Second Temples. *Not to mention the anniversary of my brother's death.*

28

Jeremiah

McLean, Virginia
October 22, 2031

GENERAL JEREMIAH WESTFIELD HAD BEEN considered a brilliant military strategist and tactician. In closed testimony before the House Intelligence Committee just before he became ill, he acknowledged the failure of the American defense establishment to successfully adapt after the end of the relatively stable Cold War arrangement between the United States and Soviet Union. During that period, deterrence had been ensured by the promise of mutually assured destruction in the event of a nuclear war, and conventional conflict had been relegated to surrogate nations or tribes in the less industrialized world. The general likened the geopolitical aftermath to a smashed crystal chessboard that had left uncountable, dangerous, sometimes invisible glass-like shards scattered about the earth.

The Chairman of the House Select Committee on Intelligence had appeared confused, noting that there had been no major attacks in the U.S. domestically or on overseas installations in the three decades since September 2001. After an unusually pregnant pause, the general had responded cryptically that, in his view, the United States and "certain" allies he declined to name faced a period of "unprecedented" military and geopolitical uncertainty. During the conquest of Pakistan by the Islamic State, the United States had apparently been less effective in neutralizing Islamabad's nuclear capabilities than had been thought. An aide then whispered something to the general and he abruptly cut himself off, declining to clarify his comments.

Shortly thereafter, he had become gravely ill, first in a delirium and then in a coma. When he woke up, he was nearly paralyzed with severe tremors and stiffness, hallmarks of Parkinson's disease. Due to the general's top secret military clearance and the effect of the illness on his mental status and judgment, he was evaluated and treated by a special team of military doctors in a secure facility. Despite multiple medical tests, no cause was identified for the unusually rapid onset of severe symptoms and, by default, it was attributed to a virus and labeled post-encephalopathic parkinsonism.

Jeremiah was a West Point graduate who, like many successful military men, had been able to bridle and re-direct insatiable internal anger and aggression into the service of his country. His extraordinary ability to put himself in the place of America's smaller, creative enemies and, with an extraordinarily high probability of success, anticipate and counter their tactics and strategy had rocketed him through the ranks. He was sometimes referred to as the idiot savant general because of his slow southern drawl and long pauses. A former West Point instructor had written that he could appear prosaic at times. His genteel, congenial interpersonal style had defused much of the rivalry, back-biting, and aggressive career sabotage that had hampered many of his other classmates and had enabled him to rise based on his merits.

His ability to see into the mind of an enemy had been a natural product of his "schizophrenic-like" background. He had grown up in an economically depressed small town in eastern central Mississippi. His mother was Jewish, but non-observant, and his father was Methodist. The local traditions of bigotry and high unemployment in the town had amplified interest in the Ku Klux Klan, of which his father was a "social," not ideological, member.

The Ku Klux Klan had become increasingly active during Jeremiah's elementary school years. The FBI, with files on many KKK members, had approached the general's father to become an informer. Although he had no use for the Klan's beliefs, he refused to inform on his friends, co-workers and neighbors out of principle. Then, one day, the Klan went too far and bombed the local synagogue and rabbi's house. Although the family were not members of the synagogue and not known as Jews, his wife's family had been endangered, and Jeremiah's father decided to "turn." Upon his father's death, the general learned that his father had secretly – for the family's protection – donated the informant fees he had received to a small college for blacks in Jackson called Tougaloo.

From very early in life, Jeremiah was privy to both sides of the coin. In one ear, the secret guerilla war and terrorist plans of his father's compatriots in the white community, and in the other ear, the secret countermeasures being taken by the FBI and its surrogates. Thus, while young and plastic, his brain had developed a pattern of being able to anticipate and counter from above the moves being made from both sides of the chessboard. Jeremiah was not angry as a young child. He only became angry later when a knock on the door came in the middle of the night and the family was hauled by masked men into the woods, where in front of them his father was tied to a tree, beaten nearly senseless, doused with gasoline, and burned to death. The family moved away from Mississippi. During the remainder of his childhood, Jeremiah's rage was nearly equally divided between the clandestine, ragtag, pathetic underground guerilla movement that had killed his father and the government that had failed to protect its own informer.

As an army intelligence officer in South Korea, Jeremiah's father had been among the first to interrogate captured Chinese soldiers. He had interpreted the signs of the impending invasion, but his views had been ignored, suppressed or buried in paperwork by the command structure until moot after the main forces of the Red Army had swept far south of the Yalu River. After the war, he was quietly put to pasture in a dead-end desk job and left the military voluntarily but was not forgotten. After his death, a Mississippi congressman who had served in the same unit, took an interest in the family and saw to it that Jeremiah received an appointment to West Point.

Jeremiah thrived in the military environment, where he could achieve the success his father should have had and where he could sublimate the helpless rage he had experienced during his father's humiliation and murder. With intelligent and tireless passion, he became the world's foremost authority on suppression of military threats to the United States from extremist underground groups around the world. Each success, be it a pre-emptive drone strike or a capture of an underground adversarial leader, served as a soothing balm against the recrimination he felt for his inability to have helped his father. But not for long. The talisman that blocked the movie that ran through his mind of that night in Mississippi would lose its power, only to be restored by another violent and more spectacular success against the enemy.

The insatiable thirst for larger and larger success fueled his meteoric rise into and through the flag ranks as the unmatched master of the post-Cold War geopolitical game. Now in treatment, Joey recognized that the critical areas of the brain, the dorsolateral prefrontal lobes that controlled internal anger and had helped the general anticipate and counter the plots of enemies, were damaged by the ravages of Parkinson's disease. *As if that were not enough misfortune for the general,* thought Joey, *the treatments for Parkinson's disease could cause aggression and psychosis on their own. A typical damned if you do, damned if you don't two-edged sword in this godforsaken field of psychiatry.*

29

Jeremiah's Visions

THE AGENCY HAD WARNED JOEY that this morning's session might be difficult. Jeremiah frowned and met Joey's gaze. With all the hubris he could muster, given the shaking palsy he had contracted of late, he thundered, "I don't want to take the G-D medicine."

"What is it that bothers you about it?" Joey asked quietly, hoping his equanimity would calm the man.

The general lowered his voice. "I don't need it."

"I think you're interpreting taking the medicine as somehow saying something about you that hurts your self-esteem."

"And what would that be, doctor?" Jeremiah asked with feigned incredulity. "Could that be because it's called an antipsychotic?"

Joey wondered how many times Jeremiah had used the Socratic method to reel in and discredit adversarial but naïve civilian questioners in a congressional hearing. *If he loses his temper, I'm going to recommend a beta-blocker*, he mused.

"Antipsychotic is an unfortunate term for that class of medicines," Joey replied.

Jeremiah's eyes widened in surprise and he sat back in his chair in a limp, subdued posture. He seemed to have been caught off guard by the unflustered reaction of calm and equanimity to his tirade.

A good sign, Joey thought. *He responds to body language, at least.*

Then Jeremiah's tone dropped an octave and he replied conversationally, without bluster, "Why do they think I need something like that?"

"It's not because of you. It's to counter the effect of the medicine you take for your tremors and shakes. The medicine has a chemical in it called L-dopa that helps the nerves that control your muscles so you don't shake and freeze up. But that same chemical, L-dopa, can cause trouble in other parts of your brain. The second medicine, the so called antipsychotic, is supposed to prevent that side effect, that's all."

"What side effect is that, doctor?"

After a pause, Joey said, "It's not unusual for the medicine you take to cause a nerve messenger called dopamine to overstimulate certain areas of your brain. If this happens, it causes unusual experiences that may seem real. Has that happened to you?"

Jeremiah looked at him straight in the eye and said, firmly and calmly, "I have had some unusual experiences but they're real."

Joey paused and subtly nodded, intending to transmit the notion that he was taking seriously the possibility that Jeremiah's unusual experiences were real and that he wanted to evaluate them objectively with no bias from the referring diagnosis of "substance-induced psychosis." The official dossier had provided few details to support the provisional diagnosis, but Jeremiah's wife had been more forthcoming.

Joey wanted to sound like he was asking fresh questions, but he was aware that Jeremiah might know that the wife had called him. He couldn't risk being perceived as disingenuous to the patient but at the same time he didn't want to betray the confidentiality of the wife, who, in addition to being a valuable source of information, had pleaded that her marriage might be jeopardized if her husband learned she had discussed his condition with his doctor.

Joey hadn't made up his mind yet whether Jeremiah was psychotic, but he knew the general was still well enough and savvy enough to hide it if he were. After a long silence, the two men locked eyes across the angle between their chairs. Something common in their experience, barely conscious, bubbled to the surface. Jeremiah seemed to feel a sudden desire to talk openly to Joey and said, "I see weird things sometimes when I'm alone."

Joey plastered his most non-judgmental look on his face and waited to see if Jeremiah would say more. The general remained silent. After a few moments, he prompted, "Can you describe what you see to me?"

"It's hard to be sure, but it looks and sounds like my father."

"You see him?"

"Yes."

"Does he speak?"

"Yes."

"Can you tell me what he says to you?"

"He says 'I'm all right.' It has the feel like he's come a long way to tell me this. He says it emphatically, like he knows I was worried. He's dressed in his work clothes, but he looks tired, like he traveled a long way. His clothes are wrinkled. He's haggard from the journey, but underneath he looks healthy, just tired, I think. It's like he can't stay. I want him to stay but he has to go, like he's afraid he'll get in trouble and went to great lengths to come here just to tell me he's OK back where he came from."

Joey felt a wave of sadness like a shadow coming over him. He recognized it as empathy for his patient. A specter-like image of Madeleine, coming forth to comfort him, darted into his imagination and left just as quickly.

"Do you speak to him?"

"Yes," Jeremiah said, no longer in a guarded tone.

"What do you say?"

"Daddy!"

"Anything else?"

"No. That's all that happens."

"How does it make you feel?"

"At first, I'm overcome with shock, and then excitement and joy that he's OK. And then I'm sad. I weep because he's gone."

"Did this ever happen before you took L-dopa?"

"No."

"Never?"

"That's correct."

"Have any of your relatives ever experienced such a thing?"

"No."

"Does it have any relationship to drinking or stopping drinking alcohol?"

"No."

"Do you have any other visions?"

"No."

"Or hear anything else you find unusual or that others can't?"

"No."

"Feel anything or smell anything unusual?"

"No."

It was obvious the general was tired of these questions but Joey had to ask them in order to write his report.

"What do you make of the visions?"

"I don't know."

"Do you think it's the medicine?"

"I never had them before the medicine, but when they're happening they seem real. Given the relationship to the medicine, I can see it's involved somehow. But it doesn't mean the visions aren't real."

In an instant in which he barely broke his gaze with the general, Joey recalled a dinner discussion with several accomplished Ethiopian psychiatrists. During Mengistu's Communist Derg regime, Ethiopian medical students had been sent to the Soviet Union for medical school. After the Communist regime fell, they had completed psychiatric residencies and fellowships at prestigious Western universities. Many had later been awarded significant grants to support investigation of specific African aspects of psychosis. In a remote area of the Rift Valley, considered one of the cradles of civilization, the

Ethiopian doctors and Joey had shared a fresh circular bread called injera covered with very spicy vegetables and rare beef. They swigged local beer and tej, a honey wine. The doctors and their staff, some of whom were Coptic Christians, spoke more freely as the night wore on, attempting to reconcile Western scientific and traditional African mystical views of psychosis. All acknowledged the effectiveness of antipsychotic medications in their practices and regularly used them. However, their explanation of the etiology of psychotic phenomena such as hallucinations and delusions was very different from the West. They felt that intrusions from the spirit world were the ultimate cause of psychosis and that antipsychotics worked by strengthening the brain's resistance to these spirits.

Joey blinked away the memories and refocused on the situation in the room. He did not want to challenge Jeremiah's implied supposition that the voices were real but wanted to draw him out further.

"Help me understand what you mean when you say it doesn't mean they aren't real."

"Who's to say it isn't some sort of representation of my father?"

"As in a spirit?"

"'Spirit' is a loaded word," Jeremiah replied cautiously, in a thoughtful, tone. "I would rather not paint myself in a corner that way."

He's wise to hedge, for the record, thought Joey. "But you see the experience with your father as some type of supernatural phenomenon?"

"That was your word, not mine." The general stiffened defensively in his posture.

Don't let him go so far as to cross his arms or the session may as well be over, Joey told himself. "I'm not trying to label your thinking," he said as disarmingly as he could. "Do you see it as a coincidence that this began after you developed Parkinson's disease and started L-dopa?"

"No, doctor," Jeremiah said, sounding sarcastic and bitter again. "I don't deny they are related." But then, in a more gentle tone, Jeremiah asked, "What if the damage from Parkinson's disease made my brain more receptive to things that were really out there? The spirit of a deceased loved one, for example, that are blocked out by something in a healthy brain, but that our ancestors or a modern-day shaman could turn on and off?"

Jeremiah seemed to collect his thoughts as if he had worked this out in his head before and then continued. "Maybe L-dopa juices up the brain, too, and makes it more receptive. For God's sake, if you can pick up a radio signal with something as simple as a crystal set, why couldn't the human brain, a billion times more complicated, pick up a signal of some kind?"

Joey observed that Jeremiah seemed to pause to gauge his reaction. His first impulse was to question Jeremiah's logic but he decided it was too risky. Jeremiah might lump him into his paranoid system, if that's what it was, with all the other doubters. He decided to try a different approach by discussing Jeremiah's theory objectively as if it were a fair hypothesis. He knew he was at risk of appearing to buy in to Jeremiah's delusion but decided to chance it.

"There have always been phenomena that are there but that we can't detect without instruments. Most wild animals, including other advanced primates, hear and smell things humans can't. If you turn on a television, you see an image that's derived from something invisible in the air. So your notion that the brain, which after all is an electrical instrument of sorts, could pick up some kind of signal may not be viewed as so far-fetched someday."

Jeremiah smiled and relaxed in his chair, pleased at the apparent collusion of the doctor with his eccentric theory.

Joey, however, felt uneasy with this and suddenly had the notion of the general reporting back to headquarters that he had agreed with his interpretation of his hallucinations.

"But that is an academic discussion on my part," he said hastily. "What's important for me to know is whether you can entertain that it may be entirely a symptom of Parkinson's disease, L-dopa-induced hallucinations with the form determined by unresolved grief on your part."

Jeremiah looked disappointed but looked like he knew what he was supposed to say to keep his important position. "It feels real when happens. But who knows? How could anyone know for sure? I would like it to be real. I'll tell you that because, after seeing the way Dad died, I need him to be OK."

God knows I know how he feels. With a monumental effort Joey forced images of Madeleine, half-buried in the rubble, out of his head. He nodded sympathetically to Jeremiah. "I can certainly understand that. By the way, was your family religious?"

"My dad was Christian and believed in the afterlife. That Jesus and all a man's ancestors would be waiting for a believer at the gates of heaven with trumpets and open arms. My mom was Jewish. Who knows what Jews think about the afterlife? They mostly say to take care of things here on earth."

"Did anyone else in your family ever see your dad come back?"

"No."

"I believe we are out of time for today."

"One more thing, doctor."

"Of course."

"I've done a little reading and this diagnosis they gave me, Parkinson's disease, usually comes on a little at a time. It came on me all at once. That seems odd, but none of the military doctors will talk about it. I know you're a shrink, but would you mind taking a fresh look at the medical records and tell me what you think?"

"You bet."

In his notes, Joey wrote: "Psychiatric Diagnosis: unresolved grief, probable L-dopa-related hallucinations with partial insight, questions their veracity, therefore not psychotic in nature. Beliefs about terrorist attacks do not rise to the level of a delusion because he is able to acknowledge they may not be accurate. Would characterize as an overvalued idea. Suggest grief psychotherapy to complete grieving over father. Psychiatric Diagnosis: Post-traumatic stress disorder and L-dopa-induced hallucinations (non-psychotic) induced by

unresolved grief. Medical Diagnosis (Provisional): Apparent Parkin
son's syndrome. Etiology unknown."

30

Sensitive Compartmented Information

McLean, Virginia
November 19, 2031

C AITLYN WAS NOW MANAGING HER second generation
of Jacobsons. She handed Joey a sealed packet containing General Westfield's previous medical records. It was marked "Top Secret."
Obtaining them had taken a week's adroit bureaucratic maneuvering
on Caitlyn's part, including calling in several favors.

She returned an hour later. "What do you think?"

He shook his head slowly and raised an eyebrow, his voice a
mix of surprise and skepticism. "Medically, it's odd, very odd. They
diagnosed acute viral encephalopathy, but he had no fever and his
spinal fluid showed no signs of infection, zero white cells and all viral
cultures negative."

"But the protein was very high," observed Caitlyn.

"Totally non-specific. No patterns associated with viral
infection."

"What about the brain wave test?"

"It was consistent with delirium, but again, no specific pattern such as one might see with herpes simplex encephalitis."

"What else can cause delirium?" she asked.

"Anything that can make the brain medically sick. The real question is, what besides an infection can cause delirium and give a person Parkinson's disease virtually overnight?"

Joey seemed lost in thought. *Parkinson's disease overnight*, he mused. He seemed to recall something about monkey experiments where a drug induced severe parkinsonism by poisoning the nerves that made dopamine. It was sometimes a contaminant in street drugs and had caused classic symptoms of Parkinson's disease in humans as well. *MPTP, that was it.* He suddenly looked up at Caitlyn. "Does General Westfield use drugs?"

Caitlyn thumbed through the chart, then answered, looking over her tiny reading glasses at Joey. "From what I can see, nothing in his dossier supports that."

Joey nodded. "I agree from talking with him. I don't think he's an occult drug user. But maybe someone slipped it to him."

"Like the poisoning of that Ukrainian opposition leader? Viktor Yushchenko?" Caitlyn asked.

"Exactly," Joey replied.

"But what would the motive be for poisoning the general?"

Joey thought for a moment. "To distract him, discredit him, to shut him up. I can imagine countless people who would have an interest in bottling up the information he had."

"Just think what would happen to the stock market if that stuff the general was saying got out."

Caitlyn was starting to sound impressed by the theory. Joey realized that, by bantering about the market, they were displacing their anxiety about the general being right and their being blown to smithereens. Gently, he redirected them.

"Now what we need to figure out is what would be the footprint of parkinsonism from MPTP poisoning versus a virus or another toxin. Can you give me a literature review on the clinical characteristics of MPTP poisoning in humans?"

In the old days, they would have driven to the National Library of Medicine in Bethesda, but now it could all be done from the office on the shiny Apple computer Caitlyn loved. An hour later, Caitlyn printed out a list of nearly 100 abstracts. Joey chose seven. Caitlyn purchased the full articles over the internet. Joey sat for a long time in his office with the articles and the general's medical dossier before inviting Caitlyn back into his office. She sat down directly across from him, looking at him expectantly.

"Well, doctor?"

Joey liked to teach. "It looks to me like there are two distinctive characteristics of MPTP-induced parkinsonism. Unlike other toxins and most infectious causes, it gives all the classic signs of parkinsonism. That fits the general. He has the tremor, the stiffness and the slowness. But even more distinctive is the signature in the brain. It pretty much wipes out the main dopamine-using motor nucleus in the brain, the substantia nigra, causing gliosis."

"What's gliosis?" Caitlyn asked.

"It's like scarring in the brain. It's sort of like tissue that grows in to fill the space when the nerves are damaged," Joey explained patiently.

"Does the general have it?"

Joey looked at Caitlyn hard. "Well, that's what is so strange. The brain imaging report seems to be missing."

"How do you know brain imaging was done then?"

"A mysterious illness like this hitting one of your top generals. You would damn sure use your top technology and at least get an MRI."

"Why an MRI?" she asked.

"Magnetic Resonance Imaging produces a much more detailed picture than a CT scan. All they have here is a CT report described as 'normal.' But the resolution is way too low to see the substantia nigra well. It could be functionally wiped out and you would never know it. Caitlyn, can you request the MRI?"

An hour later she returned, looking puzzled.

"What happened?"

"I went through all the electronic records and you were right," she said. "They ordered MRIs, but not just one, a whole series of them as if they were following something."

"Did you request the scans? I'd like to look myself."

"I requested both the reports and the scans through the secure electronic record system we always use for the brass."

"And?"

"It said the MRI reports were unavailable."

"Did the system verify our top secret clearance?"

"It did but this was apparently a higher clearance. I called to be sure. The general's MRI reports are 'Sensitive Compartmented Information.' In other words, 'need to know only,' and you are not on the list."

31

An Early Winter

I T HAD BEEN AN UNUSUALLY heavy early December snow-storm. Joey met Bevy, Noah and Teddy for dinner in Old Town Alexandria. Lined by nineteenth century townhouses, the wide streets blanketed in several inches of fresh snow seemed strangely empty. The powdery snow seemed to dampen and filter the sound of footsteps and the occasional tire spinning to variations of dull thuds. Teddy packed a snowball between his gloves and hurled it at Noah's chest. Noah turned his back, showering his neck with powder.

"Aighhh, Teddy!" Noah scooped up a handful of snow and dumped it down Teddy's collar.

"Noah, that's not fair, I didn't even get it in your shirt."

Both twins were laughing. Bevy, her arm around Joey's shoulders, rolled her eyes cheerfully. The four strolled on, charmed by the novelty and beauty of the setting, until they turned onto a small unsigned side street, more of an alley than a street. They then turned onto another small street or large alley until they were parallel with the Potomac River. At the end was a very thick antique door with an oversized brass knocker. The address on the mailbox was 0, signifying that it was the establishment at the end of the street adjacent to the river.

"Jesus, Joey, where are you taking us?" Bevy asked optimistically, having benefited many times in the past from his ability to find out of the way restaurants with unusual atmospheres and outstanding food.

"To a hole in the wall. What did you expect?" They rang a buzzer. Teddy noted the video camera overhead, and when the door buzzed open, he remarked good-naturedly, "I guess we passed," and charged in curiously.

None of his siblings was prepared for what they saw. Inside was a bustling, country-style restaurant that specialized in simple, family southern cooking. In the bar, where the sound was well insulated from the restaurant, a country music singer/guitarist took requests. In contrast to the deserted streets, the place was packed and noisy.

Bevy took off her knit cap, shook her long auburn hair over her shoulders and slid into the worn leather booth. Joey hung his overcoat and fedora on the hook and sat down next to Bevy. The twins slid into the other side, their eyes fixing momentarily on Joey's salt and pepper hair. They exchanged quizzical glances. Bevy watched, handed Joey a menu to distract him, frowned at the twins and mouthed "later." She managed to kick both twins under the table without Joey noticing and asked, "Are you hungry or hawngry?"

The three boys laughed at the old family joke. "Hawwngry!" they said in unison.

A tall, middle-aged waitress in cowboy boots and a denim jacket appeared as if on cue. "Speaking of the devil," Noah quipped.

"What can I get y'all?" she asked warmly as if she had known the Jacobson clan for years.

They swigged cold draft beer from frosty mugs and munched hot fried pickles out of a plastic basket lined with a paper napkin. Next came platters of crisp fried chicken, catfish and hushpuppies. Noah and Teddy talked about how technology and personalized medicine were changing their practices, but they loved their work. A play Bevy had produced had just opened at Ford's theater to excellent reviews. Their children and spouses were well.

After they devoured a freshly baked blackberry cobbler topped with huge scoops of homemade peach ice cream, they moved from beers to shots of bourbon. They closed the bar down, just as they would have ten years earlier. It was snowing big fluffy flakes when they stepped outside.

Noah's eyes shined. "Great choice, Joey. This place could have been transplanted straight from Nashville."

Joey's eyes took on a faraway look for a moment. "It's very similar to a dive I frequented with Madeleine just down the street from Vanderbilt Hospital." Bevy put her arm around him and gave him a kiss on the cheek.

"I remember, I met the two of you there when I visited right after you got engaged."

Joey looked into Bevy's hazel eyes and nodded. Then he took a deep breath and stood up straight. "Where to now, guys? Are you up for some blues?"

Noah and Teddy whooped and hollered in agreement. They walked ahead, throwing snowballs and horsing around as naturally as they had when they shared a bedroom as kids. Joey noticed that Bevy kept their pace around 20 yards behind the twins. *Sound carries over dry snow. She wants to talk about something in private.*

"Joey, I had wanted to ask you how it was working out living at the McLean house."

"The rent is right, if that's what you mean," Joey said dryly. Their brother was buried there. The house they had grown up in had been left in trust to all four living children after their mother's death.

"It must be lonely there sometimes."

"Very much so, but I love the house, the pond, the woods."

"It's hard to imagine being there without Mom."

Joey nodded several times in agreement.

"Actually, I'm not home too much. It seems like I spend more time at the office or on the road for work than home. When I'm alone, I'm lonely, and all kinds of things come into my head. Safer to be busy."

"Don't you think it's time you started to go out?"

Now the real topic she wanted to discuss privately. Joey suddenly felt gratitude for his sister. *She really does care about me.*

"I guess I'm the same as Mom. She never dated after Dad died, no matter how much people hounded her," Joey said.

"I never agreed with that. I hounded her too. What's the point of being a grief saint? From what I remember and everything people told me about Dad, he would have wanted her to be happy."

"She was happy and she considered herself married to him until the day she died."

"There was something else though, some other kind of bond," Bevy said. "Near the end, she hinted that Dad had made some kind of bargain, like a sacrifice they had both benefitted from. But anyway, your situation is completely different. You were just married, you never had a chance to have children or a life."

Joey nearly tripped on a slick spot.

"Are you OK?" she asked, steadying him with her arm about his waist.

"My ankle turned a bit on a slick spot. I'm OK. It's only been a couple of years. I feel as married to her as the day she died."

"Has there been any woman since Madeleine?"

"No."

"Is there anybody who at least turns your head?"

Joey sighed. "One, and I don't feel good about it." He looked at Bevy. Her face was covered with frost, but he thought she looked pleased. *She really does care about me.*

"The spy girl?" Bevy asked.

"Yes, Katharina."

"You said she was smart and pretty."

"Very good at her craft, but also very manipulative. She was my handler on a number of missions overseas. There were times when the only safe place to talk was her room."

"Did you…?"

Joey cut her off, "No."

"Did you want to?"

"Yes, I wanted to and I still feel bad about it."

"Do you still see her?"

"I only saw her for work and it was only required overseas. I'm not traveling much these days."

"Will she be back?"

Before Joey could answer, Noah said, "We're here, guys." The twins were already beating the snow off their coats in the entrance.

Bevy squeezed Joey's hand through his gloves. "It's a start," she whispered.

Joey whispered back, "Leave it alone."

Bevy frowned and hit him with her fist playfully in the ribs.

Joey smiled, "I love you, sister." Bevy laughed.

Inside, a band from Greenwood, Mississippi, crooned and danced sentimentally. Joey ordered a shot of Jack Daniel's, Bevy a White Russian, Noah and Teddy Talisker Scotch on the rocks. Noah swirled the Scotch over the ice and sipped as if tasting a delicacy and set it down.

Bevy picked up Noah's glass, took a tiny sip and screwed up her face in disgust. "It tastes like a peat bog!" She stuck her tongue out and set the glass down again in front of Noah.

Joey chuckled. "It's only nasty at first. It mellows as the ice melts."

Noah and Teddy clinked their glasses and sipped. Teddy said, "Touché." Noah nodded.

Teddy eyed Bevy's glass. "What's in that concoction?"

Bevy stirred with her finger and tasted a drop. "Ummm, Kahlua and cream and vodka. The vodka gives you the buzz and the caffeine in the Kahlua keeps you awake to enjoy it."

"May I taste it?" Teddy asked politely.

Bevy set the glass in front of him. Teddy took a little sip. "It's good." Then he took another, leaving his lips white.

Bevy laughed. "Wipe your lips."

Noah reached for the glass. "May I taste it?"

"Sure, go ahead," said Bevy.

215

Noah took a little taste, then a long draw. Joey caught Bevy's eye and winked. They both smiled.

The sharp-eyed waitress spied the empty glass and was over in a flash. "Can I get you another drink, ma'am?"

Bevy looked at Noah and Teddy, "Actually, I think we need three!"

The twins nodded eagerly.

The waitress asked, "Are you guys twins?"

"Yes," they said sequentially.

"Identical?" she asked.

"That depends, who do you think is more handsome?"

The waitress spoke to Bevy, "You're their sister, I can tell."

Bevy nodded.

The waitress turned toward Joey. Her eyes roved over his graying hair, the lines in his face, his posture. "Is he your daddy?"

Joey threw his head back and laughed. Bevy blushed.

"I mean your big brother, not your daddy," the waitress added hastily.

The twins hesitated. The waitress stammered, "It's last call. I better get those drinks before the bar shuts down at midnight."

After the waitress hurried away, the twins and Bevy exchanged glances in a concerned way that Joey thought was a little conspiratorial.

"Joey," Noah began, "the waitress was right in a way. I feel like you look like our much older brother, not our baby brother. Don't take this the wrong way, but every time we see you, you look older. Are you OK? What's going on?"

Joey felt the lightness and mirth of the little reunion dissipating like the air out of a balloon. "We've had a very nice evening. Are you sure you want to go into this now?"

"We're not trying to bum you out or anything. We're just concerned about you," Teddy added. "We just want to make sure everything's all right."

"You can't judge a book by its cover," Joey joked feebly. Then he sighed as they looked at him skeptically. *No cheap theatrical exits tonight*, he thought. *I'm going to have to talk about it.* Bevy, Noah and eddy weren't just his siblings. They were three of his best friends. He ecided to level with them.

"Since Madeleine was killed, it's like I've aged forty years," he aid quietly. "They say hair can turn gray overnight, but in my case he hair was just the tip of the iceberg, the visible. It should have hade alarms go off about what was happening inside me. Her death riggered something inside my body."

The siblings looked at Joey with concern, studiously avoiding he temptation to glance at one another to see what the other was hinking, knowing such a look might make Joey conscious of just ow bizarre the conversation was turning. For now, the whiskey was alking and they wanted to hear what it had to say.

"I procrastinated about seeing a doctor. I know too much about ur limitations, our motivations, our faults." Then he paused.

The twins, he knew, had doctors as patients. They saw through im immediately, recognizing denial.

"You were afraid," Noah said, looking him straight in the eye.

"Afraid of what?" Joey asked in a low monotone that sounded erfunctory. He knew full well what Noah was thinking.

"You were afraid they would find something."

Joey pursed his lips and said nothing.

"No?" asked Teddy mildly.

"Not exactly," Joey said. After a moment's silence, he conceded, Well, maybe. Unfortunately, I was right."

"What do you mean?" Bevy asked, alarmed.

"Once they started looking, they found everything." Joey pursed is lips and shook his head slightly, releasing a long sigh through his ostrils.

"Everything?" Noah asked.

"Well, enough."

"Enough for what?" Noah persisted.

"Enough to ruin my confidence about the future."

Bevy frowned. Teddy interjected softly, "What exactly happened?"

Joey collected himself. "Virtually every organ system in my body went bad at once. I had a bicuspid valve since I was a kid, and all of sudden, it stops working and the blood starts flowing backwards, and my pancreas slows down, making insulin, and my sugar goes up. And then they start poking and looking around, and my kidney is full of holes. They tell me benign holes, thank God, but they want to watch them, and in the process they see a spot on my pancreas and so forth."

Joey saw Noah, a gastroenterologist, wince when he said "spot on my pancreas." He pre-empted Noah's question. "No, not exactly cancer yet."

Noah and Teddy visibly relaxed. Once pancreatic cancer was diagnosed, it was usually too late for a cure.

"The only things that still work right are my brain and penis," Joey quipped, trying to lighten the atmosphere.

"That's because you've got so much redundancy," Teddy said with a wink. Bevy blushed.

"Well, I can still work, thank God. I can do what I want to do, which is practice psychiatry. But I have to keep my mind busy."

"I've never known your mind not to be busy," said Noah with a sympathetic smile.

"But sometimes now, when I should be listening to my patient – you know, sometimes they drone on and on – my mind wanders."

"Has anyone complained?" Bevy asked, looking concerned.

"Not yet. When they're on the couch, I sit behind them."

"What do you think is going on?" Noah asked intently.

"The diseases that run in our family, which usually come on in old age, are coming on all at once in me before middle age. Something turned on the aging genes early or they were programmed wrong to begin with."

Bevy wiped away a tear. "Do you think it was the stress of losing Madeleine?"

Joey sighed. "That might have been the trigger. Men, older men at least, don't do so well after they lose their wives. But even after the severest psychological trauma, you just don't see this degree of accelerated aging unless something else is wrong."

"Have you seen a geneticist?" Teddy asked.

"Well, I was a little nervous about getting worked up. Confidentiality, you know. Everything gets reported as an insurance code and the medicines you take can be found by anyone. So I saw someone out of the country."

"How did you find them?" Teddy interjected incredulously.

"It's an odd thing. Mom knew him through the mohel at the temple, of all people."

Bevy's brow furrowed. "The mohel, Izzy Rosen, the guy at the temple who does the bris?"

"Small world, what can I say? Izzy knew a very old doctor in Prague who apparently has seen quite a bit of this."

"Did the Prague doctor diagnose some type of premature aging syndrome?" Noah asked. Teddy looked on intently.

"He seemed pretty confidant of that and it was confirmed by the testing. There is a biological clock of sorts at the end of a chromosome called a telomere. Mine were close to midnight, like an old man. He wanted to start genetic therapy but it's experimental. He said it had worked for some others who were in the same boat as me. I'm thinking about it. Mom seemed to think the world of this guy."

32

Snowed In

McLean, Virginia
December 11, 2031

A S JOEY WALKED ALONG THE deserted, snow-covered streets back toward his SUV, he felt a sense of satisfaction and closure from his conversation with his siblings. Although years apart in age, they had shared the "joie de vivre" despite the loss of their father and brother. He had followed in the footsteps of his brothers, sharing many similar experiences in their medical training. They had struggled through mountains of book learning in the early years and trusted their classmates to take care of each other's patients under exhausting conditions of thirty-six hours on call, twelve hours off, thirty-six off for weeks at a time. They had eventually become certain enough in their skills so that the fatigue had not been a threat to them.

"We could do it in our sleep, if we had to," the brothers often joked.

As for Bevy, she was like a physical reincarnation of her mother:

tall, athletic and pretty on the outside, funny, brilliant and warm on the inside. She had been a bottomless source of comfort and good advice to him after the loss of his wife.

During dinner, he had received a call from the security system indicating that they had received a low-probability signal of an entry at the office, but not to worry because this was common during heavy snow and was unlikely to be valid. He had not wanted to disturb his reunion with his siblings and had thought of calling Caitlyn and asking her to go in. He decided against it because of the icy roads and checked back with the security company, who had sent someone over but found no sign of a break-in. He felt sufficiently reassured for the time being but, given the sensitive situation with the general, he wanted to have his own look before retiring for the night.

He found that, on the block of his office, the city power had gone off, most likely from a branch heavy with snow falling on a power line. The natural gas backup generator was functioning properly. He had reluctantly invested in it after the remnants of a hurricane had knocked out power to the area for seven days the previous summer. Tonight's brief interruption in electricity had apparently triggered the signal to the alarm company, as it often had in the past during thunderstorms.

The digital clocks in the office blinked uselessly, stuck on the time the power had been interrupted. Joey switched on a lamp by his chair but did not turn on the main lighting. The room was warm and the parrot slept undisturbed in its cage under the hood. He had wondered if patients might be nervous having a parrot in on their private sessions. Instead, he found most patients were not only OK with the parrot but actually found its presence comforting. The room had a ghostly hue from the reflection of the lamp on the frost-coated windows and skylights. The datura was a nocturnal tree. Its white blossoms were fully opened and Joey was taken aback by the thick sweet fragrance. Without the heating action of sunlight, the daytime acrid odor of the Ethiopian wedding dresses had been reduced to a distant must.

Joey suddenly felt very tired and sat for a moment in his analyst's chair, intending to check his appointment book for tomorrow. There was something penciled in illegibly in juvenile cursive for the morning. It was written to the side like a note. He couldn't tell what time it was or the name. He felt aggravated. *That's not like Caitlyn*, he thought and looked closer. He blinked and shook his head. It reminded him of his own childhood writing he had seen in a scrapbook.

I'll close my eyes for just a second and then I'll be on my way, he said to himself.

He remembered morning rounds in medical school after being up all night on call, propping his head up and holding his eyelids open as his eyes swam in his head. That was how he felt now. He looked up at the canopy of the datura tree and saw countless trumpet-like white blossoms staring down at him. They blurred. *They look like eyes*, he thought. *God, the fragrance is strong this time of night. No wonder the parrot didn't wake up.*

Then he lost consciousness.

When he awoke, he felt as if he were pulling himself up from the bottom of a deep well. He looked at his watch. It had stopped sometime during the night. *Curious*, he thought, *it's self-winding. It must have gotten wet during the storm.* He pulled himself to his feet and peered outside. There was some light, but the snow pelted the window and had intensified to the point where he couldn't distinguish night from day. The drifts looked to be over 2 feet. The sleet mixed with the snow made a persistent tapping sound on the skylights.

Periodically, the wind would pick up, whistling distantly through the thick anti-eavesdropping glass. There were no lights on in any of the buildings across the street, no cars or pedestrians were to be seen. He couldn't discern the road from the sidewalk under the heavy blanket of snow. He didn't know how long he had slept. The generator droned on and on in the background.

Caitlyn will never make it in today, he thought. The datura blossoms, responding to the faint light filtering in through the snow-covered glass, had closed a notch but still exuded their thick fragrance, although not as strongly as in the dead of night. He felt sleep drunk. His legs were like rubber. It was all he could do to get back to his chair. Then he decided to lay down on the couch.

He left his hat in the chair and shuffled to the couch, lying on his back with his head slightly elevated on a pillow. *I'll just rest for a moment.* Just as a delicious feeling of numb sleepiness seemed to take away his breath, there was a light tapping on the door between the waiting room and his office.

He raised his head and listened. It wasn't the timid knocking of an adult, he decided. It sounded like a child. That was absurd. *A tree limb, perhaps, blowing against the building.* Tap-tap TAP tap-tap.

It seemed to wait to see the effect, then repeated louder, but still timidly. *I don't think it's a limb*, Joey concluded. *Who could be in the waiting room in a storm like this?*

He tried to stand up but could not. His feet would not move from the couch to the floor. It felt like his legs had gone to sleep. He attempted a less ambitious maneuver of raising himself to a sitting position, but his muscles wouldn't obey him. He felt self-conscious but had no fear for his safety. *I can't be seen like this*, he thought. If he had been fully alert, he would have recognized this as the type of denial patients describe when they're having catastrophic medical disasters such as a heart attack or stroke. Then another thought crept into his head. *Had they given me some toxic drug like they gave the general?*

He felt something in the pit of his stomach and his shoulders tighten in a moment of panic, but it was quickly replaced by a more comforting thought. *Sleep paralysis. That's it. I'll just go back to sleep* and as he started to doze, the knock came louder, more determined. Bam-bam bam bam-bam. He managed to open his eyes.

"Come in," he said in a low voice that conveyed uncertainty and would have been barely audible on the other side of the door. Then he got a hold of himself. "Come in," he said in his usual decisive voice, as if he had been expecting the visitor all the time.

The door opened and a little boy of around 7 years old appeared. He looked vaguely familiar. There had been an entry in his ppointment book he couldn't read. He realized he had no idea what me it was and tried to conceal his befuddlement.

"Have you been out there long?"

The child seemed to consider several answers but said nothing. Ie walked into the office and seemed uncertain where to sit. The urniture was too big for a 7-year-old.

Joey silently recalled a supervisor's admonishment to the interns: It never benefits the patient to share your confusion."

"Did you have trouble getting here in the storm?"

The child shook his head and smiled faintly.

Joey studied the child from the couch, unwilling to trust his legs ɔ carry him to his chair. "Please sit down."

The child climbed into Joey's chair instead of the patient's chair. Ie assumed a relaxed posture, with his hands resting on his knees, nd seemed to wait for him to speak.

"Are your parents with you?" Joey tried to formulate a plan for iterviewing the parents without revealing his abject ignorance about /hy they were here. The child shook his head decisively, indicating e was alone.

Who would drop a child off alone in weather like this?

He had half a mind to make an excuse to get a glass of water or omething out of the waiting room to see if the child was really alone, ut his legs still felt rubbery and he didn't trust them to stand. He arely saw children without their parents. He was not board certified n child psychiatry and was cautious to stay within his areas of pro- ɛssional expertise. He wondered if the child had been scheduled by nistake. *There must be extremely important issues for the family to have isked an accident driving on the nearly impassable snow-covered roads,* e thought. *An overseas State Department or Agency case, perhaps.* He uddenly wondered if the child spoke English.

The child had a winning smile, poise and a certain magnetism bout him that was beyond his years. Joey was baffled by a vague sense ɔf déjà vu. As if that wasn't enough, the child had sat in Joey's chair s if he had been there before. *Perhaps his father has such a chair.* The child carried his neck a little stiffly as if an old injury had healed, but imperfectly. Otherwise, the child appeared physically and neurologically healthy. He appeared to have been doing homework of some kind in the waiting room and had brought in a piece of paper showing what could have been a complicated series of interrelated math operations that were beyond his years. They looked like differential equations and integrals. *Must be an older sibling's work*, Joey reasoned.

The boy is looking at me sympathetically. He knows I'm not well. I suppose he could tell I had been sleeping when I was supposed to be working and inferred something was wrong with me. No, there is something more sophisticated in the way that boy looks at me. I believe it's empathy.

Joey tried to return the child's comfortable gaze, feeling a strange sense of connection. He felt comfortable in the boy's presence saying nothing but decided he had best find out why the boy was here. But then he changed his mind again, reasoning that the silence must be meaningful. *Well, I can analyze the counter-transference*, Joey thought. *If the boy makes me feel this comfortable, he must have the same effect on others.* He waited for the boy to speak, hoping his own silence would exert subtle pressure on the boy to speak just as it had on hundreds of patients before him.

But the boy didn't speak. It was snowing intensely again and the natural light had faded. The datura blossoms hung open, their sweet fragrance filling the air. Joey suddenly felt very tired. He dozed briefly, then awoke with a sense of panic. Had the boy seen him sleep? The boy seemed to sense his concern and nodded sympathetically with a faint, reassuring smile. The futility of the session, even Joey's falling asleep had been OK, but the boy's smile seemed to be saying something more meaningful.

He thinks I'm old, Joey realized with a start. *He's being kind.* Now the boy was nodding as if he read his mind.

Joey tried to analyze this as transference. *The boy must have a loving relationship with a grandfather figure.*

The boy looked at his watch. *A little young to wear a watch*, Joey mused, wrinkling his brow slightly. But everything else about the boy seemed precocious as well.

"It's time for us to go," the boy said, peering directly into Joey's eyes without any pretense of rising to leave.

Joey heard the boy clearly but assumed he meant to say, "It's time for me to go."

"Excuse me," Joey said, trying not to appear as discombobulated as he felt. "I couldn't hear you." Although in the back of his mind, he knew the boy had spoken perfectly clearly.

The boy looked directly into Joey's eyes as if he had expected the question. In exactly the same voice, he repeated, "It's time for us to go." He nodded softly in a way that was intended to be reassuring. Joey was struck by another wave of déjà vu, this time from the distantly familiar prosody in the child's voice. He felt a pang of regret and sorrow somewhere deep in his belly and swallowed hard. He tried to analyze the counter-transference, the feelings and memories aroused in him by the dynamic with the boy. Something in the boy had triggered an overpowering feeling of loss in his own psyche, but he couldn't place it.

As a psychiatrist, he was trained to use his emotional reaction to patients to try to understand their hidden lives. *Had the boy experienced a trauma of separation?* Joey closed his eyes for a moment and tried to open his mind to the other associations he had to the boy. He had the vivid fantasy, almost memory-like, of a muffled snuffle, the breaking down of an emotionally strong boy who tries not to cry, but whose denial is being overwhelmed by a grief so staggering as to defy words. *The grief of permanent separation from his family, perhaps his whole world.*

Joey felt the loss he attributed to the boy intensely. It surprised him. He identified strongly with the boy. He would have to explore that factor. Vaguely, he recalled that, after hitting his head on the side of an airboat when he was barely a young man, he had thought he saw a boy under the water. The feelings it had evoked were eerily similar to what he was experiencing now. But his grandfather had told him that he had been confused, that it was only his reflection.

For a moment he lost his breath, as if it had been knocked out of him. The sensation frightened him and he panicked for a moment, nauseous, feeling the room spin. He closed his eyes. He heard the door to the waiting room open and close deliberately and gently. Then the door to the street opened and closed.

"He can't go out there by himself," Joey said to himself in a raspy tone as he attempted to rise to his feet. He tottered and fell back to the couch, struggling futilely to support his weight on his legs. "He can't go alone," he said in a whisper, his voice cut off by a gasp for air, and then he was overpowered by sleep.

He awoke before dawn, switched on the light and stood slowly, testing his legs. They were stiff but held him and he walked awkwardly into the kitchen. He plugged in the coffee machine and frothed just enough milk for an espresso macchiato. He walked to the shelf behind his desk, carefully stepped on the stool, tottered for a moment, and steadied himself. He reached up high and pulled down a thick picture album. He settled back into his chair, blew dust off the cover, coughed, and wiped the cover clean with his handkerchief. He thumbed through the album until he found his favorite picture. It was the family's first overseas trip together, taken just a few weeks before the accident. Underneath, his father had scrawled, "Châteaux D'artigny, Loire Valley."

He chuckled and thought out loud, "Typical of a doctor's handwriting." The family was standing on a balcony overlooking a green pasture dotted with yellow mustard blossoms. Looking triumphant, his mother and father held long-stem wine glasses high, clinking them just as the camera shutter opened. His brother, Joey, stood in the foreground, his head cocked to one side and mouth open wide in a huge grin, almost a howl. Bevy wore a yellow sundress, her strawberry blond hair brushed back, her expression pleased and mischievous. Noah and Teddy stood under their parents, looking a little bewildered. He understood how, in naming him Joey, his parents had tried to fix the unfixable, to restore the family to how it had been before the accident.

To the side of the picture, his mother had printed in clear block letters, "joie de vivre."

He recalled how he had been told that after the accident, his mother couldn't so much as lift a finger or roll herself over in bed. But as long as he could remember, she had been able to walk with a brace, drive and do everything she wanted to do. Bevy said their mother had trained her muscles, millimeter by millimeter, through countless indescribably exhausting hours of physical therapy.

He thumbed through more of his mother's pictures, smiling at her often mirthful expression. His father's pictures struck him as more of an enigma. He was struck by the deep expressions of love and something like gratitude in his father's eyes that ran through the family pictures. But there was something else he couldn't put his finger on, something in his father's eyes. Maybe his posture too. The shape of tension in his father's shoulders waxed and waned, but it was always there in the pictures. Joey knew that his brother had been very ill and had miraculously recovered. Had that scarred his father? Had he had premonitions of his own death?

Joey sat back in his chair and stared into the distance for a moment. He felt a sense of closeness and connection with his dad even though he had never met him. That was partly why he had followed in his footsteps and become a psychiatrist. Caitlyn had stored his father's chair and couch after his death. When Joey had gone into practice, she had them re-covered with the same colors and patterns. She said they were the heart and gyroscope of a psychiatrist's practice. She stored the busts of Freud and Kraepelin, allegedly hewn from sacred stone in Prague, as well. When he had a difficult patient like the general, he often asked himself what his father might have said and done. It was mostly a rhetorical question because he had never met his dad. But not entirely. Caitlyn had saved some of his father's office notes and he had eagerly studied them. They had been particularly helpful in understanding the strange bond between himself and the general. His father's notes suggested that unusual bonds between patients and psychiatrists often resulted from similar unresolved issues.

He had concluded that the general's primary drive in life was seeking absolution of his helplessness in saving his father, beaten to death by the Ku Klux Klan before his very eyes. In turn, Joey, who often in tandem with Madeleine had saved many lives, had been unable to save hers.

He shifted in his chair and the room suddenly seemed darker, like the sun had gone behind a cloud. *No*, he said to himself. *I'm not going to succumb now.* He took a deep breath and sat up straight again. He thought to himself, *The reason I was able to bond with Jeremiah when no one else could is that, at some level, he knew I could really feel what he was feeling. Otherwise, I would never have been able to diagnose and treat him properly. Dad said the books were right in that patients often develop feelings for their doctor like they do for their dad. If that's right, Jeremiah at some level may seek absolution for not saving his father from terrorists by saving me from the bomb. If there is a bomb.*

He set the album on the coffee table, still open to the same page, and stood up. His legs were steady now. He walked to the kitchen, made another espresso, and returned to his father's chair. His mind felt clearer than it had in months. His hand on his chin, looking up at the parrot, he thought to himself, *There's something else that bonds me to Dad, I think, just as it bonds me to Jeremiah. The three of us were all unable to save the most important people in our lives. My brother died in Dad's arms, Madeline died in mine.*

Suddenly, Joey felt the room spin as he remembered. He closed his eyes and grimaced, eyes shut tight. With the skin on his forehead and cheeks squeezed into lines, his lips pulled away from his teeth, "Nooooo," he heard himself shouting in Nice, "nooooooo." Then he did the only thing that worked when the memories came. He closed his eyes and thought of the mantra, quietly at first. Then his head rocked back as the mantra thundered louder, louder even than his memories of his shouts, the "noooos" when he found Madeleine under the rubble, when he saw the angle of her neck, when he couldn't make her breathe. His own breathing seemed to stop for a moment, all was quiet, then he gasped for breath.

He opened his eyes slowly. He felt calm. The room felt peaceful. Thoughts of consolation replaced the intense sadness. *If I can't bring*

er back, I can give her life through our children. He thought of the
*w*in embryos, Maddy and Joey, he had made from his sperm and
*e*r eggs. He smiled and felt as if part of a load were taken off his
*s*houlders at the prospect of carrying on with the children they had
*d*reamed of.

There's a way forward, he said to himself. *They'll know their mother.*
I'll keep her in our lives.

Suddenly, his quietude was shattered by a more sobering
*t*hought. *If Jeremiah was right about the bomb and it was big enough,*
*t*he freezers down in Fairfax might go out for good. He made a note
*t*o have the embryos transferred to the generator-powered freezers at
*Q*uantico. *It's a military base. There's risk of loss of confidentiality, but*
*a*t least I'll know they're safe. The Agency shouldn't care. There's nothing
*b*lackmailable about in vitro fertilization. Maybe there was thirty years
*a*go, but not now.*

He lifted the album off the coffee table, still open to the family
*v*acation picture. His eyes focused on his brother, Joey. *So ecstatic*, he
*t*hought, smiling. Then something struck him as odd and he turned
*t*o another picture of his brother, then to a picture of himself at the
*s*ame age. Then back to his brother.

The Agency had provided their contractor doctors facial recog-
*n*ition software to weed out enemy spies posing as patients. It was
*r*isky to use it. The Agency could monitor the chip if it wanted to.
*C*uriosity got the better of caution and he zoomed in and scanned the
*f*aces of his brother and himself at age 7 with his iPhone. He emailed
*t*he pictures to the desktop in the reception area, downloaded the
*i*mages, and digitized them into the software.

The system responded with a greater than 99.99 percent likeli-
*h*ood they were identical.

That's weird. What are the odds of that?

He chose two more pictures of himself and his brother and got
*t*he same result.

"No freakin' way," he said out loud. He felt hyper alert now
*a*nd his hand was trembling. *An experiment has to have a control*, he

thought. He took a picture of Noah at age 7 and compared it to his brother. The system reported "no match." He repeated the procedure using his picture and Noah's. Again, the system reported "no match."

He recalled how, when he was a child, everyone had marveled how alike he and his brother, the first Joey, had looked. The Agency's facial recognition software was state of the art. An exact match meant an identical twin. He sat up in his chair, fully alert now. He rested his chin between his thumb and forefinger and looked up at the skylight as he sometimes did when brainstorming. He thought out loud in a low whisper, "How could this be? My brother was born ten years before me."

Having recently created embryos from his seed and Madeleine's frozen eggs, he was acutely familiar with in vitro fertilization. If an embryo divides, it produces genetically identical twins, or triplets or quads, for that matter. If the division occurs in the laboratory before implantation, parents sometimes freeze the extra embryos as an insurance policy in case the implanted one dies.

Maybe Mom and Dad froze me, then defrosted me when my twin was killed? That would explain why we look exactly the same and why Mom and Dad gave us the same name.

Then it dawned on him.

It all fits. He sat back in his chair and let out a deep breath, relieved to understand what was happening to his body. He looked up toward the skylight. "Mom, why didn't you tell me?"

Mom must have been embarrassed about the in vitro procedure so she never told me. It wouldn't be a stigma these days. But it was her secret and I'll keep it her secret. That's the psychiatrist in me, I suppose. He smiled. He felt his shoulders relax and walked lightly over to the computer. *Maybe it explains a lot of things*, he thought. *My premature aging, Mom's cryptic references to genetic therapy, maybe even those damn dreams of that little boy.*

He entered "complications of in vitro fertilization" into Google Scholar. He found a long list of injuries to the genome that could occur from the freezing and thawing process. He printed several references, then googled "anomalous communication among twins." Several writers claimed to have witnessed unexplained sharing of feelings and long-distance communication between twins. *So maybe the little boy I see in my dreams is my deceased twin,* he thought. *If we came from a common embryo that split, maybe we share the same soul?* he mused.

Exhausted, his head bobbed, then nodded back in his chair. As he fell asleep, his brow unknitted and his cheeks rose as he seemed to hear the words of his favorite analytic supervisor. "Insight releases energy and gives the patient a sense of control." Then his face fell again as the voice continued, "But it doesn't necessarily cure the symptom."

33

Pet Therapy

BY 11 A.M., WHEN CAITLYN arrived at the office in a borrowed four-wheel-drive pickup truck, many of the main roads had been plowed of snow, but most of the secondary streets were still impassble for all but the highest ground-clearance vehicles. There was a steady dripping sound outside the windows where the sun had melted water along the sunroof. The datura blossoms had long since closed. The parrot chortled and fussed cheerfully underneath the sunlit cover of his cage. An acrid smell of dusty old leather and sweat overlaid the subdued floral scent of the closed flowers. The city electricity had been restored and the emergency gas generator had shut off.

Caitlyn was surprised to find him asleep on the couch, fully clothed with his shoes on. Open in front of him on the mahogany coffee table was an old family picture album his mother had put together showing the lives of each of her children. Caitlyn looked at the pictures that he had apparently been perusing when he fell asleep. The proud father fishing and hunting with his first born son.

A tear came to her eye and she closed the album hastily but clumsily. It slid off the well-polished wood, pictures of the child scattering on the floor. Joey shifted position fitfully but settled back into sleep without fully awakening. She glanced at him with a sympathetic look much like maternal affection. She had worked for his father and known Joey his entire life. Her expression abruptly changed to one of concern as she seemed to notice how old he looked.

She put on a pot of coffee in the kitchen for when he woke up. Then she tiptoed over to his chair, picked up the day's schedule and tiptoed out again. She gently closed the soundproof door, turning the knob slowly so that the locking mechanism made only a dull, barely audible click as it released.

She sat down in a stout but comfortably padded chair at her desk in the administrative area and checked the voice mail, carefully checking off each appointment on the scheduling calendar. Everyone had cancelled due to the storm. Then she rebooted the computer and allowed the bionic security system to scan three fingers of both her hands and the retina of both her eyes. Next, she entered a complex series of passwords and answered four security questions about her childhood in order to log on to the secure server. She entered a document room reserved for their office and checked the status of Joey's appeal for the general's MRI results. It remained denied.

She downloaded dossiers for the patients who had been scheduled to see Joey today. She logged off the secure server and booted up the computer used for routine business matters. Forty-seven unread emails downloaded. She sighed heavily, yawned, and then raised the blinds in her administrative office, seeking the stimulation of the sunlight. She quickly scanned the subject lines, opening several, then closing them and marking them "unread" again. She read an amusing article from *The Onion* about the Prague airport. Then she ordered a copy of *The White Hotel* by D.M. Thomas for herself on Amazon, went to the bathroom and returned to continue scanning the day's email. A red-flagged message from an insurance company with the subject heading "Payment Denied!" caught her eye. Her posture tensed.

"Shit," she said under her breath. She googled the insurance company and searched for the page that described the credentials of the company's medical and psychiatric reviewers. There was nothing posted.

"No freaking surprise," she said quietly, shaking her head angrily. She thought hard for a moment, lips pursed with determination. Then she returned to the insurance company's home page and clicked on the "Our Team" icon and searched "Medical Reviewer."

"Bingo!" she said just audibly as the page opened inviting applicants to apply with a minimum of high school education. The byline read, "Brief Training Course Required" and "Work from Home." Over the years, billing insurance companies had required steadily more paperwork while payment was reduced to a pittance. In order to make ends meet in private practice, most offices had cultivated "insiders" within the insurance companies who could help them cut through the labyrinthine red tape.

Caitlyn thumbed through the antique Rolodex she kept alongside the office's computerized directory. She pulled out the business card of a "friendly" contact who worked in the approvals office. A handwritten note on the card reminded Caitlyn to ask about the woman's aging Labrador retriever.

Caitlyn's contact sounded harried when she answered the phone but became friendly and helpful after she recognized her voice. Caitlyn asked what code was on the insurance claim submitted, noting it should have been "fifty minutes psychotherapy, MD, advanced training."

"Uh, no," the voice on the other end said, rummaging through papers. "That's the code submitted for the visits that were paid. But the one visit that payment was denied was actually coded as 'Pet Therapy.'"

"Pet Therapy?" Caitlyn asked incredulously. She felt a kernel of anxiety growing within her. It puzzled her.

The woman on the other end went on to say in reassuring tones, "We do cover 'Pet Therapy,' but at a lower rate of reimbursement. Our Standard Operating Procedures for Pet Therapy requires documentation of the provider's credentials and training, and that adequate professional oversight was provided. I believe the patient said the provider at this visit was a parrot, not the doctor."

Caitlyn glanced through the patient's chart. The notes described a woman trapped in a marriage with an unfaithful husband. She lacked the financial means to leave him and start anew. The woman had been unable to grieve over her disappointing marriage and fluctuated between anger, despair and denial, but never detachment. Before the trouble with her husband, she had never been treated for a psychiatric disorder. The note said Joey was considering starting an antidepressant to try to break the stalemate in psychotherapy and blunt her depression.

Caitlyn had been worried about the long hours Joey worked. Was it possible that he had nodded off at the end of a long day listening to a patient who he could not help much and the parrot filled in? Caitlyn had read that parrots were highly intelligent, could understand abstract concepts like the number zero and could have vocabularies of more than a thousand words.

Caitlyn heard papers rustling on the other end. "Well, this only came up because we are required by the regulatory commission to audit claims periodically. So we randomly ask a patient to describe their most recent doctor's visit and a reviewer determines if the patient's description substantiates the billing code. According to the patient, near the end of the last session, she asked the doctor something very specific that couldn't be answered by the usual analytic-style counter-question like, 'What do you think?' or, 'How does it make you feel?'"

"What was the question?" Caitlyn asked.

The administrator chuckled, then apologized.

"What time is it?" asked the administrator.

"Do you have to go?" asked Caitlyn.

"No. I mean that was the patient's question to Dr. Jacobson," said the administrator good-naturedly. "Dr. Jacobson didn't answer. So she repeated the question and then sat up and looked at Dr. Jacobson and he was sound asleep in his chair. Then she saw the parrot and realized that, if Dr. Jacobson was asleep, then the conversation during the session must have been between her and the bird. She said the parrot looked like he had been busted and wouldn't say another word."

"Jesus," Caitlyn whispered to herself, shaking her head incredulously, eyes widened.

"Well, don't worry. The woman wasn't mad. In fact, she was very protective of the doctor," the administrator said reassuringly, sensing Caitlyn's consternation from the uncharacteristic pause on Caitlyn's end of the line. "She pointed out to us that parrots are among the most intelligent animals, quite capable of associating words with meaning and abstract concepts."

Before Caitlyn could compose herself and speak, the administrator said dryly, "The doctor's just lucky the bird was working that day or we wouldn't have been able to pay at all."

Caitlyn appreciated her friend's unstated charity and wit and decided it was a good time to bail out of the conversation. They exchanged stories of their dogs' play in the recent snowstorm and ended their conversation cordially, with a mutual promise to get their pets together for a playdate, both knowing they never would.

Caitlyn stuck another Illy capsule into the espresso machine and pressed the button. "Ahhhhh," she said, sucking in the fragrance as the steamy shot squeezed out. Gingerly grasping the ring of the tiny espresso cup between her plump thumb and forefinger, she squeezed into her desk chair and rolled herself over to the computer.

She had just opened the Style section of the online *Washington Post* when an email in Czech came in. Startled, she sat up straight, nearly overturning her coffee. She drank it in one gulp, set the cup down, and opened the message. It appeared to be an advertisement. She printed the message, deleted it and emptied the trash file. Then she tiptoed over to the door to Joey's office and peeked in to be sure he was still sleeping.

Satisfied, she sat down at a different desk and scanned the message into her personal computer, a secure MacBook she never connected to the Internet. She shredded the printout and walked into the kitchen. Hanging by a magnet attached to the back of the refrigerator was an SD card. She inserted it into her Mac, opened the program, and waited for it to decode the message. It read, "JJ to rendezvous with Dr. Z. at Hotel U Prince. Staromestske Namesti 29, 6 p.m., 9th of Av, to initiate genetic therapy protocol."

"Thank God," she said to herself. "Not a moment too soon."

Caitlyn recalled how Rachel, shortly before her death, had shared the secret of Joey's cloning and laid the groundwork for Caitlyn to subsequently meet with Izzy Rosen, the mohel. Despite his cataracts and poor hearing, the mohel had immediately recognized Caitlyn from the family brisses decades earlier and agreed to see her.

At their meeting, Izzy had opened a dusty old bottle of grappa and poured generously into two tall, narrow glasses.

"How is Joey doing?"

He took a long sniff from his glass, savoring the aroma. His eyes lit up behind his heavy cataract glasses when she told him he had become a doctor. He wept and blew his nose loudly when he heard of Madeleine's death.

"What of the children?" he asked.

"There aren't any," Caitlyn said softly. "She was killed on their honeymoon."

Izzy looked up at the ceiling and said something unintelligible that sounded to Caitlyn like a short prayer in Hebrew. While he spoke, Caitlyn drained her cup of grappa.

"Do you mind?" she asked, refilling her glass.

"No, not at all. Please help yourself. Did he remarry?"

"No," she said, shaking her head and pursing her lips.

The mohel nodded for her to go on.

Caitlyn pulled a small pack of Kleenex from her purse and dabbed her eyes. "I think in his heart he considers himself still married to Madeleine."

The corners of the Izzy's mouth turned sharply down. "Does he te?"

"No. He could, of course, but he doesn't want to. He still feels nnected to her."

Izzy shook his head and blew his nose into his handkerchief. ter a long pause, he said, "He's too young to live that way. He's a ychiatrist. He knows this isn't right. She wouldn't want it for him her."

"He knows. He knows all of that. But there's another piece of it at makes it a little less irrational."

Izzy set his glass down and waited, looking intently at Caitlyn.

"He still fantasizes of having their children. Well, it's not just a ntasy. He has a plan."

The mohel looked startled, wide-eyed. "How?"

"Well, first I saw the bills."

"The bills?"

"He gets a bill every month for egg storage. Madeleine trained obstetrics and gynecology. She loved helping infertile parents and inging children in the world. It was common in a lot of OB-GYN ining programs, I think, for the residents to anonymously donate eir eggs to a bank for women who couldn't conceive. After her ath, the department called Joey to see if he wanted Madeleine's eggs stroyed. But he didn't. Instead, he had them shipped to the Fairfax yobank. I know from the bills that he's tried to make embryos with adeleine's eggs and his sperm."

Izzy's eyes took on a faraway look for a moment, then he broke to a smile, searching Caitlyn's eyes for affirmation.

"He wants to live their dream."

Caitlyn shifted in her chair, but her smile was more reserved an the mohel had expected. "It's been very difficult, using a form of vitro fertilization."

"I'm not surprised the cloned boy's sperm has trouble getting to the egg. But if they inject, it seems to do OK. Intra-cytoplasmic erm injection, they call it, or ICSI. They can even choose the sex of e offspring by selecting a boy or girl sperm."

241

"Well, it worked. I asked him about it after I saw the bills. F said he has two embryos in storage and he's even named them, Jo and Madeleine." Caitlyn saw the mohel sit up with a start. He look alarmed. She wondered if he was troubled by the names. Then s dismissed the idea. There were so many other problems with wh Joey was trying to do. Even if he found the right surrogate moth and the twins came to term, what of a single man raising them? Wh of Joey's health?

"If you saw Joey, you'd think you were looking at a much old man."

Izzy listened and nodded for her to continue.

"His hair is silver. Not a trace of brown left."

"That doesn't bother me. We see a lot of premature gray. But he healthy?"

"I would say yes and no. I file all of his documents, including h medical records, so I see hints of things. His blood pressure is high He has little tumors here and there they have to watch. Each one h a 10 or 20 percent chance of malignancy. When you add it up, tl odds aren't good. But nothing malignant yet."

"Everybody has those. Everybody will die sometime. But we s them much earlier in the clones. The clones age prematurely, so tl same tiny tumors that show up in many of us when we're 70 or & show up in the clones thirty or forty years earlier. Good progress h been made in reversing this using snippets of genes delivered by virus. But Joey will have to go to Prague to get the treatment. Nothir is approved by the regulatory agencies here so it has to be in secret."

"Thank God something can be done about the aging. May you can help with the visions too."

"Visions?"

"Visions, dreams, flashbacks. We're not sure what to call ther He falls asleep in his chair at work and they come. They're so viv and the sense of déjà vu is so strong, he doesn't know what to mal of them."

"That's also something we see in the clones, but it usually tak

242

drug or poison to push them over the edge." He looked at Caitlyn
ard.

Caitlyn shook her head. "He definitely doesn't use drugs." She
ondered if the Agency was slipping him something, but that couldn't
e discussed with the mohel. She would run a toxin screen on Joey's
rine next time. Another thought occurred to her. Sometimes when
ne scent was heavy from the datura tree in the office, she felt a little
oopy. She recalled that she had googled datura and read about its
allucinogenic properties shortly after the Agency guy had delivered
. She had assumed it had to be smoked or eaten to be toxic. Now
ne wondered if there was enough toxin in the heavy scent to tip a
ulnerable brain like Joey's into delirium.

The mohel waited patiently for Caitlyn's attention to return to
im. "Some clones report memories they could only have been ex-
osed to in their first lives."

Caitlyn looked up with a start. "How do you explain that?"

"The religious among us argue that such memories could only
e carried by the soul. I'm more inclined to look to science. What is a
nemory? It's an electronic circuit among the brain cells. What codes
or circuits in the brain? Genes. So, couldn't memory be coded in the
enes and passed on at some level by cloning?"

Caitlyn shrugged her shoulders, looking unconvinced.

"Look at the animal world. There's knowledge that animals are
orn with. If it's not stored in the sperm and egg at some point, where
ould it come from? How does a lone bird find its way on its first mi-
ration? How does a salmon find its home to spawn? What is instinct
´ not genetically coded memory?"

Caitlyn nodded.

"There are very basic experiments that support this. If a flatworm
subjected to shock each time a light comes on, it will curl up in
esponse to light. If you cut the flatworm in half, the part that grows
new head will somehow remember and curl up to light without
ver having been shocked. It proves memory can be stored outside
he brain."

Caitlyn listened intently, though she was not convinced.

"Human memories are much more complicated and their tim⟩ course could be jumbled if extracted from genes. Even in non-clone⟩ flashbacks almost never occur true to the original event. Memory, eve⟩ in normal people, tends to be distorted over time by a process calle⟩ elaboration. This is why witnesses in crime cases are so unreliable. A⟩ this may sound metaphysical or academic, but it's important becaus⟩ otherwise a clone's flashbacks may be interpreted as mental illness."

Caitlyn nodded.

The mohel reached for the bottle of grappa and refilled bot⟩ their glasses. "If he waits much longer, it may be too late. He shoul⟩ schedule an appointment in Prague as soon as possible."

Caitlyn nodded vigorously. "I'll take care of that."

Izzy asked, "Does he know he's cloned?"

"No. Rachel felt it would be too traumatic psychologically. Sh⟩ mentioned a doctor in Prague who specializes in genetic therapy ⟨ premature aging though." Caitlyn's eyes held Izzy's and she nodde⟩ toward him subtly. "Maybe it's time to tell him."

Izzy shrugged and sighed. "Unless I can show him proof, he'⟩ just think I'm a crazy old man." He squinted up at the ceiling ⟩ moment, mouth agape, then back at Caitlyn. The color returned t⟩ his face and a faint smile broke on his lips.

"Maybe I have just the right thing."

Caitlyn nodded nervously. She wasn't so sure.

34

Malach HaMavet

McLean, Virginia
December 29, 2031

T HE LAST RAYS OF SUNLIGHT danced on the canopy of the datura tree. As Joey watched, the parrot shifted his feet restlessly on his perch, preening as if in anticipation of his next case. Caitlyn knocked gently. When she opened the door, she was met by a waft of datura-sweetened air.

"I've really got to speak with you about that tree," she muttered. She saw Joey's head jerk up. He had been dozing. He seemed confused for a moment. "Are you OK, Doc?" she asked gently.

"Thanks, Caitlyn," he said, trying to sound alert. "Just leave a little coffee on. I'll see you in the morning."

"Did you know your final report on General Westfield is due tomorrow?"

Joey tried to suppress a look of surprise and a feeling of consternation. He had thought he was done for the day.

"You've got to slow down and take care of yourself, doctor," she said protectively as she walked toward the door.

Joey smiled. Caitlyn seemed immune from aging and was eternally good-natured.

The natural light had passed. The room was lit only by the muted light of an old Prague crystal fixture. Joey felt a little high and pleasantly drowsy. It reminded him of the effects of a light anesthetic drug just before one passed out.

His head fell back against the back of his chair. His eyelids felt as heavy as lead. He moved his hands to prop them open, but his fingers felt numb. His tongue felt thick, his breathing shallow. *Just enough air exchanging to keep me conscious*, he thought. *Did Caitlyn put something in my coffee? Caitlyn knew my father. She would never turn*, he thought, reassuring himself. Then he recalled that a colleague from the Cuzco station had warned him that the datura tree was hallucinogenic. He had been careful to avoid its sap and nectar. The fragrance was very heavy tonight. Could the scent alone have overpowered him? His head slid down on his shoulder and he gasped for air spasmodically as he lost consciousness.

In a stuporous dream, he heard several sharp knocks on the door that led from the waiting room to his office.

Bam-bam bam bam-bam. *I remember that knock*, he thought.

The door to the dimly lit waiting room opened and, his face wrapped in a scarf, the same child who had visited the night of the blizzard hurried past him into his office. Joey was a little taken aback but had recovered his sense of authority by the time he stepped back into his office and gestured toward the comfortable leather chair that sat at a forty-five-degree angle from his own. The child walked straight past and sat on the couch.

"Do you mind if I lay down?" he asked, not waiting for Joey to answer. He reclined, with his back to Joey.

Joey caught himself before he could say, "I usually take the first few sessions face-to-face. Later, if appropriate, you can lie down on the couch." Instead he said, "You seem very comfortable here." He took his seat behind the boy, curious, trying to learn what he could from the child's strange behavior.

The parrot, he saw, sidled over on his perch closer to Joey and peared to study the boy, turning his ear toward the conversation, tening intently. The last sunlight flickered out in the utmost branch the datura, the petals at its mid trunk, straining upward, opening ghtly as if drawn up by the string of a shade.

"We were on the beach," the boy said in a voice so familiar that startled Joey. His head jerked up and his brow wrinkled. He felt rtunate he was sitting behind the child. Judging by his forwardness, e child apparently had been in some kind of therapy on a couch fore.

Damn the dossier. I need to make a note to complain about the lack history. Who was filling these things out anyway?

Although the boy's back was to him and his head was partially dden by a scarf, Joey noticed that the boy still carried his head at a ckeyed angle. His brow wrinkled. *Must have been a serious injury,* · thought. He had intended to explore this at the last visit but had ought better of it. He would normally have taken a full history from e parents, but the parents had never shown up.

The parrot moved to the center of his perch and preened his athers nervously.

"How can I be of help to you?" Joey asked.

The boy began to talk about his "last trip."

"My father took my sister and me to Wellfleet on Cape Cod. ie first night, we went to a drive-in movie. We had popcorn and w a shooting star. The next day, we went to a nature reserve and w all kinds of birds. Then we had lobster and clams for lunch and ad pulled us in a trailer behind his bike in the afternoon. When got hot, we stopped for ice cream. We had a flat tire on the trail the woods by an old cemetery but Dad fixed it. It was late in the ternoon by then, but there was still enough light to go to the beach. iere were lots of steep steps, but Dad held our hands and helped down. We built a sand castle and decorated it with shells and put y soldiers on the walls. Daddy took lots of pictures. The tide came and started to wash away the castle. We frantically tried to protect id rebuild it. But the sky turned purple, the wind came up, and the aves got behind it and washed it away."

Joey interjected in a low, raspy voice, "Did protecting the cast mean something special to you?"

"It was just a game. But after that, it seemed to get dark all once and, without the castle to orient me, I got separated from m father and sister. It was a moonless night, but the stars didn't mal much light, and before I knew it, it was pitch-black. My shorts we wet. I couldn't find my shirt and the steady wind was cold. The didn't seem to be anyone left on the beach and I started to get scare

"I called for my sister. There was no answer. I was worried. Wh if she had wandered into the water? What if she was alone, lost?"

"What did you do next?"

"I called again and again for my father. There was no answer."

"Then what happened?"

"I was beside myself, but I forced myself to think. Where we the steps? It was dark, but I thought if I walked in the opposite d rection of the water, I would eventually come to the bluff. And if followed the edge, there would eventually be stairs up to the parkir lot. I started to make my way toward the dunes when I heard a woma call my name. I answered, 'I'm here!'

"The gray silhouette of a woman seemed to appear from n where. She said, 'Come with me. I'll show you the way.'

"She took my hand. From her voice, I expected her hand to fe warm and soft like my mother's. Instead, it was cold and leathery. drew back but she wouldn't let go. I expected her to take me to m father or at least up the steps to the Coast Guard station, but sh walked toward the water. When we stepped into the water, I asked h whether she had a boat tied up out there.

"She held my hand even more tightly and quickened her pac After the water rose over my waist, I asked, 'Who are you? Do yo know my father?' It was hard to hear with the breeze and the surf, b she said 'Malach HaMavet.' I thought she sounded Jewish and I fe comforted, but the water got deeper and deeper. Just before the wav closed over my head, she said, 'Don't be afraid.'"

Joey startled in his chair when he heard "Malach HaMavet Trapped in a dream, he couldn't rouse himself to open his eyes.

At dawn, the datura blossoms closed and Joey slept peacefully without dreaming. At 8 a.m., Caitlyn gently woke him. She made him a double espresso and, after a few moments, he felt the strength returning to his legs, pulled himself to his feet and made his way cautiously to his desk. He unlocked the file cabinet and reached for the general's file. It was missing.

35

Hot Day in June

McLean, Virginia
June 5, 2032

JOEY HAD BEEN SURPRISED TO receive the invitation from visit Izzy Rosen to his home in Georgetown. Izzy had been a close friend of his parents and an almost legendary figure in the Washington, DC, Jewish community, so Joey felt he couldn't decline the old man's hospitality.

Supported by his cane, the mohel stood as straight as he could and motioned to Joey to sit down. Judging by the way his clothes fit him and his gnarled posture, Joey guessed he had been tall once. The room smelled of black licorice, flowers and mildew. The old man raised his lips over dentures that seemed to dangle precariously from his gums, his eyes twinkling behind thick glasses.

He's happy to see me, Joey thought. *It must get lonely at this age.*

Izzy motioned for Joey to sit down.

"Whoa," Joey said, despite himself, as he sank far deeper into the overstuffed couch than he had expected.

"Would you like a drink?"

"Sure," he said. *Why not? How long has it been since I had a drink? He probably wants to reminisce.*

Izzy filled two long-stemmed, conical crystal glasses with a green spirit from an unmarked bottle. He handed one to Joey. "Do you want me to add water?"

Joey shook his head. He watched curiously, unsure what he would be drinking, but trusted the mohel. "I'll follow your lead."

"It's better with water," Izzy said, pouring a silvery strand of water from a small crystal pitcher first into Joey's glass and then into his own. He stirred with a long silver spoon and the clear green spirits foamed up white.

"L'chaim!" the mohel said.

"To life!" Joey said.

Their glasses clinked.

Joey drank half the liquid in the glass and shuddered involuntarily, his expression bemused. *Wow, that's bitter. Makes me want to wretch. Like ouzo, but worse.*

Izzy dispatched the contents of his glass in one gulp, set it down and smiled faintly, his cheeks radiant. Then he looked at Joey and noticed his grimace. "I forgot to offer sugar," he said, motioning toward a little silver bowl and spoon.

Joey waved it away. "No thanks." His pancreas was getting old faster than the rest of him and he was watching his sugar intake to stave off diabetes. Joey squinted at the bottle but couldn't read the label in the dim light.

"Absinthe," the mohel said, watching for Joey's reaction.

Joey recalled that absinthe was rumored to be hallucinogenic. *What was the active ingredient? Wormwood?* He wasn't sure. But he had to drive a car today. He set his glass down. *Does he keep up with all his former clients?* Joey wondered. He made a mental note to ask his brothers. *Next is he going to ask me to take off my pants so he can follow up on his work?* He imagined a scholarly article. *What would it be?* he mused. *The Journal of Circumcision, A 30-year follow-up of 20 men circumcised with Metzenbaum Scissors.*

Izzy poured himself another glass. This time he didn't add water. ey looked at the old man's red, bulbous nose. *Stigmata of alcohol. o bad*, he thought. Izzy motioned with the bottle at Joey's glass.

"I'm good," Joey said. "No thanks."

"You never knew your daddy, did you?"

Joey knew the mohel was well aware of this. *He's using this as an trée to tell me something about my parents*, he thought. *Why not go ong?*

"No. He passed away the night I was born," Joey said.

"He was a special doctor, you know. He took more time with lks than anyone else, explained everything in plain words they uld understand. People always left him feeling better than when ey came in, even if he had bad news for them. If folks couldn't pay, ur daddy would keep seeing them just like anyone else. People tell e the same thing about you."

"Thank you." He felt his head spinning from the absinthe on an npty stomach. He glanced at the bottle: 140 proof. *Thank goodness didn't finish the glass.*

"When your brother and mother had that accident, he never t on what he was feeling inside. People would ask your dad how he as doing and he would just say, 'It's not about me. You should be orrying about my son. He lost his life. And Rachel, she's fighting ralysis and lost her baby.' He saw it as his mission to give you all the e you would have had without the accident."

"He must have had a lot of balls to keep going after all that." iddenly, Joey's face fell. "I wish I had known him."

The mohel said the most comforting thing he could think of. our father would have been very proud of you."

"He would have been proud of me being a psychiatrist like him. ometimes wonder what it would be like to be in practice with him."

"And your mother, folks said your mother's recovery was a iracle. And it was, but not a divine miracle. Your mother made it ppen. My God, what determination and character, all done with it and jest. At first, she couldn't so much as move a flicker below her oulders. Do you know what she had to do just to roll over in bed?

She fought back one millimeter at a time, until she could go hom[e]
Then despite it all, she brought the joy of life back into your house[.]

Joey nodded and smiled. He could hear the mirth in his mot[h]er's voice, see it in her face. The mischief in her grin. It had bee[n]
infectious and all the kids had grown up filled with the joy of li[fe.]
That is, until Madeleine died.

Izzy seemed to sense what he was thinking.

"Joey, I know you know what loss is like. Loss that turns t[he]
world black."

It didn't take much to bring back Joey's grief over Madelein[e.]
Suddenly a sullen shade fell and stole the warm sun of a Saturd[ay]
meant for siblings.

Izzy drove the nail in further. "Loss that you feel in every cell [of]
your body."

Joey was starting to feel impatient. *What was the point of this?* H[e]
wanted to make an excuse and leave, but the absinthe on an emp[ty]
stomach was making him lightheaded. He clenched the end of t[he]
armrest with one hand and a cushion with the other to steady himse[lf.]

The mohel studied Joey with his eyes and seemed satisfied wi[th]
the chilling effect of his words. He poured himself another half gla[ss]
of the green spirit, drank it in one gulp and paused like he was mu[s]tering his resolve.

"That's how your parents felt when they lost you."

Accustomed to keeping a poker face, Joey squinted and wrinkl[ed]
his brow, studying the old man. *What was the point?*

"You would no doubt do anything to give your Madeleine t[he]
life she deserved."

"Yes, of course."

"Or the children she would have had?"

Startled, Joey abruptly sat up straight. *Izzy knows about the em*[*]
bryos. How?

"I would give her the life she should have had in any way [I]
could, of course. If I can make her children for her, by God I will."

"And may it be God's will that you succeed."

The mohel pointed the bottle at Joey's glass. Joey let him pou[r] an ounce or so. Izzy poured a few ounces in his own glass. Joey inked his glass against the old man's. It made a loud, solid sound. hen they both drank. Izzy took a deep breath. "Did you know that ur parents took the same approach when your namesake died?"

"Some type of extreme life support?" Joey asked. He felt a little ritated. *Why was he bringing this up now?*

The mohel sensed Joey's impatience. He pointed at a yellowed anila envelope on the table next to Joey's chair. "Open it carefully."

"Is it from my parents?"

"Yes."

"Is it something emotional?"

"To the extreme."

"To the extreme?" Joey repeated. He searched the mohel's untenance for a clue but learned nothing. He had a conference call heduled with the Agency at noon and it was after 11. *Besides, if it's motional, I would rather open it in private*, he reasoned silently.

"Do you mind if I open it back in the office? I have a noon eeting."

The mohel's mouth opened to protest, but Joey was already anding. He picked up the envelope carefully, lest it disintegrate in is hand. He gave the old man time to rise on his cane, shook his and hardily, and walked out the door. He squinted in the blinding nlight but felt invigorated by the fresh air.

Inside, the corners of Izzy's mouth turned sharply down. He abbed his handkerchief at the big tears that rolled under his glasses nd down his cheeks. "May the words in that envelope bring you eace," he said in Yiddish.

In the safety of his office, deserted on a Saturday morning, Joey arefully tore open the yellowed envelope. Inside were faded photo-opies of two letters written in his father's handwriting and a consent orm for a medical procedure. He settled into his comfortable chair, but his shoulders rose tensely and his brow furrowed. His hand shook as he switched on the lamp and donned his newly acquired reading glasses.

> Dear Joey,
>
> There are no words to express how much your mommy and daddy and brothers and sister love and miss you. Do not worry that we would ever forget you or you would diminish in importance to us. Your place at the dinner table is still yours and your room is as you left it. When Noah and Teddy play a game, they play for you too. Bevy reads your world atlas for you nightly. Mommy orders your California rolls for you when we eat sushi. Each afternoon, I sit by the old campfire site next to the pond at dusk as if you were with me and watch the greatest show on earth as the sky changes, the wind comes up and the birds fly home to roost.
>
> Before you went to sleep, you may have known that Mommy was badly hurt. We want you to know how courageously she fought her way back. She can walk now with a brace.
>
> Our beloved son, we don't know what you experienced, what you knew, what you were conscious of when you left us. Our worst thought is that you may have been afraid.

Joey stopped reading, shut his eyes and rocked his head back against the soft headrest of his chair. He felt his heart hammering in his chest. He stifled a scream. He imagined his brother, 7 years old, in the dark in the wilderness, his body crushed, his mother paralyzed a few feet away. What terror had his brother experienced in those last moments on the precipice between life and whatever death held?

Mentally exhausted, Joey sighed, rose slowly, walked to the cooler and filled his glass. He drank the chilled water quickly, returned to his chair and read on.

But I know that your strength and re-sourcefulness would have buoyed you, Joey, in whatever you felt was coming next. You would have known that Mommy and Daddy's love would reach you somehow. As your father, Joey, I will always be haunted by my inability to save you. What gives me strength to carry on is a mission to make our family like we were before. When your mommy and I realized you were going to be taken away from us after the accident, I whispered to you that we would find you.

Dearest beloved Joey, we are coming for you the only way we can. After there was no hope of saving you, I took a piece of flesh from your ear. We have found a doctor in Prague who is willing and capable of cloning you from the skin cells we preserved. Today we leave this note in the remains of the wall of the Second Temple in Jerusalem. Many Jews believe messages left there will reach heaven. We pray its words will find you. Tomorrow we fly to Prague, hoping to recreate your body in a laboratory in the ancient synagogue there. We pray with tears and joy, son, that your soul will reenter your new body and live the life with us that was intended.

With all our love,
Mommy and Daddy

The second letter was much shorter.

Almighty God, please return the soul of our beloved Joey to the body of his we recreate by cloning. With reverence and awe for You, Lord, I affirm my vow to sacrifice my life for my son's.
Joseph Jacobson

The medical consent form vaguely described a procedure involving placing an embryo created in the lab inside his mother. Joey was struck by two things. Firstly, the list of adverse effects seemed to address the embryo more than the mother. His eyes stuck on "premature aging," "flashbacks," and "unforeseen complications." Secondly, in addition to his mother's signature as the patient, there were two witnesses. He recognized his father's handwriting and the name of the old mohel, Izzy Rosen.

A cold sweat dripped from his brow, his heart thumped and then seemed to flutter. He stood, felt nauseous and light-headed, then hot. He collapsed back in his chair. Ever since he had gone into practice, it had been his locus of control, his gyroscope for stabilizing his world.

He composed himself, struggled to his feet and lurched toward the bathroom. He stopped in front of the mirror, staring at his face. *Who am I, what am I? I'm a piece of my brother's ear.* He suppressed an impulse to smash his image in the mirror with his fist. *Why didn't Mom tell me? She couldn't tell me. It would have freaked me out. The little boy who comes to my office is my brother. But he's also me. How can I be two people? I died forty-one years ago, but I'm alive.* He looked into the mirror again. *I'm old like Dolly, the cloned lamb, and I'll die early like she did. Maybe not, maybe the old doctor in Prague knows what to do.*

He felt his heart racing and tried to slow his breathing. *Hyperventilating will only make it worse.* He stumbled back to his chair, closed his eyes and tried to meditate. *It's always calmed me.* But instead of the familiar whispered chant, each repetition of the mantra crescendoed into a prolonged shout, his head tilted toward the heavens. Colored light exploded in the darkness behind his lids, coalescing into specter-like images. He saw the face of the boy under the surface in the Honduran swamp. *That's my face.* Then he saw the same boy, crushed under an ATV, his neck askew, head pressed into the grass. He heard the helicopter land in and take off again. *Without me.* He saw his face on the boy on the beach with Malach HaMavet. The Angel of Death in the form of the old woman coaxed him into the shimmering waters f the Shenandoah River. As the water closed over his head, she said, Don't be afraid." And he wasn't.

The thunderstorm that had darkened his psychiatry office and lowed the datura blossoms to open had passed. The sound of water ripping off the eaves could be heard faintly in the background. The in broke through the clouds and beams of light danced through the oom. Joey awoke to the sound of the parrot chortling gibberish. *I feel iore relaxed than I have in years.*

Then he looked at his watch and sat up straight with a start: 4:00. evy and the twins were coming over for a swim at the family house McLean where Joey lived. Joey's mother had set up a memorial oundation, which Bevy now ran, giving scholarships to young, as-iring playwrights. Bevy had just been awarded a MacArthur "genius rant," and the siblings planned to celebrate. *I'm late. They'll be there hen I arrive. We'll have a lot to talk about.*

It was an unusually hot day for a summer that had followed a very ool spring. At Joey's home in McLean, Bevy and the twins waited out ie storm on the tin roofed porch overlooking the swimming pool nd their brother's grave in a copse at the side. In Bevy's lap was a usty album of photographs open to a picture of two 4-year-olds with rightly colored plastic light sabers battling a laughing 7-year-old.

"Do you remember him?" Bevy's voice was loud, to carry over ie din of the rain.

"Star Wars was his favorite game. Even though we were younger, e always included us," Teddy shouted back.

The intensity of the rain waned to a sporadic tapping.

Bevy pointed to a photo of Joey crouched on his legs, engrossed a book. "Gosh, that boy loved to read. That's the picture Mom used s the logo for his memorial foundation."

"Her last heart attack came so soon after she'd set it up," Teddy

said mournfully. "You know how proud we are of what you've don
with it, Bevy."

Bevy gave Teddy's hand a little squeeze.

At the other end of the couch Noah pointed to a photo of hi
father, framed by snow-capped mountains, holding a high-powere
rifle, dressed in a red parka, standing next to a mottled gray mar
"That's the hunt where he brought home the elk head."

"You guys are going to hunt up there with Joey next fall, right?
Bevy asked.

"Yes!" Noah responded. "The Washakie Wilderness area, lef
fork of the Shoshone River. A full day's horseback ride from the near
est road. No phones, except by satellite. You're joining us this yea
right, Bevy?"

She snorted. "When pigs fly."

The sun came out and the swampy Washington, DC, heat re
turned. Bevy moved to perch on the tip of the diving board, danglin
her toes into the sun-dappled blue water and sipping a Kir Royale
Noah and Teddy circled the pool with nets on long poles, fishing ou
dragonflies, bees and leaves.

Joey threw open the gate and appeared before them, red eyed
disheveled and pale. Bevy stared transfixed, then stammered, "Joey
you look like you've seen a ghost."

The corners of Joey's mouth jerked up and down in a feebl
attempt at a smile. He handed Teddy the brittle, yellowed letters. "Al
three of you had better read this sitting down."

Bevy and the twins pulled up chairs and huddled together. The
were sobbing after the first few paragraphs. Bevy blew her nose o
a paper napkin, stood up and hugged Joey, tears streaming onto hi
shoulder. She raised her head and their eyes met,

"Oh my God, Joey, it must have been hell to read this alone
There's so much pain in this letter. Mom and Dad never shared th
agony of their loss until now. They were so stoical. It was like bi
brother was never gone."

For a moment Joey's eyes widened and darted back and forth

He closed his lids, took a deep breath and looked his sister in the eye. "That's because he wasn't gone," he said.

Bevy took a step back, nearly stumbling over her chair. The twins caught her, then returned to their seats, grimacing, eyebrows knitted. They stared at Joey, mouths agape, waiting for an explanation.

"You probably think I need a shot of a Haldol. Before you put me in a straitjacket, finish reading." He smiled, looking macabre. "You haven't gotten to the meat of it."

Bevy and the twins exchanged worried glances, crowded together and continued reading.

"Oh my God," Teddy shouted, wide-eyed.

Bevy shrieked, her glass fell from her hand, exploding on impact with the pebbly terrace.

Noah looked up at Joey and said calmly, "Where'd you find this crap? It's obviously a fake."

Joey flashed a knowing smile. "You're in denial, brother, but who wouldn't be? Before Mom died, she left it with Izzy Rosen for safeguarding. It is indeed Dad's handwriting. That was easy to verify. But the cloning checked out too. I borrowed high tech facial recognition software from the agency and compared photos of the first Joey and me at the same age. The chances of our being different people," he paused, "zilch."

Teddy stuttered, "Why, why would Mom and Dad do something like this?"

Bevy sniffled and dabbed at tears. "It's all in their letters, Teddy. They wanted to give our brother his life back. They wanted to make our family whole again."

"Dad never got to enjoy it. No sooner than we got Joey back, we lost him," Teddy said mournfully.

Bevy wrapped her arm around Teddy's shoulder. "He had to have been at peace, though, knowing what he accomplished."

Joey shot Bevy a pointed look. "Did you know I was a clone?"

"No," she said, shaking her head decisively. "Joey, I can't begin to fathom what you've gone through today."

261

"It's not every day you find out you're a clone," he said acidly.

"Joey," Bevy said. She bit her lip and stepped forward to hug him.

Joey stepped back, as if rejecting pity. "Life will go on," he said bitingly. *But for how long? What's the expected life span of a human clone?* He felt queasy again. *I need space.* He looked pointedly at the broken glass at Bevy's feet. "You guys are barefoot. Don't move. Let me get a broom and dust pan."

Bevy blurted, "Don't go yet." But he had already turned and stalked into the house.

"We're screwing this up, royally," Noah said. "Our brother's just had the shock of a lifetime and we're sitting around like deer in the headlights."

"He looks terrible. He must be having a mammoth identity crisis," Teddy said. "The way our society stereotypes cloning, he must feel like a freak. He's got to be afraid that we'll reject him, that the world will reject him as some kind of Frankenstein character."

"Or an exploited character like in 'Never Let Me Go,'" Bevy added.

"Forgive me if I sound clinical here," Noah interjected, "but a little cognitive therapy may be just what the doctor ordered for Joey. We need to get our shit together and show him cloning doesn't amount to a hill of beans as far as we're concerned, that he's the same old Joey to us. Screw the world, they don't need to know."

"A little levity won't hurt either," Teddy added.

"Amen," Bevy said, slapping both boys' hands in an emphatic high five.

"This may help." Teddy pulled a bottle of prosecco from the icy slush in the cooler at their feet.

Joey returned wearing swim trunks and sandals. He assiduously swept the glass fragments into a dustpan. Bevy handed him a glass of cold sparkling wine.

"I can use that" he said, his voice congenial now. He closed his eyes, chugged the drink and shrugged.

Bevy eagerly refilled his glass but tipped the bottle too far, the suds overflowing the edge. "Joey, I've been thinking, this whole cloning thing is overrated. It's stupid. It doesn't matter."

Joey listened with a bemused expression. *They're going to humor me now.*

Bevy shook her long auburn hair back from her face. "I want the stage rights. 'Boy cloned by parents after ATV accident.'"

"It'll cost you," Joey said, looking up at his sister, eyebrows raised, smiling slightly.

"If you donate the stage rights to the foundation, you can take an in-kind tax deduction," Bevy said dryly. She flashed a deadpan smile and gave a little wink. Then she jumped into the pool, making as big a splash as possible. Noah and Teddy quickly followed and commenced to wrestle at the shallow end.

Joey treaded the pebbly bevel comprising the edge of the pool, dabbling a net on the end of a long extendable pole under a bloated but still alive frog submerged just out of his reach. He lowered himself into the water, net in hand, submerged, and netted the frog. "Got it," he said as he climbed out, turning the net inside out. The frog plunked into the flower bed.

Joey poked it a little to be sure it was alive. It moved. Noah hopped backward onto the side of the pool, kicking jets of water toward Joey. When he got Joey's attention, he said, "I just don't think this cloning is a big deal. From a moral perspective, why should there be a distinction between a person created by cloning and a person created by in vitro fertilization? In both cases, the embryo is created in a laboratory petri dish. Long ago, test-tube babies were stigmatized. Nowadays they're mainstream."

Teddy nodded. "What moral difference does it make whether the baby comes from injecting a sperm into an egg or cloning a cell?"

"True," Bevy mused, sloshing her legs back and forth through the water. "Acceptance of human cloning is probably just a little bit behind other means of assisted reproduction on the moral clock."

Noah added, "But actually, the difference is that the in vitro methods combine sperm from a man and an egg from a woman, mimicking natural reproduction. Cloning takes the entire genome from one parent and can bypass reproductive cells altogether. Instead of re-sorting the genes of the two parents into something new, it produces a duplicate."

Joey rested his chin between his forefinger and thumb. He cocked one eyebrow. "Uh, kind of like budding?"

Bevy and the twins looked at him blankly.

"Budding's what they call asexual reproduction in hydras and sponges. A new one forms by budding a piece off," Joey said with an anxious smile.

No one spoke.

"Call me Bud, folks," he said, anxious to keep the conversation light.

Bevy's face lit up. "I love the pun!"

Noah raised his glass. "To Bud, our oldest and youngest brother."

Teddy and Bevy raised their glasses high. "To Bud."

Joey threw back his head and laughed.

"Not really a duplicate, though," Noah added. "There are so many epigenetic influences."

Teddy growled, feigning annoyance. "Cut the technical mumbo jumbo."

"Some things never change," Bevy said, hurling a beach ball toward the twins' heads. The twins leaped apart a split-second ahead of Bevy's missile.

"Bevy!" Teddy said indignantly.

Noah contrived a frown. "Jesus, Bevy."

The twins broke into big grins. Teddy hurled the ball back at Bevy, who caught it and gave the boys a "don't even think about" look. Joey laughed with the others, but their lithesome movements made him think of his limp.

They aren't changing, but I am, he reflected. He thought of their bodies, muscular and fit, their smooth ruddy complexions, the vibrant color of their hair. *I could be mistaken for their father. Yet, chronologically my body is younger. Mom and Dad must have known that cloning would have a price*, he mused. *But at least I'm alive, and a damn good life it's been.* Then he felt his heart sink. *Until I lost Madeleine, that is.*

Noah threw an exaggerated, beseeching look at Joey and Teddy regain their attention. "May I continue?"

Joey blinked back the painful thoughts and shook his head back to the present. He nodded to Noah to go on. Teddy feigned a little ow. "By all means," he said.

Noah said a few words under his breath to Teddy, then spoke the manner he used when teaching educated patients about their nesses. "Epigenetic means influences that occur on embryos and ildren from the womb or post-natal environment. For example, entical twins start with the same genes but can end up 5 inches fferent in height."

Suddenly, Noah looked up as if he had had an epiphany and his ice took on more energy. He looked at Teddy, whimsically. "Speakg of twins, the process by which identical twins are made is not so fferent from cloning. The fertilized egg, the zygote, divides, producg a genetically identical duplicate." Looking at Joey and nodding assuringly, he said, "In essence, no different from a clone. So, really, oned humans should have the same legal and moral standing as the entical twin that budded from the original zygote."

Noah looked at his siblings. All three nodded.

"That means one of us is a clone, Teddy."

They all were silent for a moment, then Bevy threw the ball at Ioah again and they all broke into laughter. "Come on!" Bevy said.

"I'm joking," Noah said. After a pause, he said under his breath, ort of."

Teddy slogged through the water to the steps and sat down. Where's that prosecco?"

Bevy lifted the most recently opened bottle. "Come get it."

Joey took the bottle from Bevy, limped over and refilled Teddy's lass. He returned the bottle to Bevy, who took a swig directly from ie bottle. She handed it back to Joey. He took a swig too.

Teddy took a moment to gather his thoughts and said, "Since ou're part of Joey, our older brother who has a death certificate, in ie eyes of the law are you legally alive or dead or equivalent to a em cell? God only knows what your legal rights are in Virginia. The bottom line is that Mom and Dad knew what they were doing whe[n] they kept this secret and so should we."

"Agreed," they all said in unison.

Bevy stood and took another bottle of prosecco out of th[e] cooler. Her eyes shone and laughed under her bangs. Underneath th[e] blinding sun, she refilled everyone's glass with the cold, frothy wine

Joey listened with the corners of his lips elevated into a fai[nt] smile. For a moment his eyes twinkled like old times from the twin[s'] banter. But the bunching of his eyebrows and the deep furrows in h[is] forehead told a different story. He stared at the tulip tree he had plan[t]ed as a child. It had been so small then. Now it was so tall. Sudden[ly] he couldn't recall whether he had planted it as the first or the secon[d] Joey. "Which Joey am I?"

"You're the same Joey you always were," Noah said quickly.

Joey smiled bitterly, "Which Joey is that?"

Bevy planted a little kiss on Joey's cheek, "You're Joey, ou[r] brother."

"Your older brother or younger brother?" Joey snapped. H[e] turned around and stalked into the house.

"Should I go after him?" Teddy asked, his voice several octav[es] lower than it had been in the earlier, light-hearted banter.

"Give him a minute," Bevy answered.

Joey reappeared carrying a stack of framed pictures. "Am I th[e] boy hunting with Dad or this boy hunting with Granddad? Am I th[e] big boy in this picture where you're playing at my feet? Or was I th[e] little boy playing at your feet in this picture?"

Noah and Teddy glanced at each other. "The young one!" the[y] said in unison.

Bevy nodded, "You were created from your brother's cells, bu[t] you're a unique person, a completely different being. Let the old Joe[y] go, live in the present!"

Then another thought jolted Joey, "Have I been dead?"

The twins and Bevy exchanged nervous glances. Bevy spoke up "From what I read in Dad's note, you were cloned from a live ce[ll]

m your first body. Most of your body died, but you lived on from
at cell."

"But what of the 'I'? Could 'I' have carried on as 'me,' the origi-
l 'me' from one cell? Are the genes in the cell that cloned me, 'me'?"

Noah cleared his throat before speaking "The seeds of a complete
rson, in this case, 'you' are in the genes of all your cells."

Joey's eyes took on a glazed over look. *The boy I see in my dreams.
ever saw his face until today. He has my face when I was 7 years old. Is
me, the first me? My first body? Or is the boy I see in the dreams the soul
the first me, the soul of my first body?* A bittersweet feeling came over
m. He realized he missed the little boy in his dreams. He longed to
k with him, to be with him. Then he shivered and tried to reject a
ought, to block it out. But no, the thought was there. For better or
rse, he longed to join him. Then, from far away, from outside his
ad, he heard Bevy repeating his name.

"Joey," she said gently. "Are you OK?" Her hand was on his
oulder.

Joey suddenly was aware that the chatter around him had
pped and he looked up. He felt each of their eyes looking at him
mpathetically. Bevy stepped down from the diving board and sat
xt to her brother on the little shelf sticking out into the water. She
t her arm gently around his freshly sunburned shoulders.

"This is a hell of a lot for you to deal with," Bevy said lovingly,
anting a little kiss on his cheek.

"Copy that," Joey said, trying to sound like he had regained his
mposure.

Bevy brushed the gray hair back from his eyes and gathered his
ze into her own. "We're your family. We're going to get through this
gether."

"Hey," Noah said, gently shaking his brother as if to awaken him
to a different way of thinking. "To hell with this legal and moral
rseshit about whether you came from one cell or two. Who cares
hose soul you have? You're our brother. It doesn't matter to us. But
u need to get your ass over to Prague, find that mad scientist, and

get that genetic therapy Mom told you about. You're starting to loc like Father Time."

Joey laughed at his reflection in the water. "It's true."

Teddy's hazel eyes looked softly into Joey's. "Do you know wh advice I think Madeleine would give you if she could?"

Joey waited. Teddy continued, "She would say, 'Figure it all on if you must, but in the meantime, live in the present.'"

Bevy shot a glance at Teddy and gave a thumbs up.

Joey nodded and smiled faintly. "I think that's right. I thir that's exactly what she would say."

36

Tisha B'av
(The 9th of Av)

McLean, Virginia
July 17, 2032

T HE TEA LEAVES HAD BEGUN to form a clear image. Congress had unobtrusively adjourned for summer a few days ago. The president's whereabouts were vague. Cots and medical supplies had been stacked as discreetly as possible in the lobbies of office buildings in a periphery believed to be safe, just outside the Beltway. The emergency medical reserve had been asked to be available for possible drill on short notice any time in the next week. Thus, he would not be able to join his family and office staff in Luray, safely shielded from DC by the Blue Ridge.

And, yes, by the Jewish calendar, it was Tisha B'Av, or thereabouts. He tried to reassure himself. *If the military were certain of their intelligence, wouldn't they have evacuated DC? On the other hand, wouldn't such a drastic step cause almost as much panic and economic damage as the bomb itself? Maybe the general really was paranoid,* he thought.

But he wasn't taking any chances. He would work at home today and had brought the parrot with him, just in case. As far as he could tell, the rear command and medical emergency stations in McLean were still in place, which meant they believed the bomb, if there was one, was relatively small, perhaps Hiroshima size. But the general had said they weren't sure. The general had said there was an almost chauvinistic tendency, racist maybe, within the intelligence community to discount this enemy.

At noon, the August light flashed brighter for a moment, as if the sun had peaked furtively from behind a cloud and quickly hidden again. Then a distant booming to the southeast, just before the windows blew out and the wall collapsed on the eastern side of the house. *Must be a megaton or more*, he thought. He ducked. Moments later, the windows blew out on the western side of the house as the air rushed back to fill the low pressure from the blast. The rushing sound of the air was deafening. Then there was silence. There was no fire. He had had the presence of mind to turn the gas off.

He opened the parrot's cage. "Fly, my friend."

The parrot looked at him uncertainly.

"Fly back to Honduras if you can."

The parrot grasped the hinge to the cage and swung himself free but didn't fly out the open window.

Joey found it hard to catch his breath. He lay down to rest. When he awoke, he didn't know how long he had slept. Hours, days, he wasn't sure. It was hard to breathe. He had had many dreams and he knew he had spoken in his sleep because the parrot repeated gibberish he knew he had never said to it before.

It feels like I'm drowning, he thought. He coughed blood into his handkerchief. *I must have radiation sickness. Pulmonary edema. The cells lining the airways turn over fast. They'd be among the first to be vulnerable to an acute radiation dose. I must have gotten 5,000 rad* more, depending on the wind, how close the bomb had been to the ound, the fallout.

Then he coughed into the handkerchief again. Big brown clots rrounded by fresh red blood. He threw up blood. He felt light-head- and lay down to rest.

When he woke up, he drank several glasses of the water he had led the bathtubs with, just in case, before the explosion. He opened e potassium iodide and choked down three pills and the same with e Prussian blue, and put the bottles in his pocket. *Pointless, but just case*, he thought. *It's nearly dark outside and unseasonably cool. Dusk?*

He made his way out to the landing overlooking the backyard. here were two ways to get down. One was a set of steep, deep stairs ith a railing, and the other a much more gradual way through a pse with stepping stones set in the ground but no railing.

He picked up a cane he never used in public and made his way own the gradual slope, using the cane for support. *It looks like it does ter a bad storm,* he thought. Downed trees were everywhere. Some d been to the west, parallel to the wind of the first blast, and others at had somehow withstood the first blast, with their canopies to e east, were downed by the blowback. It was very difficult crossing e yard and he had to stop and climb over trunks and pick his way rough branches. He was very weak and short of breath. The parrot uttered clumsily from limb to limb alongside him, his muscles weak- ed from his long captivity. But Joey had taken care to let him out doors and he had not forgotten how to fly. He was exhausted when e reached a grave with a large stone marker freshly cracked by the unk of a huge tulip tree. The English words read:

Joey Jacobson
Born November 10, 1990
Died July 31, 1998
Son – Brother – Grandson
Friend – Scholar – Hunter

He lay down in the still-warm earth over the grave. He ha[d] always felt an affinity for this spot. He felt oddly content there. *Hom[e] somehow*, he thought. The yardman had kept the grave neatly weede[d] and only strawberries and petunias – a favorite of his father's moth[er] – broke the warm soft earth. His parents' graves were on either sid[e.] His maternal grandparents were next to his mother. Just a little dow[n] the slope was a separate area where Shane lay. The softness and swe[et] aroma of the ground felt strangely soothing. *I'd be comfortable*, h[e] thought, *if it would envelop me, swallow me up and take me beneath [to] mingle with the bones of my brother. Strange, I would welcome it.*

He began an assessment of his life. It had been short, but h[e] had loved his brothers and sister, and they should be able to tak[e] care of themselves. They were safe in Luray with their families an[d] six-month's supply of food, fuel and weapons. There were enoug[h] of them to make a formidable force against the inevitable lootin[g] and anarchy that was to come. He had contributed to his countr[y] and helped many patients. He had never been deterred by whether [a] patient could pay. He had had fun, kept his commitments and don[e] everything he wanted to do. Everything except live out his life wit[h] Madeleine. He shuddered for a moment at that thought.

He didn't want to go. If he survived, he would find a surrogat[e] mother and raise the embryos he had created from Madeleine's egg[s] and his sperm by in vitro fertilization. She had believed people live o[n] through their children. It was the best he could do for her. He gaspe[d] again for air. *Like I'm drowning*, he thought as he passed out.

The cicada sound reached a loud din as the peeper frogs bega[n] their sweet chorus, first one here and there, then a few, then a ca[-] cophony. There was a loud plop in the pond. The cicadas and peepe[r] silenced, then gradually started again, louder than before.

A great blue heron stood like a statue in an inch or two of wate[r] cleared of green algae along the bank of the pond, hunting. Its gra[y] blue and white feathers blended perfectly into the mosaic of mud an[d] foliage along the bank. Near the middle of the pond, the algae sep[a-] rated in an ever widening circle where air bubbled up from the sprin[g]

Something moved in the underbrush. The heron sensed danger, picked up its spindly legs and walked deeper into the pond, wary but unafraid, continuing to hunt, partially obscured by the heart-shaped leaves of a broken tulip tree hanging low over the water.

On the shore of a cove off the main pond, a Canada goose tenderly preened blood from the feathers of his mate. Her long black neck dangled over their down-covered nest a few feet from the water's edge. He nudged her snowy white cheek gently as if to raise her from sleep. Unable to rouse her, he buried his head in her breast feathers as he used to do on cold evenings. Alarmed by the absence of her heartbeat, he abruptly checked the nest for the goslings.

Finding them absent, he stood erect, sounded four low-pitched warning honks, and half-ran, half-flew along a trail of downy feathers to the fox den. He pumped his neck menacingly and hissed into the narrow opening. When the fox didn't emerge, he flew low over the fallen trees and debris to the center of the pond, where he swam in small circles until he was too exhausted and hoarse to paddle or cry out. Then he floated motionlessly, as if mortally wounded by hunters. When his energy returned, he raised his head and spread his wings slowly a few times as if to test them, then skimmed over the water back to his mate. He stood by her body for a few moments, clucking and murmuring softly, and then checked the nest to be sure he hadn't missed a surviving gosling. When he was sure it was empty, he took to the air, circled the pond where he had lived monogamously with his mate for twenty years, and flew north toward the Potomac.

After the last trace of sunlight had disappeared, a silvery fox with a long, bushy, black-tipped tail emerged from a hidden but well-worn path through the dense blackberry shrubs and brush next to the pond. Smiling craftily and sniffing the air, it scurried toward Joey, sensing vulnerability.

A distinctly human voice seemed to warn him away. He scampered back into the brush and crept to within sight. The fox saw a large green and blue bird standing over Joey. The strangely colored bird coughed blood and spoke again, but the voice was distinctly human. The fox had never seen such a creature, and with its natural fear of both humans and birds of prey, it leaped for the safety of its den.

The Agency had compiled a list of civilian assets to be rescued and transported to rear command centers well outside the periphery – those considered at greatest risk for radiation exposure. Joey was on the short list, but medical and surgical specialists had been prioritized above psychiatrists.

Due to the current emergency, Katharina had been temporarily reassigned to the command center at Quantico Marine Base coordinating air rescues. Her beauty and charm had aged well, like a fine wine. In the dark command center, she sat very close to the aging general and peered at a screen showing the location and availability of the helicopters at their disposal. The general placed his hands firmly on the edge of his chair to suppress the marked parkinsonian tremor. Katharina ran a well-manicured finger slowly up and down the neck and around the lip of her Diet Coke bottle. The general pretended not to be distracted. Then, using the cursor, Katharina highlighted a recently renovated Agusta 109E Power night-vision equipped air ambulance in Charlottesville that had just returned to base and been refueled.

Katharina typed the GPS coordinates of Joey's home in McLean and hit "send." She looked at the general. He nodded decisively, overcoming his infirmity. "Get me Pegasus," he shouted into the radio. For a moment, his voice became clear and authoritative like it had sounded before he became ill.

The parrot had slept fitfully that night. He awoke to a whirling, beating sound. Joey did not open his eyes.

"Helicopter," the parrot said in a voice indistinguishable from Joey's.

Joey awoke to the sound of Madeleine's voice. "I didn't expect to see you so soon," she said, her blue eyes misty.

She washed Joey's body carefully with a warm rag and dressed him in white pajamas. It was dark, but Joey thought he could make out her outline in white too. When she finished, Joey stood up slowly, testing the strength in his legs. He felt young and healthy again.

"We never got to say goodbye," he said, embracing her. Then he brushed her faintly moist lips with his, drawing her breath deep inside his lungs, holding it in like a drag. The effect was much the same, like a shot of adrenaline and endorphins. Then he looked into her eyes and kissed her deeply, as if incorporating her into himself so he could always keep her safe—as if by kissing her this way, he could lock their fates together so they would never be separated again.

After the kiss, Joey rested his head on Madeleine's shoulder, his eyes closed, his expression blissful, like he had been lost and just found his way home.

The EMT on Pegasus barked orders with confidence and authority. "Suction him. Give him oxygen. Hurry!"

Something like a vacuum cleaner sucked dried blood from Joey's lungs. It made a sound like the dentist's office. Then cold oxygen blew in. Joey felt a burst of energy. There was the whirr of a generator and a floodlight switched on. He tried to open his eyes but could not, and then he was floating in an almost irresistibly delicious somnolence.

37

Pegasus

KATHARINA ARRIVED IN CHARLOTTESVILLE JUST as Pegasus touched down on the pad at the University of Virginia ospital trauma unit. She bent over Joey's lifeless body, caressing his lt-and-pepper hair, still thick. She nuzzled him cheek-to-cheek, cks of her sandy brown hair mingling with his. She hugged him ard, dabbed away her tears, and pulled the sheet up over his head.

"*Gay schlafen*," she said.

She knew of his cloning. The Agency had heavily monitored sets like Joey and had been anxious to learn the vulnerabilities of oned humans, fearful that cloning might be exploited by the na-on's enemies. Of more personal interest to Katharina was Joey's plan find a surrogate mother to posthumously bear Madeline's and his iildren.

She thought to herself, *I'm in my late 30s. I don't know how many tore chances there will be for me to have a baby or if I could ever commit* to one man. But I could bear Joey and Madeleine's children, be a good mother to them.

Epilogue

KATHARINA AND BEVY HUDDLED AROUND the wood-burning stove in the aging Jacobson vacation home near uray, the embers still glowing red. The infants Joey and Madeleine ad fallen asleep at Katharina's breasts. "I think their stomachs are ill," she said triumphantly.

Bevy gave her an appreciative look, then put her last tile down n the Scrabble board. "Hasta la vista, baby."

Katharina ran a chipped fingernail around the edge of her cock-il glass. "*Verdammt*," she said with a smile. She drained the last of he vodka.

Despite the shortages of everything since the bombs, General Westfield had kept them adequately supplied with food, weapons and odka.

"Time for evening patrol," Katharina said.

"I'll flip you for it," Bevy said.

"Ha, you couldn't hit the broad side of a barn with a 12 gauge full of buckshot," Katharina quipped, good-naturedly punching Bevy in the shoulder.

Bevy feigned an exaggerated frown. "Be careful, OK?" she said gently lifting Joey and Madeleine from Katharina's breasts and placing them in their makeshift crib.

Katharina poured two more fingers of vodka into her glass and chugged it.

Bevy gave her a genuine frown this time.

"Got to keep warm," Katharina said, lacing on a pair of high rugged boots before standing, shrugging on her heavy parka, and slinging an M-4 carbine over her shoulder. She picked up one of a pair of walkie-talkies, opened the door, stepped out and whistled. A few moments later, a humongous, snow-covered black German shepherd bounded to her side. The guard dog had also been provided by the general, surreptitiously reassigned from perimeter patrol duty at Quantico.

Bevy called after her, "Have fun with the *hund*. I'll have a cup of hot tea waiting when you get back." Katharina mouthed thank you and blew her a kiss.

Bevy shut the door. "Brrrr," she said, checking the wood box. *Empty.* She placed a second blanket over the infants, donned her winter coat and gloves, stepped outside and slogged her way to the woodpile. The blowing snow made it hard to see and chilled her exposed neck. She brushed the heavy snow from a log and carefully swung the axe, splitting the wood into quarters that would fit into the wood-burning stove they relied upon to heat the cabin. Back inside she filled the wood box and stoked the fire to a small inferno. *I'll just close my eyes for a moment, then I'll make tea.*

With the fuel shortages, highway transportation had virtually ceased for all but military use. The landing on the river had become the primary entry point to their land of desperate and sometimes violent gangs searching for food, shelter and in some cases vulnerable women. Bevy and Katharina had been as generous sharing food with their neighbors as they could. But there was no organized protection in the region from vandals.

When Katharina emerged from the woods into the meadow, the dog sniffed, then growled softly, looking into Katharina's eyes for instructions. *Stay with me,* she motioned with her hand. Together they crawled through the snow to the edge of the bluff overlooking the river landing. The dog's fur bristled. Katharina unslung her carbine and scanned the water's edge with the infrared scope. There were human shapes, lots of them. Her eyes widened and her body tensed, jolted by adrenaline. "Oh my God," she whispered. She pressed the silent button on her walkie-talkie and dialed the code that would warn Bevy to flee to safety. She would cover the landing with a withering fire if necessary until Bevy and the babies had an adequate head start, then rendezvous at the deer hunting cabin at the old apple orchard deep in the national forest.

The three tones rang out on Bevy's walkie-talkie and woke her with a start. "I didn't hear that, I dreamt it," she said out loud, trying to contain her anxiety.

Ten seconds later, the three tones repeated. She felt her heart race and the blood rush into her face. She punched in the acknowledgement code and hooked the walkie-talkie onto her belt. She looked for the heaviest coat she could find and donned her father's old winter hunting parka. She slung the heavy backpack full of emergency supplies over her shoulders, scooped up her niece and nephew and strapped them firmly into a pair of tattered twin Bjorn papooses. She grabbed a picture from childhood of the family beaming with anticipation the day they had bought the Luray property and stuffed it into her satchel. She looked sadly at the Scrabble set that had helped Katharina and her pass so many days since the bomb. *What else?* She glanced at the light 30-30 deer rifle in the corner, hesitated, then slung it over her shoulder, stuffing her pockets with cartridges. She blew out the lanterns to help conceal the cabin and stepped out into the storm.

There were explosive sounds muffled by the snow from the

direction of the river. *Katharina's buying us time.* She looked down at the sleeping babies hanging from her chest, took a deep breath, and stepped resolutely uphill toward the forest. Then she stopped suddenly, hesitated as if undecided, ran back to the house, and pried the last remaining mezuzah the family had brought from the old home in Smolensk from the door frame. She zipped it into her backpack and ran for the cover of the forest, hoping the blowing snow would cover her tracks. *I'm not superstitious, but if this mezuzah helped Fanny and Sarah survive the pogroms, it can help me survive this.*

She found the path leading up the mountain that she and Joey had played on in the happy days before the accident. It would take her around the deep ravines and dense foliage up the mountain to the fire road along the ridge and through the national forest to safety.

She maintained a steady pace uphill, bent against the wind and snow, indifferent to the heavy load of the backpack, babies and rifle. She passed under the rope tied to the trap door of one of the decaying deer stands where her father and Joey had hunted deer, then through a clearing with a few older trees whose contorted branches looked eerily human. As children, Joey and she had always felt a vague but unsettling sense of danger here. She quickened her pace until she passed through a narrow opening in a barbed wire fence, past a faded granite marker of some kind and onto the fire road along a high ridge in the George Washington National Forest. She slowed her step to a fast walk along the overgrown, pitted road. Massive trees with gnarled trunks, their limbs burdened heavy with snow, towered on both sides of her as far as she could see. *We're safe for now.*

She stopped and listened. There were faint tapping and popping sounds from the direction of the house. She thought she recognized the sound of Katharina's carbine. *Thank God, she's still alive.* She unhooked the walkie-talkie from her belt and punched in the code for "proceeding to rendezvous point." A high-pitched single ping coded for "Roger" rang out. Bevy thought she had never heard a sweeter sound. She blew a long sigh of relief, hooked the walkie-talkie back on her belt and checked the babies to make sure they were still warmly ensconced in their coverings. She walked at a comfortable speed now,

dging the snow-covered pits and fallen trees along the decayed
ad. She estimated that before dawn she would reach the hunting
bin at the old apple orchard. If all went well, Katharina would join
r shortly thereafter.

She thought of her children and husband, who had been on
kibbutz in northern Israel that fateful summer. It was Katharina
ho had first been privy to the news that, when the credibility of the
iclear bomb threat had been established, the Israelis had exploded
electromagnetic pulse device over Tel Aviv, disabling the nuclear
plosive's triggering device.

It had thrown the city into the Stone Age by crippling all of its
ectronic technology but had saved countless lives and preserved the
ty for the future. She thought of the lives snuffed out before their
me in the attacks on DC, the panicked evacuations of New York
d Chicago, and the reprisals. She recalled her mother's confused
mblings near the end of her life, "The Angel of Death comes in
any forms."

The wind had died down and it seemed to be getting warmer. A
assive white moon rose over the snow-covered ridge, illuminating
eir path in an otherworldly light. She felt her spirits rising. She
me to a strand of old growth chestnut oak and thought of a hike she
d taken on this ridge with her father and Joey as a little girl when
e world was like a basket of candies, each a delightful surprise wait-
g to be sampled. The twins, awake now, dangling in their papooses,
ared ahead wide-eyed attentive, as if they were on a buggy tour.

"It's a rare thing, two full moons in one month," she announced
d then began crooning, "Bluuuue moon…."

A wizened rabbit with a white tail froze in the trail in front of
em, seemingly staring at Bevy. They stopped. The rabbit tensed.

Bevy spoke softly to Joey and Madeleine. "See that old bunny? It
ust be confused by such bright light at this time of night."

Bevy waited. The rabbit bolted into the forest.

Looking down from the ridge, her eyes fell upon the South Fork
f the Shenandoah River snaking through the valley. She spied the
end where the shimmering waters abutted the Jacobson's meadow

but couldn't find the house. Then she saw pillars of gray smoke billowing from the site where her home had stood only hours ago.

She felt a chill, then a sense of resolve, and quickened her pace, eager for the shelter of the cabin where she could build a fire. She thought of her brothers and their families. They should be safe on the Pearl River family farm her grandparents had left them. It was a safe distance from Jackson, where post-bomb chaos and rationed resources had flared tensions between the urban and northern suburban communities into pitched battle. She recalled the moss-laden, short-leaf pine forests and the soporific smell of topsoil in the fields. She had always been unsettled by the South's Confederate history, but the sanctuary offered by the family farm was alluring to her now. Katharina had said she thought the general might help them get there. From there she would find a way to her own family in Israel, somehow.

Katharina's voice crackled over the walkie-talkie.

"Put a pot of tea on for me, honey."

Bevy breathed a sigh of relief. *If Katharina had taken the shortcut along the river, she might arrive in time for the twins' morning feeding.*

"Brrrrr," Bevy said to the twins, who were avidly watching her every move. "This cabin is cold." She wrinkled her nose. "And smelly."

She squatted in front of the cast iron stove, lit a match, and gently blew the little flame under the teepee-shaped pile of tinder into a small inferno. When the larger, damp branches had begun to crackle and smoke, she collapsed into a hardwood chair nearby.

She eyed a faded marionette her father had brought her from a business trip to Italy and then she saw the stack of dusty, mouse-nibbled American Girl and Star Wars books splayed out on the shelf. She recalled playing with Joey inside the cabin while her father hunted deer in the apple orchard below. She opened her satchel and took out the family picture from that fateful day when they had bought the weekend home in the mountains. In the flickering light from the ancing fire in the stove, she looked from young Joey's eyes to the vins' eyes and back again. *Who could have any doubt the same soul nhabited those mysterious spaces?* Then she heard the familiar excited ark of the German shepherd and broke into a big toothy grin.

Book Club Questions

1. Rachel and Joseph go to extreme lengths to give their son the life they feel he should have had. If cloning were possible today, do you think it should be allowed? Is it right for grieving parents to make these decisions? Are there times of grieving in your life when you think you would have explored it? Would it have been the right decision? Are there special circumstances in which it would be more or less acceptable?

2. Many parents believe they would sacrifice their lives for their child's. How many would actually do it? Would it be the right decision? What about the other children who would lose a parent? Is it right for a father of three to sacrifice his own life to save one of his children?

3. Scientific research suggests certain experiences can actually make tiny changes to our DNA. The cloned Joey experiences flashbacks from the first Joey's life. Do you believe that is possible? What does this indicate about how memories may be formed? Do you believe people have souls? And if so, are these memories indicative

of a person's soul? Is the soul unique to the body or to the body's experiences?

4. Was it right for Rachel and Joseph to keep Joey's cloning a secret? Were they protecting him, or themselves?

5. The original Joey was the oldest of his siblings, but the cloned Joey was the youngest. What role does birth order play in who a child becomes? Do you think the cloned Joey becomes who the original Joey would have been? If not, does this make Rachel and Joseph's quest meaningless?

6. When Joey and Katharina are in Butajira on a mission, she attempts to seduce him. Although he resists her at first, the combination of the vodka and her perfume seemed to be wearing down his defenses. The next thing we know, they are waking up in separate quarters. What do you think happened in between? Did Joey succumb to Katharina's advances, or did he politely decline?

7. What role did spirituality play in Rachel and Joseph's decision to clone their son? Do you think people's faith would make them more or less willing to consider cloning?

8. Is cloning humans moral? Should the government be the arbiter of whether cloning humans is allowed? Would it change your answer if cloning inherently led to the complications Joey experienced?

9. It could be argued that a major theme of the book is the consequences of living in the past. Both Joey and his parents are consumed by loss. Are we better off in a world where we are forced to let people go and move on with the grieving process?

CPSIA information can be obtained
at www.ICGtesting.com
Printed in the USA
FFOW02n2249101116
29239FF